An Informal Arrangement
by Heather Gray

an Informal Romance novel

Janet —
May you be blessed
by the story!

Heather Gray

in celebration of my Savior
in memory of my daughter
with pride in my son
with gratitude for my husband

But He said to me, "My grace is sufficient for you, for power is perfected in weakness." Therefore, I will most gladly boast all the more about my weaknesses, so that Christ's power may reside in me.

2 Corinthians 12:9

One

"No, no, *don't flush the toilet!*"

Maddie ran into the room, assessed the situation, and placed her hand on the patient's shoulder, shaking him lightly. "Mr. Jenkins. Mr. Jenkins, it's just a dream." This was her first day working with him, but he'd been on the unit for a while. Nothing in his file indicated a history of night terrors or bad dreams.

The man in the bed groaned and thrashed. "Not... albino... horned toa'... Please, no." Was he talking about toes or — a shudder tore through her — toads?

Had he seen one? She fought a shiver as she searched the immediate vicinity. No toads — horned or otherwise — in sight. He was obviously dreaming, but still... What did a horned toad look like, anyway? Not a frog with antlers, surely.

Every off-white nook and cream-colored cranny of the room came under careful scrutiny as Maddie continued speaking to her distressed patient. "Mr. Jenkins, wake up. You're having a nightmare."

His eyelids fluttered for a moment before opening. When he saw her, Mr. Jenkins' eyes grew wide. A remnant of sleep slowed his voice. "Is everything okay?"

What was she supposed to say to that? Tell the poor man he'd awakened her deep-seated dislike of all creatures not cute and furry? Or worse, explain how that dislike had been birthed?

"You, uh, were having a dream." Brilliant response.

"I was?" He scratched along his stubble-darkened jaw, emanating a masculinity that belied the days he'd spent in the ICU. "I kind of remember it. Was I talking in my sleep? I do that sometimes." He glanced around and licked his lips before whispering, "Is there a reason you seem so alarmed?" His voice, smooth like hot apple cider on a cold winter's day, warmed her.

Maddie blinked. She shouldn't have let her mind go down that path. Some thoughts didn't belong at work. "You mentioned something about a toad..." Her remark hung between them like a two-day old helium balloon.

The worry wrinkles on his forehead faded away, melting into his hairline and drawing her eyes to light chestnut hair that couldn't seem to make up its mind whether it wanted to stand at attention or lie down and take a nap.

"Umm, I guess I remember. Huh. I wonder where that dream came from." If his nonchalance was anything to go by, he had to dream about toads on a regular basis.

"And you mentioned the toilet." Maddie took a deep breath and went about her morning routine. Shift had just started, and she still needed to do her patient assessment.

She put the blood pressure cuff on Mr. Jenkins as he told her about his dream. "There was an albino horned toad that got out of its terrarium. It was in the toilet for some reason, but because the commode was white, nobody could see it. Which doesn't make sense. Albino animals aren't pure white, but what can I say? A hand reached for the lever to flush, and I panicked. That's when you woke me."

After she charted his blood pressure and listened to his heart and lungs, she asked, "What exactly is a horned toad? I'm picturing something froggish."

Mr. Jenkins laughed, disturbing Maddie's attempt to count his pulse. He reined himself in, and she began counting again. "Frogs and toads are different, you know, and a horned toad isn't even a toad. Not really, anyway. It's a lizard."

Her eyes darted around the room again. Maddie worked with people — and not animals — for a reason. "So toads and frogs are different, but a horned toad isn't a toad."

"That's right. The people who discovered and named it must have been confused."

Maddie held up an index finger. "Hold on a second." Then she marched over to the small attached bathroom. An empty toilet had never been so beautiful. She stepped back into the room. "Whew. All clear."

When her patient chuckled, she knew she'd hit the mark.

"Are you sure you're not the one who's confused? A toad that's not a toad?" She quirked her eyebrow as laughter sparkled in Mr. Jenkins' eyes.

"I'm never going to live this down, am I?"

"Are you aware you've been the talk of this unit?" Maddie kept up the banter as she continued her assessment.

"We're in the ICU. Being talked about might not be such a good thing." The strain of his current health situation didn't bleed into his congenial voice.

Some patients were better than others at compartmentalizing. They put their problems aside, lived in the moment, and in some cases wouldn't even acknowledge whatever illness, predicament, or condition had landed them in the hospital. Maddie often associated such behavior with men, but Mr. Jenkins was taking it to a new level. She decided to prod. "You're improving more rapidly than anyone here expected. We're all happy for you."

"I didn't do anything. All the credit goes to God." As if an afterthought, he added, "And the medical staff here, of course."

Maddie turned away. It wasn't his testosterone-dominated brain at work. Faith was to blame. Her stomach lurched. "So if it's not a frog or a toad, what is it?"

Mr. Jenkins graciously allowed the change in subject even though he'd already told her once. "A lizard. The cool thing about it is how, when it feels threatened, blood shoots out of its eyes."

Maddie made the mistake of trying to picture a blood-shooting lizard atrocity. She didn't get far in her attempt before dots danced in front of her eyes and she realized her mistake.

Poor Mr. Jenkins shot a look at the monitors that showed the readings from the various pieces of medical equipment attached to him. Obviously she hadn't kept her reaction from showing. His eyebrows drew together as he studied the data. A second later, he lifted his hands, palms out. "You're, uh, losing color. It's not as bad as all that... Is it?"

Blood shooting out of eyes wasn't bad? Nothing in his chart indicated early-onset dementia. Perhaps she should review the list of medications he was on.

"You'll likely never come across one around here, anyway." His placating voice asked forgiveness while his confused eyes said he didn't know what he'd done wrong. "They're mostly in the southwest."

"Mr. Jenkins, how are you doing today?" Dr. Sage stood in the doorway, his tall form and imposing physique a contrast to the patient in the bed.

"Good, thank you. Please call me Holden." His eyes shifted to Maddie. "You, too."

"Of course," the doctor replied before turning to her. "How are his vitals?"

"Steady," she told him. "Heart rate was elevated, but he'd just woken from a dream. It quickly came back down to normal."

Dr. Sage raised both eyebrows. "I do believe, Holden, that patients all the way over in the next wing are now afraid to flush."

Color crept up his neck and into his cheeks. "Was I that loud?"

"Not at all." The doctor's tone was drier than the Sahara during drought season.

Holden winced.

A chuckle softened the stern lines of the doctor's face. "But you did add a little spice to our shift change this morning. To be honest, if a patient is going to yell at the top of his lungs about something, I'd much rather it be the toilet than the care he's receiving."

Holden shook his head. "You've all been great. Having said that, I can't wait to get out of here, and I hope I never meet any of you again. At least, not under these circumstances. No offense intended."

"None taken." The doctor tipped his head to the side. "On that note, I've got some news. We'll be transferring you out of the ICU later today to a bed on the main floor. You've got a long recovery ahead of you, but you're no longer in imminent danger."

"Do you know yet what caused all of this?" Holden waved a hand to indicate his body.

The doctor frowned. "There are still several tests pending. At present all we can say for certain is that you presented here at the hospital with Transverse Myelitis, apparently subacute. You didn't suffer a stroke or obvious spinal injury, and we could find no tumor, slipped disc, or other abnormalities to indicate the cause of your problem."

Holden wanted to know what had put him in the hospital. Maddie was pretty sure he didn't want a list of everything that hadn't landed him in their care.

The doctor cleared his throat. "Sorry. We're a teaching hospital. Sometimes I forget to take the teacher hat off." With a shake of the head, he began again. "We're still considering a viral cause. Have you heard of viral meningitis?"

Color drained from Holden's face as he nodded. "Is that different from transverse…?"

Dr. Sage held up a hand. "Sorry. You don't have viral meningitis. It's just an example of how perfectly ordinary viruses, when they get into the wrong places in our body, can cause devastating damage."

"So I got a virus?"

The doctor's head bobbled back and forth for a second before he answered. "The problem for us is that, while there are a few main culprits when it comes to Transverse Myelitis, the sheer number of known viruses makes it challenging to pin down the cause. We're also running genetic tests to look for certain markers that might help us pinpoint underlying causes. It may be several weeks before we have a definitive answer."

"What sorts of underlying causes?"

Maddie gritted her teeth. Sometimes less information was better for the patient's peace of mind.

"I'd rather not worry you until we know something." The doctor studied Holden for a beat before continuing. "And I have to be honest. We might never know. Test results aren't always clear-cut."

Holden opened his mouth, but before he could speak, the doctor's pager went off. He glanced at the device and read the screen before shaking his head. "I have to run. Maddie can answer some of your questions, or your doctor when you get out on the floor. If I don't see you again before then, I wish you all the best." The doctor held out his hand, and the two shook.

Dr. Sage rushed from the room and Maddie was left staring at a none-too-happy patient.

"Is it always this hard to get answers?"

Tact could be overrated. This wasn't one of those times. "Sometimes we run tests for diseases that would terrify most people. If we're checking you for every imaginable horrifying illness known to man, do you really want to know that?"

"I have a right to know."

"Of course you do, but you weren't entirely coherent when most of these tests were ordered. Dr. Sage wasn't trying to hide anything from you. That's not the kind of doctor he is. He probably just didn't know how to answer the depth and breadth of what we've looked at so far."

"Can you give me an overview?"

"Sure. You're in your early thirties, so most of the age-related causes are off the table. You don't have HIV or systemic lupus erythematosus. We found no evidence of varicella zoster, herpes simplex, hepatitis, or rubella. They haven't ruled out Devic's disease or multiple sclerosis as underlying causes yet, and some of the virus tests are still outstanding."

He ran a hand down his face.

"Do you want me to stop?"

Holden nodded. "I think I've heard enough for now. What happens if they can't narrow down the cause?"

Maddie offered a half-shrug. "Your official diagnosis would become Idiopathic Transverse

Myelitis. Idiopathic just means the cause couldn't be identified."

One of the other nurses stuck her head into the room. "Maddie, they're waiting on you to give report on your patient in 203."

"I'll be right there."

She turned back to Holden, who waved her off. "Go ahead. I'm fine."

With her thoughts moving ahead to her other patient, Maddie gave him a distracted nod. "I'll be back in a little bit to get breakfast ordered and take care of anything else you need."

She heard his soft "Thank you," as she slipped out the door.

When Maddie walked back into his room, Holden's eyes were closed. Curtainless windows framed the tips of bare trees. January in northern Virginia was stark, grey, and frigid.

She stepped closer to the bed to check on her patient, trying not to wake him if he was sleeping. As she leaned in, his eyes popped open, and she jumped. Her reaction had little to do with his sudden movement, though. In truth, the crisp emerald green of his eyes caused her unexpected response. How had she not noticed their gem quality earlier? Oh, that's right. She'd been too busy checking the room for reptiles. In the intensive care unit, no less.

"I'm sorry," he said. "Did I startle you?"

"Your eyes are the same color as a frog." Maddie fought the urge to grimace. Holden would have every right to regale the floor nurses with tales of his frog-toad-lizard obsessed ICU nurse.

He didn't, however, take advantage of the chance to mock her. "I get the feeling you don't much care for them."

A shudder moved up her spine and shook her shoulders. "I'm not fond of any animal without fur on at least some part of its body." How did they keep ending up on this topic? Maddie needed to change the subject, and she reached for the first question that came to mind. "What would you like for breakfast? Anything in particular?" Hopefully she could prove there was more to her than a phobia he likely thought silly. Not that his opinion mattered. She wouldn't see him again after he left the unit.

"Bacon."

His gusto tugged a reluctant smile from her. "Once you're out on the floor, you won't get to order your meals whenever you want. You'll need to submit your requests a day in advance, and you won't have as many choices. So let's make the most of your last day in intensive care."

She skimmed the menu before picking up the phone and calling down to the kitchen. "This is

Maddie. I'm the nurse for the patient in room 723, Mr. Jenkins. I'm calling to order his meal."

"Mr. Jenkins, room 723… All right, go ahead with your order."

"He would like the bacon breakfast burrito, with pork bacon instead of turkey. And the bacon breakfast sandwich, also with pork bacon, but without the egg, cheese, or English muffin, please. Orange juice to drink and…" Tossing a saucy grin at Holden, she said, "You know what? Go ahead and add a side of bacon to that. Pork, though. Not turkey."

The man taking the order sputtered for a bit before asking her to hold. A supervisor's authorization was required before the order-taker could approve such a gluttonous combination. The kitchen was supposed to serve healthy meals. Go figure. The bacon-fest of an order she'd placed jeered at such constraints.

Maddie whispered to Holden, "You'd never be able to do this, but I might get away with it." She gave him a playful wink as the order-taker came back on the line and rattled something off. "Yes, I understand, but we need to get some calories into him. He's lost a lot of weight." The gentleman again consulted someone else before coming back on the line.

The phone wasn't even back in its cradle before Holden, eyes filled with glee, asked, "Well?" His body practically vibrated with eager curiosity as his hands clutched his blanket and he leaned forward in bed.

Laughter tap-danced along Maddie's skin and through her voice. "They asked if you'd like bacon ice cream with your meal. It's something new they decided to try, but apparently none of the patients will eat the stuff."

He looked like he'd just taken a swig of curdled milk.

"Is that the face I made when you talked about that critter shooting blood out its eyes?" Moving to his bed and dropping the side rail, Maddie said, "Okay, let's get you over to the bathroom. I'm assuming you need to go, but if you don't, you can at least brush your teeth and splash some water on your face. That ought to feel good after so many days in this bed." Maddie began disconnecting the various monitors attached to her patient.

Holden glanced from her to the lavatory and then back at her. "Were you planning to come in with me?"

Maddie had witnessed many different reactions over the years, but Holden's blushing uncertainty pulled on her heart strings. "First things first. Let's get there. Then you can tell me if you think you're able to manage on your own."

Mutiny swept briefly across his face.

"You're still in the ICU, Mr. Jenkins, and you're in my care. I won't take chances with you. Let's see how steady you are on your feet by the time we've made it to the bathroom. Then we can argue if you want."

Holden swung his legs down over the side of the bed, and with her support slid off the edge of the mattress, planting his stocking-clad feet on the floor. They were hospital issue stockings, too, complete with non-skid bottoms, one-size-fits-all shapelessness, and a must-have-been-on-clearance nauseating green color. He swayed back and forth before getting a handle on the appendages once again doing their job of supporting him.

"We can take our time. No rush." Maddie had been briefed. She knew the history of his illness. Holden had brushed it off, assuming it would pass. Until his legs had begun to fail. He'd taken his symptoms seriously then. By the time he could get an appointment with his personal physician, though, his mobility had further deteriorated. The culprit was most likely a virus, but with the way it had ravaged his body, it was a miracle Holden stood at all.

"Do you want the walker?"

He eyed the folded-up item leaning against the far corner of the room.

"No." His answer came through gritted teeth. Holden's progress across the room was slow, but he made each step under his own steam. A safety harness was in place around his waist, and Maddie had a hand on it in case he needed help, but he never faltered.

By the time they got to the bathroom door, beads of sweat shone across his brow. The question wouldn't be welcome, but it needed to be asked. "How do you feel? Will you be okay in there on your own?"

"I'll be fine." The reply was short, but not unkind.

She offered him a reassuring smile. "Let me give you a hand over the threshold. There's a little step up there, and I don't want you to trip. Then I'll leave you to see to matters. You've even earned yourself a closed door. I'm going to be right here outside the door, though, so if you run into any trouble at all, speak up."

An inscrutable expression met her words.

"Don't let embarrassment get in the way. If you need help, ask. This is my job, not just something I do for jollies. Besides, it can't be any worse than asking for help with a bedpan."

As soon as the door closed, Maddie swept a hand across her face. She wouldn't be surprised if he locked the door. *For jollies?* Where had that unfortunate phrase come from?

Two

Holden settled back into his bed. Maddie gave him an awkward smile-grimace before slipping out the door.

For jollies?

He gave up the battle and let the snort of laughter come.

He'd seen his share of nurses over his time in the ICU, but today was the first time he'd been assigned Nurse Maddie. She was something else. Unique. A little bizarre, sure. Then again, this was the first time he'd greeted a new nurse by screaming about toilets and horned toads. When it was all said and done, he couldn't fault her for being skittish around him.

The fragrance of salted paradise on a plate reached Holden ahead of the voice.

"I don't know what you did to warrant such treatment, but whatever it was, I hope some of it rubs off on me." An older gentleman stood in the doorway holding a breakfast tray.

Hunger gnawed at Holden, and he smiled. Weeks had passed since his appetite had last visited. He welcomed it back like an old friend. "You might just be holding the best smelling thing in this hospital."

The gentleman laughed softly and stepped over the threshold. "Tell my wife. I arrive home from work, and she takes one sniff before waving me off to go change my clothes. Says she won't allow the smell of overcooked broccoli and antiseptic at her dinner table. Can't say I blame her."

Holden picked up his fork in expectation but set it down again before taking a bite. Starving, yes. Callous enough to forget the God who'd seen him through thus far? He hoped not. With one eye still on the utensil, he asked, "How long have you been married?"

"Fran and me? We'll be celebrating forty-five years next month. She's the kind of gal a man can't wait to get home to."

A new type of pang took root in Holden's gut. Surely he couldn't be jealous of the man delivering his hospital meal. "Forty-five years. Wow. What's your secret?"

Right before he stepped back out the door to head on to his next delivery, the gentleman answered, "Kiss her like you mean it at least once every day."

Kissing? Holden could imagine his mom's horrified reaction. But then, her advice centered on landing him a wife. He wanted to find the woman God had for him and settle down. It still irked, though, when his family treated him as if he were incapable of convincing a woman to marry him. Hence all their outdated but well-intentioned counsel.

Head bowed, Holden prayed. *Thank you for the meal, Lord. I give you all my fears and insecurities. Pour out your strength on me and help me fight the good fight and be grateful for the battles along the way. And maybe not so worried about the future. Not losing my company would be nice, though, if you could see a way clear to make that happen.* Holden sighed. Worry was going to win out if he didn't wrap it up soon. *Amen.*

He lifted the lid from the plate, and a puff of bacon-laced steam escaped into the air. Thankfulness came easy sometimes. The sublime texture of that first piece of bacon was enhanced by…

"Dr. Pink, report to the lobby. Dr. Pink, report to the lobby." The nasal voice blaring over the intercom disrupted the moment, but Holden didn't let it ruin the mood. His breakfast was waiting.

"All right, Mr. Jenkins. Are you ready to go for a trip?" Maddie stepped through the door, but her attention wasn't on her patient. She was frowning at the stack of papers she carried.

"Holden."

She peered at him.

"Call me Holden."

Maddie's head bobbled in what looked like a shrug and a head shake doing the tango. "Sorry. I was making sure everything is in order with your chart. They have a room prepared for you down on the floor."

Panic nipped at the back of Holden's throat. "Am I ready?" His question was so much bigger than that, but the words to express his tangled thoughts escaped him.

She gave him a blank stare before setting the papers down. By the time she glanced back up, her earlier distraction was gone. Holden felt like an unprepared student called on by the teacher. There was no escaping the attention she cast his way with eyes that looked like a tangle of gold, brown, and smoky green. "You can breathe on your own, and you're able to feed yourself. Walking is still a problem, but you made it to the bathroom and back without your vital signs tanking. The immediate danger has passed, and you're ready for the main floor. What you need is an opportunity to build up your strength, which you'll do through physical and occupational therapy."

The irony wasn't lost on Holden. Hadn't he earlier asked God to give him strength? Still... "They can't come see me here?"

A half smile tugged at her lips. "They came to work with you more than once, but you were too out of it at the time to realize. We need to free up this bed for somebody who's sick enough to require constant monitoring, and that's no longer you." Her head tilted to the side, and compassion leaked into her eyes. "You can do this."

"Nobody will talk to me about long-term prognosis." There. He'd said it. The heartbeat echoing in his ears was louder than any of the hospital's monitors.

"Okay. What have you been told?"

Holden held himself as if in traction, stiff and unyielding. "I got a virus, and it attacked my spine. Viruses usually go away, though, right?"

For the briefest moment, Maddie rested her ungloved hand on his forearm. She withdrew it, though, before he could take a full breath. Then she glanced at the door before looking back at him and answering. "The tests all say your virus is gone. When it got into your spinal column, though, it caused swelling. The swelling, in turn, interrupted the signal from your brain to your lower extremities, which is why you first started having trouble with your legs. The longer your virus went untreated, the more impairment it caused."

"So this problem with my legs is permanent?"

"The nervous system is complicated, and at this point, only time will tell how lasting the damage

29

is. Problems like yours can clear up in a matter of days, weeks, months… or not at all. One of the reasons people are so reluctant to talk about your long-term prognosis is that nobody knows. More time needs to pass before anyone can gauge what your permanent condition will be."

"Is anybody laying down odds?" A cringe worked its way through Holden's middle. The idea of people gambling on his future wasn't exactly a reassuring one.

Maddie chuckled. "Not a one. But that's because we're all aware of something you are yet to discover. Once you get moved into a residential rehab facility where the therapists can work with you for longer periods each day — that's where you'll experience the real progress. Until then, we can only guess at what kind of recovery you'll make."

Holden grimaced. "So basically, be patient. That's what you're telling me?"

"Pretty much. Give therapy every ounce of your effort. We've seen it do amazing things for people."

"And if the worst happens and this is as good as it gets? What happens if I never get any better?"

Her frown returned. "The worst? You've already escaped that fate."

"You mean death? I suppose…"

Maddie's lips thinned. "That virus likely would have found its way up to your brain if you'd waited much longer before coming in. The damage it could have wrought there… It's just my opinion, but death isn't the worst a person can suffer."

Holden's breath lodged itself in his throat as he tried to get the words out. "Thank you for your honesty. I needed the reminder."

She acknowledged his words with a nod as two transport technicians came into the room.

"They're here to move you down to the floor."

Holden took in the duo's appearance, including their empty hands. "Should I have a wheelchair?"

"We're a first-class operation," said one of the men. "We take you, bed and all. Mr. Jenkins, you won't even break a sweat."

Maddie began unplugging different cables and placing various bits of equipment onto his bed. When she tucked the face mask with the bag attached to it between his thick chart and the side rail of the bed, Holden had to comment. "How necessary is all this gear?"

She spared him a quick glance, but her face said her concentration was on the task at hand rather than him. The notion smarted, but he quashed his reaction. He wasn't usually the irrational type. The effort she was going through was entirely for him. Besides, even if she didn't want to give him the time of day, it shouldn't bother him in the least. They barely knew each other. He had to be more anxious about being taken out of intensive care than he'd realized.

"It's hospital policy." She pointed to a piece of paper taped to a cabinet door across from his bed. "That's a page-long checklist, and I'm responsible for completing it before you can go anywhere. Nobody expects you to end up in cardiac arrest while we're in the elevator, but we're required to carry all the necessary equipment with us just in case."

"Ah." Bureaucracy. "It *would* be bad form to let a patient die in the elevator of a hospital."

The transport technician who'd spoken earlier rubbed his hands together. "Like I said, you're traveling first-class. You get all the amenities for this trip."

A short while later, Holden looked around his new hospital room. It was the same size as his last one, but instead of the plethora of medical equipment he'd previously bunked with, this room had an empty space where another bed would eventually go. The sterile smell was no different than in the ICU, but the window in this room had vertical blinds to block the sun. He sighed. Sure, it was a step up, but he'd rather not need to be in the hospital at all.

Maddie, who'd stepped out into the hallway to confer with his new nurse, popped her head back through the doorway. "You're in good hands here, Mr. Jenkins."

"Holden."

Laughter touched her eyes. "Holden. Old habits and all that. The staff here will take excellent care of you, and occupational and physical therapy should come by on a regular basis. Do what they say, and they'll whip you into shape to get out of here and on to the next step of your journey in no time."

Uncertainty about the future continued to demand more attention than Holden wanted to give it. He shoved the doubts back into a corner of his mind and smiled at Maddie. "Thank you for looking after me today, and for the bacon. I appreciate it."

She waved and slipped away, leaving him alone with his troubled thoughts. The nurses had all done a good job of diverting his attention whenever he'd begun to worry. Maddie had by far been the most distracting despite the professional mask she hid behind. What, though, was she hiding from?

For jollies.

Holden chuckled as he sank into the pillows and closed his eyes.

Three

Ten Days Later

Maddie's shift was over, and exhaustion dragged her shoulders down and prevented her from lifting her feet all the way off the floor. She didn't want to visit with anyone. The day had held too much turmoil to put her in a conversational mood. Home, a hot meal, and a long bath were all she wanted.

Yet she'd somehow developed the habit of visiting Holden at the end of her shift each day, and the idea of going home without seeing him settled in her stomach about as well as a glass of sour milk.

When had they become friends? She'd only cared for him that one day. Ah, but at the end of that day she'd stopped in to check on him, and he'd suckered her into helping with a crossword puzzle. Who knew word puzzles could be so entertaining? Or that she'd feel at peace around a man who spoke of God and toads?

No. She definitely didn't feel like socializing today. And yet…

She was at his door before she made up her mind not to visit, and a sigh escaped. The hallway, a victim of ambitious acoustics, took her small sigh and amplified it into a rolling echo.

"Maddie?" The sound of his voice drew her which, in turn, made her uneasy. Vulnerability wasn't a cloak she wore comfortably.

Taking a deep breath and stuffing the emotions of the day back down where they wouldn't be visible, she pushed the door open and stepped into his room.

Holden wasn't alone. "I'm so sorry." She started to back out. "I can come back another time."

"Nonsense. I was hoping that was you I heard. It'd be pretty weird if I called your name and Hank from PT came in. Have you seen him? Big guy, burly, looks like he should be a professional wrestler?" Holden waved at the remaining empty chair. "You've earned a sit-down after a long day of hard work." His voice comforted, like a favorite blanket. He waved toward a man on the other side of his bed. "This is Joshua. He leads a Bible study I attend."

The man, with more salt than pepper in his hair, dipped his chin in Maddie's direction. His smile was friendly enough, but she was glad he didn't reach over the bed to shake her hand. If they were in the ICU and she was greeting someone visiting one of her patients, she'd be fine. Outside her domain, though, the prospect of meeting new people wasn't a happy one.

Joshua pointed to the wrapped package in Maddie's hand, his faded-denim blue eyes twinkling. "A gift from a patient?"

Ready to bolt at a moment's notice, Maddie perched on the edge of a chair near Holden's bed. "I went to the bookstore on my day off and saw something I thought you might like." She handed him a book covered in brown paper.

Holden reached for the parcel, his eyes still intent on her face. "Do I get to open it now?"

"If you must," she said, "but don't plan on showing me. I wrapped that bad boy to keep it from staring at me every time I opened my locker."

His bark of laughter drew her gaze back to his eyes. The animation dancing in their emerald depths pulled at her like the strongest magnet. He was so… happy. And peaceful. Her vocabulary didn't extend far enough to cover what she saw in Holden, but even if she couldn't put a name to it, she began to understand why he fascinated her.

"Now, that's a gift for the history books." Joshua's delighted laughter echoed in the room.

Holden's fingers traced the image of a horned toad on the cover. "Thank you, Maddie. This is a wonderful gift. A bit unexpected, too." A grin marked his face, but it was a tired one. He appeared as worn out as she felt.

"My friend here told me about what a dramatic first impression he made on you." Joshua's relaxed posture put her at ease. He changed the subject back to the book in Holden's hands. "How did you come across such a great find?"

"I was perusing the bookstore shelves. Then I turned around, and this gruesome monster-creature was inches from my face. By the time I screamed, jumped, and knocked over a display of cat books, I managed to convince myself it wasn't alive. But I still made one of the clerks in the store carry the book to the register for me so I wouldn't be forced to touch it."

"How did you manage to wrap it, then?" asked Holden.

"Sterile gloves," she answered impishly. "Plus, my cat helped hold the paper down while I taped."

Joshua laughed. "A cat person, eh? I'm partial to dogs myself. I've developed a theory about people and their animals. What people name their pets says a lot about them. What's your cat's name?"

Heat scorched her ears. "Mr. Fish Breath, but I call him Fishy for short."

Holden choked on the water he'd just sipped. Joshua jumped up and patted him on the back. The Bible study leader waited until the gasping patient caught his breath before saying, "I guess I've done enough damage for one evening, eh? I'll get going now."

He reached out to shake Holden's hand. "You're in my prayers, Brother, don't you doubt it for a minute." Stopping by Maddie's seat, he held out his hand to her, too, and she didn't mind shaking it nearly as much as she'd thought she would. "It's been a pleasure to meet you, Maddie."

After Joshua left, she tilted her head and squinted. "I can't quite place his accent. Where's he from?"

"America, but he grew up in Canada. His parents were missionaries and moved there before he was old enough to start school. He came back to the States in his late twenties, or somewhere around there."

His answer drifted in the room's still air while she decided whether to stay or go. The remnants of the day must have still been visible on her face, though, for Holden's smile faltered.

Concern was a ribbon wound through and around his words. "What happened?"

Without permission, tears flooded her eyes. Holden struggled to a sitting position in bed and looked as though he would try to get up and come to her. With a hand held up to still him, she stood and took a step back toward the door.

"Don't go." He exuded quiet confidence. "If you want to take a minute to freshen up, the bathroom's right there." A wave of his hand indicated the closed door. "But please don't go just yet."

Maddie dashed into the bathroom and shut the door behind her. She leaned against the solid surface of the faux-wood bacteria-resistant door and gulped for air. As soon as her panic began to abate, her trembling legs carried her to the sink where she splashed cold water on her face. Using the cardboard-smelling paper towels from the dispenser, she patted her face dry and looked at herself in the mirror. Ugh. Crying did not improve her appearance at all.

When she stepped back into his room, Holden was sitting on the side of the bed, his legs dangling. The nurse in her took note of the sweat beading his brow. He wasn't strong enough to sit up without assistance yet, but he should be. He'd been out of ICU for ten days. Fatigue must be getting the better of him.

"You shouldn't overexert yourself." Her inner medical professional would not be turned off. "I won't be responsible for you setting your recovery back."

His eyes searched her face, but at least he didn't remark on her blotchy appearance or red-rimmed eyes. "Do you want to talk about it?"

Her hair swirled about her face as she shook her head. She opened her mouth to say *no*, but the words "We lost a patient" came spilling out instead. Wanting to dismiss the subject, she hurried on. "She wasn't one of mine, but it's always hard anyway."

"I can't imagine doing your job."

Something about Holden's voice made her muscles relax and the stress of the day bleed away. It didn't matter what he said. The magic was in his voice. He could make podcasts of himself reading old phone books, and people would still pay good money to hear him.

"How do you handle it when you lose a patient?"

"Badly."

A sound came from the back of his throat, half exasperation and half chuckle. "I mean, what do you do to cope? What helps you deal?"

She shrugged. "Some are harder than others. If a patient's brand new to us and I don't know them or their family, it's easier somehow, which in turn can make me feel guilty if I let it. When someone's been on the unit for a while, though, and I've met their spouse, children, parents — that makes it harder. Then there are the ones…" Her voice faded. Drat. Those last words were supposed to stay inside her head.

"The ones that…?" His partial question demanded a response.

Maddie blinked hard. "The ones you like. They're good people. Funny, kind. They pull you in without even trying, and before you know it, you care more than you should."

"Is there such a thing as caring more than you should? Can we really care too much about another person?"

His words went straight to her heart, but she couldn't deny the pain of her job. "I don't have an answer. But sometimes a patient's death hits so hard, you question everything you've ever done."

Nursing was what Maddie knew, and she cared more about her patients than she showed. She was uncomfortable around most people — she hadn't even wanted to shake Joshua's hand when she first met him. She thrived at work, though. That's where she felt the most natural, where she was the most confident, and where connecting with people came easiest. She wasn't ready to explain that to Holden, though, especially not with her emotions so close to the surface.

"You get to touch so many lives," he started to say, but she held up her hand to cut him off. His pause was infinitesimal. "Would you rather a different subject?"

Grateful for the reprieve, she nodded.

"Tell me why you don't like lizards." His conversational voice was inviting.

With a self-derisive smile, Maddie said, "It's a long story."

"I'm not exactly short on time."

"My parents were a bit unorthodox." She steeled herself against the anxious flutter of her heart. "They loved me, but they made some bad choices and didn't get to keep me. I was put into foster care. After that, my parents pulled it together, and the state

42

returned me to them. It was a cycle for us. Every time they got in trouble, I was put back into the system. One of the foster families kept terrariums. Snakes, lizards, spiders — the whole gambit. If it was terrifying to little girls, they called it a pet."

Maddie ran a shaky hand through her hair, fluffing the short mop of curls. She hoped the motion would hide her shiver, but it was unlikely. Holden's eyes hadn't left her face even once since she'd started talking. The attention unnerved her. "One night I woke up to discover a snake wrapped around me. I was six or seven, and the snake was huge. Terror choked my voice off. No matter how hard I tried to scream, no sound came out." The horror on his face made her hesitate.

Whether intentional or subconscious, Holden's hand moved to cover the picture on the cover of the book. "I can understand why you're so terrified of the creatures."

What would he think if he knew the rest of the story? "Anyway…" She liked a person who wasn't inclined to pry. "I should get going. I'm on shift again tomorrow and need to get some sleep."

"Of course." His voice rumbled with warmth behind her. "Thank you for stopping by to see me, and for the book, too."

Maddie was halfway home before she realized Holden hadn't mentioned God. He'd seen she was upset and been kind to her, but he hadn't preached. A smile touched her lips.

Four

Holden clasped the book about horned lizards. He ran his hand over the cover while he stared at the empty doorway.

Maddie hadn't told him the whole story. If he'd not reacted so strongly when she got to the part about the snake in her bed, she probably would have continued. He would need to more carefully guard his reactions in the future.

Closing his eyes, he pictured Nurse Maddie. Average height. Sun-kissed hair with enough body to make her the envy of his straight-haired sisters. Hazel eyes filled with secrets. The horror on her face at his first mention of the horned toad was unforgettable. A part of him had wondered if she was squeamish in general. Some women were, after all. Look at his sisters. It hadn't taken him long, though, to realize she was anything but. Maddie handled her job with matter-of-fact precision, which meant she dealt with blood, vomit, and other bodily fluids on a regular basis. He would be willing to wager there wasn't a squeamish bone in her body.

She didn't strike him as the type who shared her vulnerability with others. She projected strength, yet she came to visit him, a man who'd witnessed the vivid fear flash in her eyes over such an innocuous subject.

Lord, I see something special in this woman, but I also see that she's hurting. I can't imagine the childhood she had. Bouncing from parents to foster homes and back again. And she stopped. There's more to her story, but she stopped. If I'm reading the secrets in her eyes correctly, the part she held back is worse than what she revealed. Comfort her, Lord, and give me the right words the next time she visits. I'd like to think...

The room phone rang, shrill in the otherwise calm night.

It was late, and he wasn't expecting any calls. Not many people knew where to find him, either.

"Hello?"

"Holden, is that you?"

"Dad? How'd you get this number?"

His father grumbled. "Some lady called to ask about rehabilitation facilities near our house since we're your emergency contact. Want to tell me what's going on?"

Audible in the background, his mom was telling his father what to say.

"Shush, Margie. Let me talk to the boy."

A smile tugged at Holden's lips. This one was no different than a hundred other phone calls with his parents.

"What's this about rehab? Do you have a drug problem we need to know about?"

"Everything's fine, Dad."

"Then why am I calling you at a hospital? Do you want to explain why some stranger was the one to tell me where you are?"

"I got sick, but I'm getting better now."

His mom's voice came again. "Find out why he needs rehab."

Before his dad relayed the question, Holden answered. "I live alone, that's why. They want to make sure I'll be okay before sending me home since there's no one to keep an eye on me."

"Should you come home, son? We could take care of you."

Every rebellious thought entertained in his teen years lurched to the surface. "No, Dad. My business and livelihood are here. Stop worrying."

"What kind of sick are we talking about, anyway? You got your flu shot, right? Is it that meningitis we've been hearing about?"

Holden released the book he still clutched and ran his hand through his hair. "Not meningitis. I got a virus, and it hit me hard, but I'll be fine." Illness had never much touched his family. They wouldn't understand. If he got into the details of his condition, it would overwhelm them. At least, that's what he told himself.

"Why didn't you call us?"

"I didn't want you to worry. Besides, you're too far away to do anything."

His father's voice dropped, the man's hurt seeping out through his words. "We could've prayed."

A gauntlet to the face would sting no less. He'd failed his parents. Again. Only a terrible son would rob them of their right to pray for him. "I'm sorry, Dad. I didn't think."

The senior Mr. Jenkins' voice, rich with untold layers of emotion, asked, "Are you really okay?"

"I'm fine. I'll be here another few days before they send me to rehab, where they'll make sure I can walk, talk, and bathe on my own. Then they'll let me go home. It's not as big of a deal as it sounds, honest." The lie was bitter on his tongue, but it would fix things. His dad wouldn't be so hurt if he thought Holden's problems were nothing major.

"Do you need our help? Your mom can fly out."

"No." He bit the word out as a flood of adrenaline washed away his guilt. He couldn't let his parents see him this way. They would panic, and then they would smother.

His father's sharp intake of breath reached Holden's ears.

"I wouldn't be able to meet her at the airport. Give me a chance to recuperate a little bit, okay? I'm not up for company yet."

"She's your mother. Family's not the same as company." Reprimand gave his dad's voice a sharper edge.

"I know, Dad. That came out wrong. Mom can't drive in the city, though. Visiting right now would be complicated. Give me some time. I'd love for you guys to come. Let me get back on my feet first, and then I'll be able to help with the air fare."

Holden could no longer hear his mother's voice. Either she'd left the room or… she was crying. Fantastic. He'd made his mother cry.

Worst. Son. Ever.

"We'll stay away, then. You'll tell us when it's okay for one of us to come? I'm not sure we can scrape together enough money for two tickets, but we can probably buy one. Say the word, and one of us will be on the next flight out."

"Thanks, Dad. I appreciate it. You're the best parents a wayward son could ask for." Holden made an effort to inject humor into his voice, but it fell flat, even to his own ears.

"You ever think about moving back home? There's plenty of work here, and you'd be close to family."

Plenty of work. Sure, but none he wanted. He'd never aspired to farm, be a tractor mechanic, or raise livestock.

"Love you, Dad. Mom, too."

"Of course, son. We love you, too. You know that, right?"

"Since the day I was born. Talk to you later."

He hung up the phone and laid his head back on the pillow. Once he had a grasp on his long-term prognosis, he could let them in. Until then, he would do everyone a favor by telling them everything was fine.

It was for the best. Nobody in his family needed to spend their energy worrying about him or how much pain he was in. He'd done the right thing. There was no reason for guilt...

Lord Above, I need you now more than ever. I need healing. No. I want healing. With an intensity that scares me a little. I don't want to be crippled. I'm struggling to stay positive, and I'm making a mess of things with my family. Face it. I'm a disaster. I could use some of Your strength right now, Lord. My life's in turmoil, and I'm losing my way.

Weariness dragged at Holden until his eyes closed. He drifted off to sleep, the book from Maddie still in his lap.

Five

Maddie had two days to herself before she needed to return and work three straight. She'd decided against visiting Holden on her days off. It was one thing to stop in for a visit when already at the hospital, but going out of her way to do so on non-work days screamed *stalker*.

On her first day back, the hours flew by in a rush of tests, bloodwork, scans, and more. Throughout the day, she looked forward to checking in on her former patient and seeing how he fared. If on target, he'd be heading to residential rehab within the week, and she was glad even if she would miss him. His discouragement showed on his face and in the stiff way he held himself. He was frustrated with not being able to do more for himself and could use some good news.

When she got to his room, she poked her head around the door without knocking. A man in his early twenties was sleeping in Holden's bed. She stumbled backward out of the room and into the hallway. A nurse reached out a hand and steadied her before they collided.

Maddie straightened her scrubs. "I wasn't paying attention. I'm sorry."

"No worries." The nurse glanced from Holden's room back to Maddie. "Were you stopping in to talk to Mr. Jenkins? If so, he's in rehab now — transferred out sometime during day shift."

"Oh." Ask which one… or let the whole thing go and accept that she wouldn't run into him again? The latter was probably for the best, even if it didn't put a smile on her face.

"You're Maddie, right? The one he calls Nurse Maddie?"

She tilted her head and gave the nurse a quizzical look. "That's me."

"Mr. Jenkins talked about you." The woman tucked a strand of hair behind her ear. "It's none of my business, of course, but when a man as fine as that one goes out of his way to spend time with me, I take notice." Hustling toward the nurse's station, she called over her shoulder, "Follow me."

Maddie stood still for a moment, the words, "He hasn't had a choice in the matter," on the tip of her tongue before her feet caught up with her brain and she scurried after the quickly disappearing nurse.

"He left something for you." The grinning woman handed her an envelope with her name written on it.

Maddie nodded her gratitude. "I wouldn't have thought to ask here."

The nurse gave her a broad grin. "Like I said, none of my business, but that's never stopped me from sticking my nose into the middle of other people's affairs. You got yourself a keeper. I wouldn't be in a hurry to let that one slip away if I were you."

Her cheeks heating, she thanked the nurse again and hurried to the exit. When she made it to her car, she slit the envelope open and pulled out a single sheet of paper.

Maddie,

> *I'll be at Lakeview Rehab. I know it's out of your way, and I'll understand if you don't visit me there — no hard feelings. But I'd be happy to see you if you do decide to drop in.*

Many blessings,

H. Jenkins

The note struck the right tone of friendly and distant. It was cordial enough that she couldn't get the wrong impression, but the fact that he wrote it told her she'd be welcomed nonetheless. With a small smile turning up the corners of her mouth, she reversed out of her parking space, ready to tackle the evening traffic.

Maddie's next day off came two days later. She got up, showered, dressed, and then stood before the mirror.

"Should I go see him?"

The reflection looking back at her had little to say and a bit too much uncertainty in the eyes for her taste. Fishy, on the other hand, mewled in agreement from his nearby perch on the corner of her thistle bedspread. Agreement to what, though, she couldn't tell. So she did what every warm-blooded mature American does when the situation calls for it. She pictured two little figures, one sitting on each shoulder. Apparel? Oh, yeah. Totally normal. One wore white scrubs, and the other red.

The white-scrubbed figure declared, "You need to get out more, and besides, he's nice. It can't hurt to pop in and see how he's doing."

Red Scrub yelled. "Are you out of your mind? You don't need attachments. That man is trouble with a capital T."

Mentally flicking the figures off her shoulders, she grabbed her clutch purse and closed the door with a snap as she stepped out of her apartment.

Maddie hit a drive-thru coffee shop on the way and got a large Mondo for each of them. Hopefully he liked his coffee strong... She arrived at Lakeview and climbed from her car while managing to juggle the two drinks and her strapless pocketbook. A brief stop at reception to get directions, then she maneuvered the hallways as she headed toward Holden's room.

Her hands were full, so she tapped the door with her foot, but the rubber sole silenced her effort. Seeing no help for it, she pushed her way through the door.

"Hey there, sweetheart. Is that for me?" A middle-aged man with a lecherous grin lay in the farthest bed.

Startled, Maddie almost lost her hold on the coffees. She backpedaled out of the room and double-checked the number. Yep. It was the right room. With a deep breath, she stepped back over the threshold.

"I'm looking for Holden."

The man with the wandering eyes scowled. "Ah, just my luck. No one sexy ever comes to visit me. Young punk kid gets all the ladies." He huffed and turned his back on her.

Young punk kid? Hadn't someone else recently called him old? *That's right.* Mentally snapping her fingers, Maddie recalled the conversation. Jacie, with all her fresh-from-nursing-school enthusiasm, had commented about Holden one day, saying, "He's such a hottie, even if he is old."

Maddie wondered what that made her. If his thirty-three years was old to the bright-eyed youth, then what would her thirty-one years be? Semi-old? Pre-old?

Hearing the man in the other bed continue to grumble about young punks, she had to ask the question. If Holden was young in this new equation, she didn't want to know what that made her. Prepubescent?

And just how many women visited him, anyway?

Dislodging the thought with a shake of her head, Maddie took another step into the room. Since the cranky man was on the far side, she assumed the bed closest to the door belonged to Holden. She set the coffees down on the nightstand and considered what to do next. Wait? Wander around trying to find him? Check back at reception?

"Mr. Jenkins," came a man's loud raspy voice from the hallway, "you are one funny man. Now I understand why they kicked you out of the hospital and sent you here. Wouldn't do for all them sickly patients to choke on their food from laughing at you."

The distinctive chuckle she'd come to associate with Holden reached her ears. Maddie stood there, awkward, remembering all the reasons she shouldn't have come.

"I thought I told you to call me Holden."

"Ah, I can't do that, Mr. Jenkins. Goes against everything my mama taught me." The voices grew closer until an orderly pushed a wheelchair into the room.

"Maddie." The word snagged as his breath caught in surprise, but Holden's eyes welcomed her.

"Now that you got a visitor, are you going to be needing me Mr. Jenkins?" The orderly stood by.

Holden's eyebrows lifted. "The clock says we have about fifteen minutes to kill before it's time to go down for lunch. Burt here was going to take me. Would you like to join me instead? The meal choices are limited, so you can eat something if you'd like, or skip the food altogether and keep me company to take my mind off the terrible cuisine I'm forced to endure."

Maddie couldn't help but be pulled toward the twinkle in his eyes. "I brought you a coffee. A Mondo, actually, which is even better in my book."

"A what?"

"Mondo. It's coffee with a couple shots of espresso thrown in for good measure."

"Whew, lady, that's the kind of thing puts hair on your chest." The relaxed cadence of Burt's voice moseyed through the room as he leaned down and whispered loudly, "Any woman who likes strong coffee is worth holding onto, man."

His eyes on her, Holden answered, "I think we're good here, Burt. We can find our way down to the cafeteria. Thanks for the ride back from therapy, though."

With a wave, the orderly left the room. The older man in the other bed still lay with his back turned to them.

"Is the food here really that bad?" Maddie cringed. Small talk was her kryptonite.

He shook his head. "Pure exaggeration. Sort of. The food's even good some days. I just figured you'd be more likely to join me if you felt sorry for me. Here, let me hold the coffees, and you can push."

Holden ended up with her pocketbook, too, as she guided his chair through the halls, following his directions. Once the hub of activity came into sight and she knew where to go, Maddie asked the question foremost in her mind. "Why the wheelchair? Isn't the point of rehab to get you up and walking more?"

Their position — him in the chair and her pushing it — hid his face from her view, but she couldn't miss the way his shoulders drooped at her words. *Way to kick a man while he's down.*

"PT is on the far end of the complex, so they insist everyone be wheeled there and back. Truth is, I couldn't walk it if I'd wanted, but I think I'm doing better. At least most days, anyway."

"I'm ridiculously good at thoughtless questions when I'm not on the job. The wheelchair caught me by surprise. I'm sure you're making phenomenal strides. Pun intended." She would have winked if he could've seen her.

They collected their lunch trays. Since she wasn't a resident, Maddie paid for hers. A small table over by the window beckoned them to sit down and enjoy the view. As though pretty greenery on the

58

other side of the glass would rid the place of its stench. What would happen if somebody bottled and sold the odor perfuming the air around them? Eau De Antiseptic and Overcooked Vegetables.

She was just about to share the thought with her lunch companion, but he spoke first. "Do you mind if I say the blessing?"

Holden's question pulled her out of the moment and thrust her back, far into the past. Maddie usually did a good job of forgetting segments of her life. Some parts were too painful, and others were so happy the loss of them cut deep. Memories got pushed into a corner of her mind until someone said something in passing that brought them all rushing forward.

More than a decade had passed since anybody had prayed around her, and the pain of the memory robbed her of breath. Her mask of protection slipped into place, and her roiling emotions hid themselves away from sight – she hoped.

"That's fine." She got the words out before bowing her head and waiting. Prepared for a long soliloquy about God's goodness, she silently chanted a familiar phrase. *In through the nose, out through the mouth.* Her pulse had begun to slow by the time Holden's voice reached across the table.

"Lord, thank you for another day of healing and recuperation and for bringing Maddie here to share a meal with me. Amen."

She opened her eyes and stared.

"Is something in my teeth?"

"You caught me off guard. Your prayer wasn't as long as I expected."

"I can pray some more if you'd like." His grin spoke to his mischievous nature.

Shaking her head, she took a bite of her salad and swallowed. "Your roommate thinks you're a young punk kid."

The sound he made fell somewhere between a laugh and a... guffaw. There was no better word. Patients at several of the neighboring tables glared at them for the disturbance. "People don't have enough fun around here. It's like they've all forgotten how to laugh." Then, pausing, he studied her, and his eyes widened. "Please tell me he didn't make a pass at you."

"Who?"

"The aforementioned roommate. He tends to say shocking things to the female nurses. He didn't... did he?"

Maddie tucked her hair behind her ear and took a long drink of her coffee. "He might have implied I was sexy. That's when I realized he must've misplaced his glasses."

"Your smile is beautiful."

His words appeared to surprise him as much as they did her, and the very feature he'd commented on slipped away.

Whether real or imagined, Maddie felt the stares of everyone in the room boring into her, judging her, and finding her wanting. Awareness of her own shortcomings bubbled to the surface and heated her skin. Accepting compliments with grace wasn't a skill she'd ever mastered.

"It's true, even if you wish I hadn't said so." Returning to his meal, Holden acted as though the moment – and her stilted response – had never occurred.

Did he honestly understand her as well as he seemed to? Or was it dumb luck that had him always knowing the right thing to say?

"You get a lot of female visitors." Maddie chomped down on her lower lip enough to make her wince. Where had those words come from? Not from the well of common sense, that was for sure. "Uh… Your roomie complained about it."

Holden swallowed a bite of… something. "Did he happen to describe the lovely ladies who stop by?"

She shook her head, losing her appetite and the high spirits of earlier that morning.

"Joshua told the Ladies' Auxiliary at church about my situation. I get homemade cookies almost daily. Not to mention hand-knitted socks and scarves."

A raised eyebrow. "The Auxiliary sounds industrious."

"They're all well-meaning women who dedicate themselves to caring for the downtrodden, and as far as I can tell, they're all north of sixty. Some by several miles."

Maddie bit back a smile. Maybe she should have been embarrassed by her assumptions – or by her possessiveness at least. Instead, she was… happy.

"So who'd you think the ladies were?"

She shrugged and answered in an airy voice. "Oh, no one. I just wondered."

He gave her a dubious look before returning to his… whatever was on his tray.

Her salad disappeared as she happily finished it off. Then she inspected her other food. With suspicion. Had she really piled those other dishes on her tray?

Holden, half done with his own meal, flashed his eyes at her. "Don't ask me what it is, but it doesn't taste as bad as all that." He waved his fork at the item she was trying in vain to identify. Her eyebrows lifted, and he chuckled. "If you want to skip the main course and go straight to dessert, I won't be offended."

"Does it have a name?" The spoon she pressed into the *food* in question was repelled, and she watched as the glob sprang back into shape with surprising speed.

"Okay, remember how I told you the cuisine here is pretty good?"

She nodded.

"I basically meant the breakfasts and salads. Sometimes dessert, too, depending. I stopped reading the signs altogether. Despite carefully examining everything they give me, I've never once found anything resembling the mental picture I conjure up based on the name. One day it read *Mexican Goulash* and I thought, 'I can do this. Taco meat and macaroni with salsa.'" He paused to take a drink. Was he trying to use his thirst to hide a shudder? If so, it wasn't working. "I kid you not, the thing they scooped onto my plate was potatoes, hot dogs, and canned peas. All cooked and stirred together until mushed into toddler food."

Nausea clenched Maddie's stomach, and she shuddered, too. "Sounds like a feast fit for a fiendish horned monster." Without an ounce of guilt, she pushed her tray aside and went for the bowl of butterscotch pudding.

Holden set his utensils down next to his empty plate. "You can come back to my room and hang out, or we can sit here and visit." The sun came in through the window and lit his brown hair, giving it a gilded look.

Turning in her chair, she contemplated the dining room as though she didn't already know her answer. "This is comfortable."

He hooted, again raising the ire of the diners nearby. "Don't want to run into my roommate again, do you?"

Telltale heat warmed her cheeks, so no good would come from denying the accusation. A change of subject was called for. "Tell me about your family."

"Well, I have two parents, a mom and a dad."

Maddie rolled her eyes.

He chuckled. "I am blessed with seven brothers and sisters, all older than me."

"Oh, my," she said. "I don't know if I've ever met anyone with such a big family before. What was it like growing up?"

"You heard the part where I said I'm the youngest, right?" Hollywood had nothing on him for all the painfully overacted drama he threw into that short statement.

When did humor get so sexy?

Holden's eyes said he'd traveled miles away from the rehab center dining room. The humor was gone. Nostalgia painted a myriad of shadows across his face. Or was it regret? "Most of my four sisters and three brothers are happily married and living the lives they want. They all live in the same small town we grew up in which is, in turn, the same small town my parents both grew up in."

"How unusual… and yet quaint." Maddie sipped her still-warm coffee.

"Have you ever been the outsider?"

Her half-shrug was as noncommittal as she could make it.

"Don't get me wrong. I love my family, and I always will. I talk to most of them weekly."

"But...?" she prompted.

He shrugged. "I couldn't live there. I needed to get out. I wanted to know what it felt like to meet someone for the first time without them saying, 'Oh, are you related to so-and-so,' or, 'So you're Marty's youngest, huh?'" Holden hung his head. "It hurt my parents when I left. My brothers and sisters, too, though only a few of them ever voiced it."

Maddie's fingers itched with the urge to reach across the table and give his hand a comforting squeeze, but she resisted.

He looked up, and fire burned in his eyes. "I wanted to be judged on my own merit. Truth be told, I craved a little adventure, too."

With a cafeteria-encompassing wave of her hand, she asked, "Is this your idea of adventure?"

A shadow crossed over his eyes, robbing them of their usual sparkling light. "This isn't exactly what I had in mind. By the time this is all done, I'm going to be wiped out. The business can suffer my absence for a while, but not long-term. In the meantime, I'm falling behind on my mortgage. My options are disappearing, and there doesn't seem to be anything I can do to turn things around."

Tilting her head to the side, she asked, "What do you do for a living? We've never talked about it."

"I run a small architectural firm." His mouth tilted up at the corner. "By *small*, I mean, me, one assistant, and a part-time secretary-type person."

"What does a secretary-type person do?"

He shrugged. "She's not skilled enough to be an admin assistant, but she tells me the word *secretary* is insulting. She answers phones, sends invoices, types up letters for me. Stuff like that."

Maddie could barely contain her laughter. "Does she bring you coffee, too?"

Holden chuckled. "Ha! I'm not that old-fashioned. I can get my own coffee, thank you very much."

"I'll bet she burns it."

He blinked. "Which is precisely why I get my own. From the shop down the street from the office."

The moment of levity passed as the sparkle slowly faded from Holden's eyes. "The thing is, if I can't work, we can't take on new clients. Miles, my assistant, can finish off the projects already underway. At least I hope he can. There's no way he can contract new commitments, though. Not without me. That's one of the reasons I waited so long to see my physician. I wanted to get everything wrapped up first in case I got laid up for a while. Without new customers and fresh money coming in…"

"How long does the doctor think you'll be in rehab?"

"Another month at least." Discouragement dropped the corners of his mouth into a frown.

Encourage without lying. It was one of her mantras as a nurse. "Have you thought about renting out your house or a room to help you get by in the meantime?"

"To be honest, I don't know what to do. Dr. Demir says she'd let me go home sooner if I didn't live alone, but since I do, she's keeping me here until I meet certain criteria. Working up to those goals will take a full month, and according to the physical therapist, probably a lot longer. I could rent out my basement, I suppose, but I'm not sure how to properly interview a tenant from in here. And the thought of letting a complete stranger into my space when I'm not around – I don't know."

He tried to hide it, but his worry was plain to see. It created creases around his eyes and dulled them from their normal emerald color to a darker smoky green. Of its own volition, a plan started to form in her thoughts and take shape.

Maddie rose. "I should probably get going."

"I have a question first."

She waited.

"What does Maddie stand for? Is it Madison?"

She shook her head.

"Madelyn?"

Again she shook her head.

"It's not," he asked with a wince, "short for Madonna, is it?"

Maddie couldn't help but laugh then. "Thank goodness, no. I never would have lived that down growing up."

"I'm all out of guesses," he said. "What will it take to get you to tell me what it stands for?"

"Coffee."

"Coffee?"

"When you get out of this hospital, you can buy me one of those fancy expensive coffees, and I'll tell you my name." Her ears had to be playing tricks on her. Had she asked him out on a *date*?

Holden watched her for a beat. She waited for him to decline the offer or apologize for the misunderstanding. Instead, he winked at her. "You've got a deal. Coffee for Nurse Maddie."

Relief swept through her, brushing her inadequacies aside. What was it about him that put her so off-kilter? "If I'm going to call you Holden, then you've got to drop Nurse."

"Hm, what should I call you then?"

"Just Maddie, I think."

His eyes twinkled. "Fair enough."

She rose to leave, but when she started to walk away, he pseudo-whispered, "*Psst*, Maddie."

She peeked at him over her shoulder.

"Next time you come, bring me something to eat."

She chuckled and called out, "I'll see you tomorrow," as she slipped out the cafeteria door.

Six

Holden let the music of Maddie's soft laughter wash over him.

I don't know what You're up to here, Lord, but I'm pretty sure I'm in over my head. Guide my path.

"Hey, Mr. Jenkins, did your lady friend abandon you here?" Burt stood there, hands on hips, affronted on his behalf.

"She had to go, and I think we were both too distracted to remember this isn't my room. Do you mind?"

"No problem." The orderly began wheeling Holden through the tables and chairs. "I don't ever mind doing something for them that's nice to me."

"I imagine you don't always get to meet people at their best, working in here."

Burt made a choking sound. "You puttin' it mildly."

"Sometimes it's hard to be gracious when you're in pain or afraid."

"Maybe so, but my ma taught me to treat people with respect no matter my situation. Not everyone learned that lesson. Some people are plain ol' mean. They're as mean the day they leave this place as they were the day they arrived."

Maddie's experience in foster care came to mind. "You're blessed to have a mother who taught you the difference between right and wrong, who wanted you to grow up to be a good man."

"Amen to that." Burt's familiar low voice rumbled. "You a believin' man, Mr. Jenkins?"

"That I am. I'm not sure how I'd handle my health issues if it weren't for the Lord reassuring me everything's going to work out."

"Ma drug me to church from the time I wore diapers. I got into some trouble when I was younger, ended up in the brig for a while, but Ma never gave up on me. Says she prayed me through it. I'll never be a doctor or lawyer or anything highfalutin, but I'm a deacon now, and that means a lot more to me than a fancy education ever could."

Back in his room, Holden used Burt as a brace as he struggled to stand after sitting so long. Once he got into his bed, he said, "I think your priorities are right on target. Take it from me, you can lose your health and your wealth in the blink of an eye. The things you do for God are the only things that can't be taken away."

"You speak truth there, Mr. Jenkins. I like the way you put that. I'm gonna remember them words." With the wheelchair safely parked in the corner on the other side of the nightstand, Burt shook Holden's hand. "I'm jus' about done for the day, but I'll see you tomorrow."

"See you tomorrow."

Holden was resting the next day when Maddie stepped through his door, her blond curls spilling across the strap of a bulky backpack slung over her shoulder. Odd as it sounded, sunshine followed her into the room.

She glanced at the other bed.

"Max is in OT for the next hour. We should have some peace and quiet for a while."

"Perfect." A muted thud landed the unwieldy pack on the bed beside his right knee.

"Do I want to know what's in there?" The last time she'd placed anything on his bed, it had been medical equipment. Not that he expected her to carry a pulse oximeter around in her backpack, but still...

Her infectious grin brightened the room. "I did the best I could. We'll see if I got it right."

The words barely penetrated. He was too busy soaking in the joy in her eyes.

She began taking items out of the backpack. First, she handed him a one-liter plastic bottle of diet soda.

"Wait!" Maddie's warning was lost, drowned out by the gurgle of carbonation squeezing itself out through the top of the bottle as he twisted the lid.

Holden sucked in a lungful of air between clenched teeth.

Thank goodness she hadn't brought him a bigger bottle. The wall behind him was covered in soda spray, the lid was who-knew-where, and his shirt was soaked.

On the bright side, she'd brought him a cold soda. Cold and sticky. Yeah. He was going to need a shower later.

That still wasn't his biggest concern, though. "Is everything you give me today going to be booby-trapped?"

"Uh, I may have dropped that one out in the parking lot before I stuffed it in my backpack. Be careful opening…" Her voice trailed off.

Was she joking with him? Studious Nurse Maddie, who took him so seriously she often missed his jokes?

"Duly noted. I don't suppose you could hand me a clean shirt from the cabinet?" He indicated a small wardrobe built into the wall across the room. Life would be easier if he could hop out of bed and get it himself. He was a long way from hopping anywhere, though.

Maddie bustled over and retrieved a white t-shirt for him. All he had were white t-shirts, the kind his grandfather used to wear, courtesy of the Ladies' Auxiliary.

Once he tugged the outdated top on, she reached into the cumbersome pack again and withdrew a large bag from BBE – Best Burgers Ever. "I wasn't sure what you liked on yours, so I got all the fixings and assumed you were man enough to pick off whatever you don't want. Without whining. The condiments are on the side, though. Picking off mustard is tricky." With that, she passed him an intimidating burger.

His eyes rounded as he took the mammoth meatwich from her. He stretched his thumb and fingers apart to mimic the height of the tower. This was a carnivore's feast, pure and simple. "I'm not sure it'll fit." His sigh was unadulterated delight. "You're an angel, that's what you are. I think I might just cry with gratitude."

He opened his mouth wide and moved his lower jaw from right to left a couple of times. "Calisthenics. You know, for the coming workout."

Maddie's laughter pirouetted through the room. "You'd best gobble it down before Max gets back."

"Are you kidding me? A burger like this deserves to be savored." With clumsy hands, he unwrapped it and applied some of the condiments. Railing against the injustice of how a virus in his spine could affect the nerves that controlled his hands would do no good. He'd already tried. So he bowed his head and offered up a silent prayer of thanksgiving for Maddie and the meal.

When he took his first bite he groaned. "Life can't get any better than this." One shoulder lifted. "Aside from the whole wheelchair thing."

"If that's how you feel..." Her hand disappeared once again into the backpack, this time pulling out a bag full of fries. "Skinny cut, fried to perfection, and salted enough to make you beg for more..."

Holden's gaze shot hurriedly around the room until he pointed to a far corner. "Grab that table. And tell me you brought yourself something to eat, too."

"I ate earlier." She pulled the adjustable table close and settled it across the bed so he could set his food and drink somewhere other than his lap.

"At least snack on some fries."

"I think I can manage that." Snagging a couple of the fried-to-perfection spuds from the brown bag, she said, "I almost got you a milkshake, too, but decided I shouldn't promote gluttony. This being your first day with real honest-to-goodness sustenance and all."

Holden's burger was half gone when he glanced up at her. "You seem different today."

"I do?"

She most definitely did. Her laugh came more easily. Her eyes sparkled, and her shoulders weren't as tense. Her face was... open. Inviting, almost.

Something had definitely changed with Maddie, and whatever it was, it looked good on her.

Seven

"You seem different…"

Holden's words echoed in Maddie's head.

She didn't feel any different… did she?

Maddie was drawn to this man even as her good sense told her to turn tail and run. He saw into those parts of her that she tried to keep hidden, apparently including parts she didn't even see herself. In the past, she would have kept him at arm's length — or further — as a result. Yet somehow, with Holden everything was upside down, and she found herself wanting to get closer to him. But was it wise to let him know the effect he had on her? No, absolutely not.

"Maybe I'm wrong. You appear to be more at-rest, though." His voice held the smallest trace of hesitation.

"Oh?" By far her most brilliant sentence to date. Not.

An eyebrow climbed northward as his head tipped imperceptibly to the side. He remained silent though, and she appreciated him all the more.

Maddie leaned back in her chair and propped her feet up on the frame of his bed. "You haven't seen me at my best. First, you experienced my extreme phobia of all animals not covered in fur. And then I was bawling my eyes out because we lost a patient. Not spectacular as far as first impressions go. Generally I'm a pretty happy person. I love what I do, I enjoy being of use to others, and I like to find things worth laughing about." Okay, so that last part was a bit of a stretch. She wasn't quite known for her laughter. Competence, yes. Good humor, not so much.

The empty wrapper on his table screamed for attention, and her jaw dropped. "What happened to relishing your burger?"

Holden cast his eyes at the pseudo-table then back up at Maddie. "I did not eat that whole thing already... Did I?"

"Of course not. There's no way that's called eating. You crossed the threshold into devouring."

"Hm..." His eyes swung to his fries. "You'd better get them now if you want any more. I can't be held responsible for my actions once I take that first bite."

She flexed her hand and snagged a few more. "So tell me, Holden, can you work from Lakeview?"

He studied her, his eyes asking for an explanation.

"I thought about what you said about your business, and I wondered if you can write proposals or do any of your other architecty stuff from in here. I realize you can't bring a drafting table in, but are there things you can do to help keep your company afloat until you're able to physically return to your office?"

"Some things, yeah, but I wouldn't be comfortable having my laptop here. Something might happen to it if I left it in my room. I don't have a place to lock it up when I go to therapy, the cafeteria, or anywhere else. That's too big a hazard."

She nodded. "I considered that, which is why I brought this today." Maddie pulled her laptop from the depths of her backpack. "I set up a profile for you. The password is Toad with a capital T. I'm not sure what all you can do, but I thought you might at least be able to check your email. I'll take it with me when I leave."

Diving back into the bag, she pulled out a tangle of cords. "I've got the adapter in case the battery gets low, but I also brought a collection of miscellaneous phone chargers I had in my junk drawer. Don't ask me why I trade in cell phones but keep the old chargers. Hopefully one of these will fit your phone. If not, give me the model information, and I'll get you a charger before I come back again next time."

His stunned expression never left her backpack. "Magical *and* bottomless."

Someone got up on the hokey side of the bed. "Yeah, I saw the movie, too."

Brow arched high, he shook his head. "Uh-uh. You can't be old enough for that one."

"Neither can you."

Once Holden finished his fries, she wiped his table-tray down and set the computer in front of him with a flourish. "Ta-da! Here's the adapter, too." With a sense of accomplishment, she sat back down and pulled out her little tablet, relaxed.

When she became aware of Holden's eyes on her, she looked up. His gaze was serious, his voice sincere. "Thank you, Maddie. I mean it."

A nod acknowledged his words, and he went on to boot up the computer.

Dismissing him and burying herself in an e-book should have been easy, but the way he'd spoken to her wouldn't be let go. With a few simple syllables, he'd made her feel precious. An unfamiliar sensation curled through her belly.

Holden started tapping away at the keyboard. Maddie, too distracted to read, switched to a mindless game instead. At least it would pass the time.

EIGHT

Holden began rubbing his eyes. Maddie asked, "Did you get much accomplished?"

He yawned. "Over a month has passed since I last checked my email. I spent more time today clearing out junk than anything else. I managed to shoot a couple of replies to people who'd asked for bids. Other than that, it was all housekeeping."

"What if they've since found someone else?" She hit on one of his fears without even trying.

"Hopefully they'll answer and say so. I told them I'd been out sick and would get back to them in more detail within the week. I'd hate to waste time and resources putting together a proposal for a job I have no chance of getting. It's the risk I run with every bid. I think about it differently now because energy is so precious — I no longer possess it in abundance. The industry standard doesn't change because of my situation, though. My priorities are what need to be adjusted."

"What's on your schedule for the next two days?"

Head resting against the pillow, Holden allowed himself the luxury of planning — something he hadn't dared attempt since he was first hospitalized. "I'm going to push myself in therapy and make some real progress. I'm getting stronger, but walking is still hard. The muscles in my lower back are weak, which is causing me more trouble than anything else. Tomorrow I'll get on the phone and talk to my assistants so I can bring them into the loop about what I'm going to do from here to keep things afloat. If they haven't already jumped ship on me."

He opened his eyes. The laptop had been replaced by a bar of chocolate and a bag of marshmallows.

"What will you do if they're gone?" She pulled a package of graham crackers out of her backpack, too.

"I can get someone new to help with the administrative stuff, or stumble along without anyone for a while. If I lose my drafting assistant, I'll be in a tight spot, possibly an impossible one. I can't put in the long hours over the drafting table like I used to. I'm not even sure how long I'll be able to sit at a desk and do my drafting on the computer. I don't want to borrow trouble, though. I'll wait until I speak with them."

"Have you talked to them at all since you were hospitalized?" Bamboo skewers and two tea light candles joined the other items.

He shook his head. "I left a lengthy message for each of them when I was first admitted, but I haven't spoken to them since. I had no idea what the future held. How on earth could I instill confidence or motivate them to follow me when I believed I'd be leading them straight off a cliff? That was just the first few days, but then I was too sick to be aware of much of anything, let alone capable of making business calls. By the time I was aware of my surroundings, my phone was dead and I had no way to contact them other than through the business number. I might have been depressed, too, which I'm pretty sure didn't help. I've called several times since I've been at Lakeview, but it goes straight to voicemail. I don't have their numbers memorized, and with my phone dead, I was stuck."

"It can't be good that no one's answering at the office." She pulled out a lighter and lit the candles, stuck a marshmallow on a stick, and handed it to him before opening the graham crackers and breaking the chocolate bar into manageable chunks.

"Is this wise?"

She grinned. "Probably not, but I won't tell if you don't."

Holden held his marshmallow over the small flame and hitched one shoulder. "I've tried not to be too doom-and-gloom about it, but I can't reach my employees, and nobody from the office has been banging my door down to reach me. All I've been able to do is keep it in prayer and trust the good Lord to have everything in hand."

Maddie frowned, and it wasn't any ordinary downturn of the lips. He'd only seen this particular expression twice before. Her mouth pulled down at the corners, her eyes took on a blank stare, and her jaw clenched. With a personality all its own, this frown was different than both her *I'm concentrating* and *I disagree* frowns.

He had to know… "Does it bother you when I talk about God?"

The easy-going atmosphere got sucked out of the room and vented into the great unknown. He had done a superb job of backing his guest into a corner she couldn't gracefully escape.

Holden scratched a nonexistent itch on his neck. "I didn't mean to put you on the spot. Maybe someday when I'm out of here, you and I can have a casual conversation about God." His marshmallow wasn't going to get as crispy black as he liked them, not with the tiny flame produced by the candle, but it was close enough, so he pulled it from its skewer and flattened it with the chocolate between two graham crackers.

She did the same with her marshmallow, but seemed to be using a bit more force than necessary to smash it.

"Not so I can preach at you, but so you can tell me what you believe. I'm interested in how you see things. Whatever you say, I'll respect your position. I don't promise to agree with you, but I won't go turning into some fire-and-brimstone preacher on you. Honest."

Maddie gave a defeated sigh and blew out the candles. "Okay. I suppose that's a fair enough request." The halo of gold that normally surrounded her pupils morphed into a dark color somewhere between brown and grey, as though it foretold a coming squall.

He had little doubt she was already trying to devise a way to avoid *that* conversation.

Nine

Two Weeks Later

Maddie put her purse and lunch up and went to scrub in. As she ran the brush over her knuckles, under her nails, and between her fingers, Holden came to mind. He'd been more discouraged the last couple of times she'd been to visit him. The light seemed to be disappearing from his eyes bit by bit. Watching February fade into March from behind the walls and windows of Lakeview hadn't done much for his disposition.

She dropped the scrub brush in the garbage pail and thrust her hands under the hot water. With a shake of her head, she put Holden out of her mind. Her attention needed to be on her patients today — her current patients.

A glance at the posted list brought a smile to her lips. Mr. Alvarado and a new patient, Mr. Williams, had been assigned to her. She went to find Rosie, the nurse she was relieving, to get the night report. This shift was going to be exceptional; she felt it in her bones.

After listening to the overnight report and conducting her preliminary exam of Mr. Williams, Maddie stepped into Mr. Alvarado's room for the same cursory inspection.

"Good morning, Mr. Alvarado. I hear you're doing better. Is it true, or is the rumor mill churning double-time?"

His smile was weak, but his color was much improved. "I'm breathing easier, even after the respiratory tech turned the oxygen down some. The doctors don't frown as much when they come around now, either."

"Sounds to me like a recipe for recovery. What do you think?"

He gave his head a single affirmative nod. "My wife wanted me to live, so I'm doing my best. Funny thing is, she's usually right anyway. If not for her, I'd have given up days ago and would be gone from this world by now."

"We all need something to live for. Family's not a bad place to start."

The nurse who'd been watching Maddie's patients for her while she was at lunch caught her in the hallway. "Mr. Williams' O2 sats and heart rate dropped some. Not enough to set off any alarms, but enough to inform the resident."

Maddie nodded. "Thank you."

She speed-walked the rest of the way so she could conduct her own assessment.

Stepping into the room, she said hello to his wife before using her stethoscope so she could listen to Mr. Williams' heart and lungs. He remained unconscious, but out of habit — and as a matter of courtesy — she still told him what she was doing. "This might be cold, but it'll be over in a second."

"Is everything okay?"

A glance at Mrs. Williams revealed red-rimmed eyes and hands that fluttered about as if they didn't know where to land. Maddie wasn't prepared to respond to the question yet, so she asked one of her own. "How long have you two been married?" She took in the woman's shiny silver hair, no doubt set by curlers, and the wrinkled white linen pants and matching jacket.

"Over forty years now." The woman replied with a smile, but her bottom lip quivered. "Is something wrong?"

Maddie had completed enough of her assessment to answer. "Your husband isn't processing oxygen as efficiently as we'd like, and his heart rate is a little lower than before. The doctor's going to come by and examine him. I'm listening for anything audible to explain this new development." She moved her stethoscope and listened again, but other than a slight crackle, she detected no change in Mr. Williams' lungs.

His wife stood by with wide eyes. "Is he going to be okay?"

Her husband's injuries were severe, and there was a fine line between giving people hope and giving them false hope. Their gazes locked. "We're doing everything we can to make sure you get to celebrate your fiftieth together."

Just then, Mr. Williams' heart rate plummeted, causing the equipment to alarm. Maddie hustled to the door. "I've got a Brady in here!" Without taking her eyes off the monitors, she strode to the supply cart and quickly began opening drawers and pulling out alcohol pads, syringes, and anything else she thought the doctor might need. Adrenaline pumped through her veins as she mentally ran through the treatment scenarios.

While she carried out her task, she kept her voice calm and matter-of-fact. "Your husband is bradycardic. That means his heart rate is lower than it should be. We don't want it to stay too low for very long because that can cause lasting problems. So we're going to take action to get his heart back up to a healthy rate." A quick glance told her Mrs. Williams was barely listening. The woman was almost the same color as her outfit, and tears coursed down her cheeks.

Dr. Sage was the intensivist — the teaching doctor overseeing the unit — on duty for the week. He raced into the room with two residents on his heels. His gaze went immediately to the screen showing the patient's vitals. "BP's falling, too. Same with his O2 saturation."

Within seconds, Mr. Williams coded. The alarm was sounded, a Code Blue blaring across the intercom system. Dr. Sage and the residents worked furiously to save him. They followed all the proper steps, administered the right medications, and fought to bring him back.

Maddie ignored the clenching of her own heart and slammed the door on the fear that tried to get in. Intensive Care wasn't the place people died. It was the place where they got better.

And her patient would prove it true.

He had to.

Mrs. Williams, thrust into a far corner of the room by the onslaught of traffic and no longer able to contain herself to quiet tears, sobbed openly. The respiratory tech tucked himself in at the head of the bed between Mr. Williams and the ventilator. The intensivist barked orders to the residents, Maddie, and the other nurses who came in to assist. Atropine, chest massage, defibrillation, epinephrine. At one point, Dr. Sage shoved a resident aside, abandoning his role as teacher, and performed CPR himself. It was with a haggard voice that he eventually called the time of death.

The fight for Mr. Williams' life seemed to go on forever and yet it ended all too soon.

People exited the room, faces gaunt and lips drawn in grim lines. Maddie walked over to Mrs. Williams and put her arms around the woman. "I'm so sorry for your loss." She held the older woman, offering the needed physical and emotional support so the heartbroken widow could walk over to the bed and say goodbye to the man she'd shared her life with for more than forty years.

This was the worst part of nursing. She'd known the job was one of highs and lows, but if she'd understood the pain of watching other people's grief first-hand, she might have chosen a different career field. By the time she had figured it out and realized the emotional toll the work would take on her, she was too in love with what she did to walk away.

Some days, though…

There were times when the thought of walking out those doors and never coming back resonated in her soul like the good idea she knew it wasn't.

A chaplain came and took Mrs. Williams from her care. A counselor from hospice was on the way up as well, to sit with and talk to her — or listen if needed — until one of her children could come for her.

Arlene Norval, the nursing director, stepped into the room and closed the door behind her. "Are you okay?"

Maddie grimaced at the intrusion. "I'm fine."

"You always say that, and I never believe you. Just tell me if you're okay to finish your shift."

"Mr. Alvarado is heading out to the floor shortly. If you need me to stay past that, I can."

"Let me check the intake report." Arlene paused before opening the door. "Stop by my office after he's settled in his new room, okay? I should know by then."

Maddie dipped her chin in response but didn't say anything. She began cleaning up the mess left by everyone's frantic attempts to save Mr. Williams. The janitorial staff would follow behind her to scrub and sanitize the room, but she couldn't stand idly by and wait. Keeping busy was as good an alternative as any. Besides, what else could she do with the time? Dwell on Mr. Williams' death? Or his widow's grief? No, thank you.

A short time later, someone from the morgue came up to collect him, and she helped move the deceased man from his hospital bed to the specialized gurney that would carry him to the basement.

Several tugs and grumbles passed until his sheet was straight and smooth. She couldn't do anything to alter Mr. Williams' outcome. He deserved dignity, though, and she would see he got it. He wouldn't leave her care looking sloppy. Speaking to her now lifeless patient, she told him, "I wish I'd been able to get to know you better." Then she watched as he was wheeled away.

Who was she kidding? He deserved a lot more than dignity. He deserved life.

Maddie needed to get a grip. The loss of a patient was always painful, but work was no place to express it. It'd never been a problem before, so why today? Why was this one hitting her so hard? Thinking back, she had to admit they'd been getting progressively more difficult the last several months. That knowledge did nothing to ease her heartache, though.

Maddie pressed her hands over her mouth until her lips were nearly bloodless, but even that couldn't hold back the keening moan.

Maddie waved goodbye to Mr. Alvarado before leaving his new room, where he was under the care of a floor nurse. When she arrived back at the ICU, she went directly to the nursing director's office.

"How are you doing?" Arlene swiveled her chair so her back faced the computer monitor. A bottle of dye kept her hair the color of honeyed ginger and fought against the age that shone in her eyes. Years of experience turned those brown eyes into pools of empathy.

"I'll be fine." Maddie forced the words out.

Arlene had an L-shaped desk, but she kept it tucked against the wall in a corner of the small office. It made the space more open, but it also meant visitors couldn't hide on the other side of a piece of furniture. Maddie, who would rather be left on her own and not coerced into discussing what happened, stood near the door.

"I believe we had this conversation already, didn't we?" Arlene indicated a chair despite Maddie's silence. "Take a seat. Let's talk."

She sank into the padded seat and considered the woman who was her boss and who had become, over the years, a sort of mentor to her. "I don't need to visit the shrink." She rebutted the question before it was posed.

"As you're aware, our census is down."

Maddie had heard the chatter. Fewer patients meant fewer nurses. People were worried about layoffs or being cut to part-time.

"I have a list of nurses who want more hours, hours that I can't give them." Arlene leaned forward.

Maddie frowned.

"You're not required to take time. Nobody's forcing you. But if you want a few days, I have a list of nurses who would jump at the chance to take your shifts."

Maddie thought about Holden and what he was going through, how discouraged he'd been lately. Even if his life didn't return to what it had once been, he was moving forward. He was getting healthier. Maybe it would do her good to invest her time in him for a while, to take a break from being in a place where people didn't always get better, where sometimes things went horribly wrong.

"Can I have sixty days?"

Arlene's eyes grew round. "That's a lot more than I had in mind when I said 'a few.'"

"I need to help someone out."

"We're not going to lose you, are we? It's not my intent to push you out."

Maddie gave her head a single shake. "I could use some downtime, and like you said, with the census down, now's a good opportunity. And I have the accrued time. I know it's short notice, but…"

Arlene sat back. "We've had more deaths on the unit in the last month than normal." Her face was drawn, her skin sallow. "I'm planning to ask one of the chaplains to come in and do an in-service or offer some counseling to gauge how the staff is doing. Not everyone handles it well." The woman reached out and touched Maddie's knee, drawing her attention. "Are you going to be okay to drive home?"

She nodded.

Arlene, who'd worked with her long enough to understand a bit about the way she functioned, offered a sympathetic smile. Grabbing a bag from off her desk, the older woman handed the crinkled brown paper to her. "Here."

Maddie lifted an eyebrow.

"You don't like to talk about it, but I need to do something to help. I bought one of every kind of chocolate in the vending machine. It might not be healthy, but if you insist on driving yourself home, I'd prefer you do so with this rather than wine."

Wine had never been one of her inclinations after a bad day. Chocolate, on the other hand… Yes, the nursing director had long ago discovered her poison.

Arlene tapped a finger against a floral wall calendar. "Sixty days, huh?"

"I'm asking a lot."

"Yeah, you are, but if I can make it happen for you, I will. As far as everyone else is concerned, though, I screamed bloody murder and chewed you up one side and down the other. Be creative."

A smile tugged at Maddie's lips. "I'll tell Sue you threatened to call security on me. By the time the story makes it around, it'll be so exaggerated people will dive for cover every time you walk into a room."

Arlene chuckled. "Fear has its proper place."

Maddie stood to go. The director rose, too, and wrapped her in a warm hug. "One of these days, my girl, you're going to have someone to go home to, and then I won't worry about you quite so much."

If she only knew what Maddie had in mind.

Ten

"Maddie, are you ever a welcome sight."

"Where's your roomie?"

"He got well enough to go home, or his insurance ran out — I'm not sure which. Someone new moves in tomorrow."

She offered Holden his coffee. After setting her own drink down, she slid her fingers into her jacket pocket and pulled something else out. "I picked this up at a vending machine. It's not a burger, but I had other things on my mind and forgot about food."

Reaching for the candy bar, his hand brushed hers. "You might just be the sweetest nurse I've met." Then, rolling his eyes, he added, "I don't always hear the puns until they come out of my mouth. Let me put it this way. You can bring me candy anytime."

"Uh…"

"I'm making it worse, aren't I?"

She nodded.

Opening the drawer by his bed, he dropped the treat in. "I'll save it for later and, with any luck, save myself from further embarrassment."

"Sounds like a good plan." She sat down and stretched her legs out, crossing them at the ankles, as she took in the white room. It was austere enough to make the hospital look like a five-star resort. The boxy wall-mounted television was the room's only luxury, and it looked like a good sneeze would bring it tumbling to the ground.

"So tell me about work. How were the last two days?"

She shrugged. "What's the word on going home?"

His head sank into his pillow. "I hate it here. When I was in the hospital, I was too sick to be aware of much. Where I was, what was happening around me — it's all blurry until that last day or two in ICU. In here, though, I get two hours of therapy each day, but those are things I could do at home. The rest of the time, I sit around accomplishing nothing. My brain is rotting." He didn't bother to tell her how much those two hours hurt or how much pain he was in for hours afterward.

His hands tightened in frustration. "I need to get my business back on solid footing, too, but much as using your laptop helps, I can't bring in new business if I can't complete the jobs, and that's just not something I can do from in here. The doc says at least three weeks before they let me go home, and that's an…" Hands in the air, he made quotation marks with his fingers. "…optimistic estimate."

Was that relief on Maddie's face?

"What are the biggest hurdles to them letting you leave rehab?"

"Climbing the stairs. They want me to be able to do that and all these other exercises without getting fatigued."

"Do you feel like you have more stamina now than when you were first transferred here?"

He shrugged. "The muscles in my back are weak. I'd hoped that was the biggest cause of my problems." Had she noticed how he'd been clenching his right hand into a fist and releasing it? Holden forced his hand to relax. "Those muscles are getting stronger, but the pain still won't release its iron grip, and now I'm feeling a new sensation. A pinching, shooting, deep-down twinge different from the muscle ache. I'm not sure how else to describe it."

"Does your doctor have any idea what's causing it?"

"I still have swelling along my spinal cord, and the MRI shows what they think is a signal interruption. Basically, the weak muscles are part of my trouble, but something else is still going on with my spinal cord, spinal column, or whatever you want to call it. All anybody will tell me is that my body needs time and it may be years before we understand the full extent of…yadda, yadda, yadda."

Maddie frowned at him. "And in the meantime?"

"In the meantime, I have to stay here and continue with therapy."

"There's no way around that? They won't let you do outpatient therapy?"

He shook his head. "Because I live by myself, no."

"What if I stayed with you?"

Whoa. Where had that come from? "I can't ask you to do that."

"I lost a patient yesterday." She gulped. "It got me to thinking. I'm taking some time off work to regroup and recharge."

Knowing how upset she'd been after someone else's patient had died, he couldn't imagine how she'd handled the death of one of her own.

She sat up and clapped her hands down onto her knees. "Anyway. I took sixty days off, and I'd like to use them to help get you home and on your feet. I'm not licensed for home health care, so it would be an informal arrangement."

Disbelief, anxiety, and hope froze his tongue.

Maddie must have mistaken his silence for something else entirely, because her professional nurse mask fell abruptly into place. "I'm not getting into a religious discussion with you, but I will say this: Are you worried about what God thinks or about what people think? Anybody who's spent more than two minutes with you knows you're no threat to me.

Even if you wanted to, which I doubt you do, you're not physically capable of being up to no good. Furthermore, if you live the kind of life where that's the first thing people suspect, you're not the man I thought."

She stood and drained the last of her coffee then threw the empty cup in the garbage. Her hands were fisted at her sides, and he needed to find the right words.

Lord, what am I supposed to do? It's a perfect solution, but what will my family… Okay, forget I said that. She's right. I need to worry about what You think and not what people think. I could sure go for a generous dose of wisdom right about now. And if You've got one, I'd love a vaccination to prevent future episodes of foot-in-mouth disease…

"I don't have any way to pay you. At least, not yet."

She waved his concern away. "I'm not worried about it. We'll work something out."

Holden bit his bottom lip. He wanted to argue, to tell her that wasn't good enough… but he couldn't. This was his chance, possibly his only chance, to get out of rehab. Even if it meant taking advantage of Maddie, could he afford to say no? "I accept your offer. But tell me, how do you plan to convince the doctor to let me go?"

"Leave it to me. You know I have a cat, though, right? Fishy's part of the deal."

"The cat's fine." Holden grasped the laptop she held out to him. "You're different from most women."

"Just how many women have been in and out of your life?" An arched eyebrow accompanied her words.

"Not many." He shrugged.

She laughed. "How can you get to be as old as you are and have so little experience with the female of the species?"

"Who are you calling old?" Not giving Maddie a chance at a comeback, he continued. "Small town. Plus, I have four sisters and two sisters-in-law. They're enough to scare any sane man away from women for life."

Chuckling, she held out the adapter to him before settling back into her chair to read. "You're one-of-a-kind, too, Holden Jenkins. That's all I can say."

He booted up the computer and began sorting his way through email again, a renewed purpose burning in his gut.

The morning quickly slipped by. The time had almost come for Holden to go to his next round of therapy when the doctor walked in. Dr. Demir was a tiny little slip of a woman and, as he'd told Maddie, looked like she was barely out of pigtails.

"Mr. Jenkins, you asked to see me. Is anything wrong?"

He saw no point in dancing around the subject. Besides, his tango was a little rusty. Or was she more of a foxtrot doctor? "I have someone to stay with me while I recover." A head-tilt in Maddie's direction indicated who he was talking about. "Can I go home now?"

Dr. Demir tapped her foot. "Now, Mr. Jenkins, we've been over this. You need appropriate care and supervision. Home nursing would be more suitable to your needs, but your insurance won't pay for it. Plus you still have a significant amount of rehabilitation to complete before you're capable of being on your own. Not to mention the fact that your transverse myelitis has been classified as idiopathic. All the tests were inconclusive and we have no idea what caused it. What if something in your home causes a relapse? You need a skilled professional with you who can handle something like that."

Maddie stood and held out her hand to the doctor, who reluctantly shook it. "I'm a nurse."

Holden bit back a smile at her take-charge voice.

"I've worked ICU the past eight years and can provide references if you require them. I am taking a leave of absence to stay with Mr. Jenkins. I'm qualified to oversee his medication, make sure he is doing his rehab, and transport him to any necessary appointments. Remaining in here will cost him his business and eventually his house. If that happens and he gives up, he has little chance of improvement. Recuperation from any illness is about a lot more than the physical steps needed, wouldn't you say, Doctor? Patients need to be encouraged and motivated as well. You can't strip a man of everything he's worked his entire life to build and expect him to fight for his recovery. There is latitude for personal judgment in these matters, isn't there?"

Maddie didn't raise her voice. She kept it professional and crisp, matching the manner and tone of the doctor who now inspected them both with studious disdain. Holden refrained from singing halleluiah when Maddie began reciting her qualifications and the doctor's eyes widened. For the first time in too long, gaining the advantage became a possibility. Never mind that his health and life were under discussion and that getting care on his terms shouldn't feel like an unrelenting battle to climb the Matterhorn.

He mentally shrugged off the remaining potentiality — that he was wrong to push so hard for release...

"Fine, Mr. Jenkins, I will take this into consideration. You," she said, pointing to Maddie, "need to provide me with at least two references and a sworn affidavit saying you will be present to supervise and assist the patient. I need proof this is not some ploy to get him out of here with the intent of abandoning him to his own devices once he's home."

It was as though Maddie sensed victory, too, for she softened her voice from drill-sergeant nurse to respectful-compliant nurse. "I have those references right here." She reached into her backpack and withdrew two envelopes. "One is from the ICU Nursing Director who hires, schedules, and reviews the staff. She's my direct supervisor. The other is from one of the ICU intensivists." She handed the letters over. "I didn't realize I would need an affidavit. I wrote a letter, though, stating what I would be doing for Mr. Jenkins." She pointed to her signature on the document. "Will that suffice?"

Burt walked in, his usual smile in place. He nodded a greeting in Maddie's direction and to the doctor before glancing at the bed's occupant. "I was told to come collect you. Is this a good time?"

Holden waved him in. "It's fine. I think they'd rather talk without me in the room anyway." Then he moved himself to the edge of the bed and, without any help from the orderly, stood and got himself into the wheelchair.

The move — pushing his limits to prove he could take care of himself — was a risky one. He kept his face averted from the doctor so she wouldn't witness the toll the action took on him. Maddie saw, though, and the intensity of her gaze scorched all the way to his bones.

"You shouldn't have pushed yourself so hard when your physician was here."

He glowered in reply.

She shook her head. "It's a good thing I'm a fast talker."

Certain he'd been condemned to life in rehab indefinitely, Holden hesitated. "Did she...?"

"She's filling out the paperwork and says we might be able to get you out of here by nightfall."

Either he was going home or Maddie was trying — badly, he might add — to joke with him. "You did your best. I appreciate the effort." It couldn't hurt to test his theory.

"Uh..." She glanced over her shoulder at the empty doorway. "Who are you talking to?"

"There was no chance Dr. Demir would agree, but it means a lot to me that you were willing to try."

Maddie rested the back of her hand against his forehead. "Huh. Your temperature seems fine. Maybe you overdid it more than I realized."

Butterflies started tap-dancing in his stomach and fluttering up into his chest. She'd done it. She'd really done it. He was going home.

"I've got most of your stuff moved out to my car. I think one more trip ought to about do it."

"You're packing for me?" That came out louder than he'd meant it to, but what could he say? If she was packing, then she'd been in his drawers. Should he explain that the tighty whities were all from the Ladies' Auxiliary and weren't his preferred style, especially in such varied sizes?

"Unless you think you're in good enough shape to do it yourself. Keep in mind — you don't own a suitcase — at least not one that's here."

She bustled about the room as he tried to think of something to say.

"I didn't want to leave the computer here while going back and forth to the parking lot, so I kept it with me."

"I'm going home."

Maddie stopped what she was doing and gave Holden a goofy grin.

Even in light of his joy, he couldn't help the question. "Doctors don't usually change their minds this fast, do they?"

Before he second-guessed himself out of his joy, she cut him off. "Not normally, so let's be content and not give her reason to change it back."

She drew his attention with a tap to his arm. "Don't ask me to pinch you, okay? Just trust me."

For days he'd been asking God to get him out of this place. Was this an answer to prayer? No other explanation made sense. Dr. Demir didn't take kindly to having her authority questioned. If anything, when Maddie had pushed for his release, the good doctor should have become more resistant to the idea just as she'd done every time *he'd* brought it up with her. Either the Almighty had stepped in on his behalf, or Lakeview's doctor was so fed up with him that she couldn't wait to push him off onto Dr. Matthews, his primary care physician. As long as she sent him home, he wasn't sure he cared why.

Maddie's back was to him, her arms full and one foot out the door, when Holden spoke. "Thank you. I mean it. I owe you more than I can ever repay." He held himself back from a dramatic declaration of how she'd saved his life or an offer to name his firstborn after her. Every word, though, had come straight from his heart.

She didn't look back or acknowledge hearing him, but Maddie's step stuttered as she exited, adding a little extra bounce to her golden curls. She'd heard him. He'd bank on it.

Eleven

With a fistful of paperwork and documentation for all the prescriptions they needed to pick up, Maddie and her new patient headed toward the exit.

Burt insisted on taking Holden to the car and getting him settled. "Now, Mr. Jenkins, you do what this nice young lady here tells you."

The urge to snort was hard to resist. Nobody had called her a young lady in more years than she remembered.

"You got to take care of yourself, yessirree," the orderly went on. "One day, when you're walking around fit as a fiddle, you come back here and show off for all the nurses and doctors. They need to be reminded that what they do matters."

"I'll remember to do that."

After situating Holden in her car, Burt shook his hand and delivered his parting words. "I'll be prayin' for you, man. God's got great things in store for you, I jus' know it."

Maddie climbed behind the wheel and snapped her seatbelt into place. Checking her rearview mirror, she started the car. Their to-do list ran through her mind as she backed out of the ergonomically slanted parking space. "I asked them to call your prescriptions in to a little pharmacy I know. Next door to it is a durable medical equipment place. The owner of the equipment shop is waiting for us. Normally they'd be closed by now, but I called in a favor, and he's got a wheelchair and walker for you."

"I don't have my wallet. How am I going to pay for this stuff? Or provide insurance information? I can't. At least not today."

"Lakeview sent your insurance info to the pharmacy for me. As far as the equipment goes, I'll cover the deposit tonight." She cast a glance his way and caught him tugging at the chestnut hair at the nape of his neck. "You'll call him tomorrow with your provider, group number, and all that good stuff. He'll let us know after that if we owe anything more or if I'm due a refund. And don't worry. I'll submit all my receipts to you for reimbursement." She threw in a wink for good measure.

To avoid any possible argument from Holden, she quickly went on to get the rest said. "By the way, the wheelchair is a rental. They'll apply your rental fee toward the purchase if you decide to buy one within sixty days. The walker is a keeper, but I'm getting you a good one."

He started to protest, but she cut him off. "I promised the doctor I'd insist you use it everywhere — including in the house — until your therapist says otherwise. It comes with a padded seat, too, so if you get tired or want to rest, you'll have a soft place to park your posterior. Make sure you engage the brake first, though." Maddie shuddered to think what would happen if the walker rolled out from under him when he tried to sit.

Silence — the comfortable kind — surrounded them as she drove until, seemingly out of the blue, Holden asked, "What does PRN mean, anyway? The nurse said it a lot when she was going over discharge instructions. I heard it in the hospital, too."

"Per Request or Need." She waggled her hand in the space between them. "In my mind, at least. It's actually Latin. A lot of medical terms are. PRN means *pro re...* Hm. *Pro re* something. In nursing school, we memorized a bazillion letter codes for different procedures, medications, conditions, and more. I made up words to go with the letters so I could remember them easier. The Latin basically translates to *as needed*, but I still think of it as Per Request or Need."

"So which of my meds are PRN, then?"

"The ones for pain. There's two of them. You may experience more tenderness than usual the first couple days because you'll be trying to do more, and you won't be able to control your environment as much. Even now, riding along in the car, I'm sure every bump I hit in the road is painful for you."

Holden's expression confirmed she wasn't far from the truth.

She shook her head at his refusal to answer out loud before continuing with her explanation. "One makes you drowsy. The other one, not so much. They work in different ways, too. We'll figure out which one is best at controlling the worst of the pain for you."

"Did you ask her if I'm going to be like this for the rest of my life?"

Her voice matter-of-fact, Maddie answered, "There's a high probability you'll endure at least a measure of lifelong pain. I think, however, doctors sometimes forget the basics of life. Once you get back into the swing of things and something besides every twinge and spasm is occupying your mind, the soreness you're suffering won't seem as significant. That's just my opinion, and I could be wrong, but sitting in bed with nothing to do but think about how much you're hurting — it's not exactly conducive to pain management. Know what I mean?"

"Do you think I'll ever get past it — the pain? You know, enough to not have to make every decision based on how much it's going to hurt. I had hoped that once I built up the strength in my back muscles again, the rest of my problems would fade away. They aren't, though. I can't help but wonder…" He shook his head. "Nobody seems to appreciate how much it hurts, and I can't help but wonder if it's going to be like this for the rest of my life."

She could hedge. She *wanted* to hedge. That wouldn't be fair to him, though. Holden was asking her because he wanted a real answer. "You'll likely experience it in some measure for the rest of your life, and if that's the case, you need to get used to it and find a way to deal with, minimize, and work around it. Whatever it takes. You can't let the discomfort — no matter how severe — stop you from living."

"I still don't understand why I'm in so much pain. It's not like I had a limb amputated."

Maddie switched lanes as she considered what she should say. "I've done some reading up on Transverse Myelitis recently. A third of patients have some measure of lifelong pain or dysfunction."

"And the other two thirds?"

"Another third recovers fully, and the other third spend the rest of their lives much worse off than you are right now."

His sigh filled the small car. "So I should be thankful."

"That's not for me to say."

"How long does your research tell you recovery should take?"

Maddie mentally ran through the different data she'd gathered before answering. "Most of what I read said that within three months of the acute phase, you will likely be recovered as far as you're going to recover, but even that's not absolute."

"Mine was subacute. Does that matter?"

"The subacute just means it came on slowly rather than suddenly. You still had an acute phase, mostly back when you were in the ICU."

"So three months…"

Holden had been in the ICU for about a week and a half before Maddie had him as a patient that one day. As she ran through the calendar in her mind, she realized he was coming up on three months from when he'd been admitted. He had to be running the same numbers in his head. "I'm not sure exactly how long your acute phase lasted, but I'd say that you've got another month before you need to invest too much time in doom and gloom."

"You really think my being at home will help? I mean, I know I'll feel better mentally and all, but do you really think it'll help physically?"

"I think a person's physical health is closely tied to their emotional and mental health, and that you can never underestimate the power of being in a place where you feel comfortable and at ease. Good things can happen."

Twelve

"Can I ask you something?" The sound of traffic surrounded them as Holden questioned her.

Maddie deftly steered her car through the rush hour. "Sure. What's on your mind?"

"Do you make a habit of moving in with strange men?" There were a hundred better ways to have asked that.

She threw him a look that made him wince. The golden threads in her hazel eyes turned dark, giving her an air of intensity that would have frightened a lesser man. He wasn't the only one who'd noticed his poor choice of words.

"No, not usually, but I don't think you'll bite. If I'm wrong, I'm pretty sure I can outrun you and make my escape."

The playful sparkle in her eyes softened the words, but still... "Ouch."

She turned in to a mostly vacant parking lot as she said, "You're an odd fellow, Holden Jenkins."

What could he do but shrug? "One of the many things guaranteeing I'd never fit into small town life. In high school I was even voted Most Likely to Run Away From Home."

She snorted. "I'll bet that makes a great pick-up line when you're trying to get a woman to give you her number."

"Come on, don't leave me hanging. You had to be voted something, too. What was it? Most Likely to Save Lives?"

Resignation in her voice, she answered, "Most Likely to Kill in Self-Defense. As if *that* should ever be the thing high school students aspire to."

"Hm. I think yours makes the better pick-up line."

Her chuckle was exactly the response he was hoping for.

Holden waited in the car while Maddie collected the wheelchair and walker, as well as the prescriptions. He needed to call Miles and let him know what was going on. His drafting assistant had been amenable to the idea of working out of Holden's house rather than an office. Now that he was going home, he needed to let Miles know it was time to make that transition.

That call would need to wait, though. Leaning his head back against the headrest, Holden silently admitted he was in considerably more agony than he'd ever been in while at Lakeview.

Am I doing the right thing, Lord? Was I wrong when I thought Your intervention got me released? It all made sense at the time, but this pain is unbearable. How much am I supposed to suffer?

A blast of frigid water in the face would have stunned him no less than his own words. Breath locked in his chest, he squeezed the armrest until his fingers became numb and his thoughts coherent. How could he complain about his own aching body when Jesus had suffered so much more for him? Self-pity was turning him into a selfish man.

Holden stared sightlessly out the window until Maddie crossed his line of sight. Then he followed her with his gaze and watched as she herded the walker and wheelchair across the vacant asphalt lot, and he realized something. He needed to focus more on being grateful.

You've given me much, Lord. An eternity to look forward to is only the tip of the iceberg. You brought someone into my life to help me during this time. Not to mention a family that, though far away, daily lifts me up in prayer. Next time I'm tempted to whine, tell me to put a sock in it.

Maddie's phone rang as she got into the car. Holden didn't intend to eavesdrop, but her seat *was* only inches away. He couldn't avoid hearing her end of the conversation even if he was gentleman enough to try. Which was questionable at the moment.

"Hey, Tom… Helping a friend… Um… Not entirely." Whoever the guy was, he said a mouthful at that point. She forced her way back into the now one-sided discussion. "I'm in the middle of something. Can we talk tomorrow?" Tom took over the exchange again, forcing Maddie to cut him off. "This isn't a good time… Of course… Yes… You make a cute mother hen… Yep, see you later."

Not that it should matter to him, but he'd assumed there wasn't anyone special in her life. Conversational inspiration struck him. "A friend?"

Maddie concentrated on traffic and pulled out from the parking lot. A couple blocks later, as he decided she had no intention of answering, she spoke. "Tom's more than a friend."

Should he ask how serious they were? What if she needed time off to spend with him? What to say, what to say?

"Oh."

Thirteen

"...more than a friend."

Good grief. What was she thinking? Maddie couldn't believe her words. If she could capture and swallowed them back down, she would. Now Holden had the completely wrong idea about her and Tom. If she went out of her way to explain it, though, then he'd think she had an agenda, a reason for not wanting him to get the wrong idea about her and Tom.

She punched the accelerator with a bit more force than usual as the light turned green.

And how would she explain Tom's presence the next day? *Hey, this is Tom. He wanted to check you out and make sure you're not a homicidal maniac.*

Holden had enough to deal with right then. He didn't need to deal with her temporary bout of social ineptitude on top of everything else. At least, she hoped it was only temporary.

Distracted by her wandering thoughts, she almost missed the freeway onramp she needed.

Tomorrow's meeting would either be funny or disastrous. Knowing her luck, it would be the latter.

Courtesy of an accident on the Beltway, darkness fell and the dashboard clock's amber glow announced the time at a quarter to ten before they got to Holden's house. It had a modest front yard that set it back from the street. The neighboring houses were close in a built-in-the-sixties kind of way, not a modern type of close where you couldn't even fit a lawn mower between properties.

Maddie pulled into the driveway and studied the cement path to the front door — and the three steps in between the two. The steps would be no problem with the chair. Her gut, though, told her he would insist on climbing them.

"Give me the walker. I can make it. Leave the wheelchair in the car."

She ignored him — something she was getting good at — and removed the wheeled contraption from her trunk.

His voice sizzled as he bit out the words. "I can do this."

With a quick stride, she moved around the side of the car and stood in front of his door, blocking his exit and casting his eyes in shadow, turning them the color of moss. "I'm not Burt. You fall while going up those steps, and I will try to save you, but I won't be able to. I'll end up hurt. Is that

124

what you want? And if I'm too injured to offer the physical support Dr. Demir seems to think you need, she might pressure you back into rehab."

She'd first thought it was ego, and she'd wanted to bite back. Staring down at him in the car's front seat, though, she saw the raw truth. Whether he admitted it to himself or not, fear had a solid grip on Holden. Maybe it did boil down to ego — how he saw himself and how he viewed his own worth — but not in the way she'd first thought.

He might have faith in a God he couldn't see, but that faith hadn't castrated him of emotion. The man was terrified of what his future held, and that was something she could confront with compassion.

ourteen

Holden wanted to argue. With everything in him, he wanted to fight for the right to walk into his own home. His desire for independence was overriding his common sense and, it seemed, his common decency, too.

Maddie's face was somber and her normally flaxen hair was swallowed by the darkness until it, too, reflected her expression. "You want to take on the world. I get it, but can we please use the wheelchair to get you onto your porch and into the house? Once you're in the house, I'll put it back in my trunk, and you can have a heyday with the walker."

The plaintive tone in her voice snapped his conscience back into place. "Please? I'm exhausted and hungry. Can we just get inside?"

Could he be any more of a heel? Not today. Not if he could help it.

She quickly pulled the shiny metal wheelchair in close and braced herself against the car to assist him from the low seat. Once up, he turned around and sank into the chair.

He'd told himself that his walking would make things easier on Maddie. What a lie. Pride had consumed him, he'd sought to rail against everything that had become of his life, and he hadn't spared her a thought.

They approached the front of his house, and she deftly spun him so he faced the street and eased him up the steps with minimal effort. The ground came into sharp focus as it fell away beneath him, the concrete path and thorny bushes surrounded by jagged gravel and a couple of larger decorative rocks on either side.

Maddie was right. Even a small loss of balance, and he could hurt her. He was going to need to learn a new way of looking at things.

She locked the wheelchair into place with its brakes. "Please tell me you have a key."

"Uh…"

Maddie slapped her hand against her forehead. "Prescriptions, check. Walker, check. Wheelchair, check. Way to get into your home? I didn't even think to ask. I'm sorry."

"It's not a big deal, really."

"Do I need to call a locksmith, or do you have a friend with a spare key?"

Holden tried to twist around in the chair to see her, but she was lost in the shadows. "I keep a spare key hidden in a ceramic frog by my back door. If you climb up on top of the air conditioning unit on the side of the house, it's easy to get over the fence."

"Are you for real?"

He patted his chest and arms. "I think so. At least, I feel real, but I suppose if I wasn't real, I might think I was anyway."

"How long have you lived around here?"

"Four years. Long enough to build a business but not so long that I've lost my countrified ways."

"Did someone forget to tell you that only crazies hide keys? People are skilled at finding those. You're lucky the place hasn't been burglarized." That had to be the same voice she used to lecture patients on the importance of brushing their teeth. Compassionate and incredulous.

Holden shrugged. "I'm notorious for locking myself out. I had a choice. Put a key somewhere outside or put the locksmith on retainer."

She hopped off the side of his porch rather than try to get back by his wheelchair. "I'm still not convinced you're for real. If it turns out you're a closet serial killer, I don't want to be groomed as your partner or anything. Got it?"

"Yes, ma'am. I'll cancel the order for the serial killer training manual."

The sound of her shoes on the air conditioning unit was loud in the still night. She grunted as she pulled herself up over the fence. Then the muttering started. "It had to be a frog. Couldn't be a cute puppy, could it?"

Perhaps this wasn't the best time to tell her that his back yard was often populated with living, breathing frogs after dark. The less she knew, the better.

Lord, please let her find the ceramic frog and not accidentally reach for a live one.

The grate of the lock sounded behind Holden, and he breathed a sigh of relief. She'd let herself in the back door and come through the house.

Maddie released his brakes and said, "We need to have a discussion about your choice of key-concealing animals."

A jostle later, he was over the threshold and in his home once again. And somehow, being in a wheelchair when it happened didn't matter nearly as much as he'd thought it would. The relief of being home outweighed the manner of his arrival.

His new companion hustled around him and out the door. When she came back in with the walker, she waved a hand around. "Your house suits you. It's comfortable."

"Is that like saying it's *lived in* or *homey* and using those as euphemisms for *disaster* and *pig sty?*"

"Now you're putting words in my mouth." She chuckled. "I just meant it feels like it would be an easy place to relax. Some people's homes are uptight. Yours isn't."

She liked his home. This probably wasn't the best time to invite her to stay permanently, but still... The last time he'd had a woman over, she'd described it as *rustic* and had looked like she'd just stepped in a cow patty when she'd used the word.

The idea he'd been processing earlier settled further into his mind. He wouldn't be responsible for Maddie getting hurt. This new way of looking at things that he was going to have to figure out — it would have to include analyzing life not in terms of what he thought easiest, but rather in terms of what would be best for Maddie.

The idea ought to unsettle him, but instead, he found it satisfying.

IFTEEN

Once she brought him the walker, Maddie stood back and waited as Holden pulled himself to a standing position. The movement was awkward, but he'd have plenty of occasion to practice in coming days.

"What would you like to do first?" His home had been sitting empty long enough to need a good top-to-bottom scrub. If luck was on her side, he wouldn't notice anytime soon. The last thing he needed was to push himself too hard on his first night of freedom.

"I'm spent and would honestly like to go straight to bed. I have to take pills, though, and I assume that means I need to eat something first."

Bed sounded heavenly. She still wasn't entirely over Mr. Williams' death, and the comfort of sleep called to her. Duty came first, though. "Will you be more comfortable in the living room or at the dining room table?"

The dining area lay directly to the left of the front door and opened into the kitchen. To the right was the living room with the couch's back within arm's reach of where they stood. Straight ahead was an open hallway that led to the bedrooms, a bathroom, an office, and the laundry room. Maddie knew that much because the back door opened into the laundry room, and she'd had to come up the hallway to get to the front door.

"Definitely couch." The corner of his mouth twisted. "Although it'll probably be harder for me to get up afterward."

"I'm going to stand back and leave this up to you. The walker is a tool and should only go where you tell it to. Keep that in mind as you maneuver past the furniture. And speak up if you need help sitting down. Once you're seated, I'll fix some dinner. Dr. Demir had a couple of things…" Her words trailed off uncomfortably.

"Hm?" Holden worked his way around an end table.

She sighed. The bossy part of nursing someone was easier at the hospital, where the parameters were clearly defined. This new role would take some getting used to. "There are some things I need to discuss with you. The doctor gave me orders, and I don't think you're going to like them, but we should address everything before you go to bed."

"Mm." His concentration was focused on putting one foot in front of the other, not on listening to her.

Once Maddie returned from the car with Holden's things, she went to work fixing something for dinner. Rummaging through his cupboards, she settled on macaroni and cheese, only to realize the refrigerator was void of milk. "Okay," she told him, "I'm improvising for tonight, but we'll need to take a trip to get groceries tomorrow."

"How can I go to the store?" His defeated words tugged at her heart, but she locked her emotions away and pulled on a cloak of cheerfulness.

Dehydrated onion and garlic found their way into the boiling water with the pasta as she answered his pessimism with her own brand of optimism. "With your wheelchair, of course. This is part of the getting-back-into-real-life thing we talked about. We can go midday when everything is less crowded if you want, but either way, tomorrow we're buying groceries."

Holden said nothing, and Maddie went back to her cooking.

A short time later, she carried two bowls of macaroni and cheese into the living room. "I forgot to buy milk, so I added some extra butter and hoped for the best." As she went to hand his bowl to him, she found him dozing, his coffee-colored hair in disarray as if he'd run his fingers through it. Silence kept her company as she ate her dinner, allowing him a few more minutes of rest. Meanwhile, she took in the warm colors and masculine furnishings of Holden's home as she wondered how to tell him about the terms his rehab physician had required her to agree to.

When she set her empty bowl on the coffee table, Holden roused from his nap. "Was I asleep?" He rubbed his eyes.

Why did people always say that? It wasn't as if he didn't know he'd just woken up.

"Here." She passed his dinner to him. "Nothing fancy, but it'll do for tonight."

"Anything's better than the food at rehab." A shudder shook his shoulders as if the recollection of his meals at Lakeview was still too horrible to bear.

Once he started eating, Maddie turned herself crossways on the couch in order to gauge his reaction as she strove for a professional tone. "I told Dr. Demir I'm in the guest room and, if I keep my door open, will be able to hear you during the night. She, uh, ordered me to sleep in the room with you for at least the first couple nights."

Holden's green eyes lost some of their sparkle. His tongue darted out to moisten his lips. Many different expressions had graced his face in the time she'd known him, but this was a new one. He seemed... insecure.

Maddie didn't know how to respond to that, so she skipped right over it and dove back into the conversation. "She might have a point. I'm not a heavy sleeper, but I don't want to take the chance I might not wake if you genuinely need me for something. A pallet on the floor will be fine these first few nights. It won't be a big deal."

"What about, like, a baby monitor or something? Then you could hear me."

"I suggested that." Her shrug was accompanied by a sigh. "She said batteries could fail and the power could go out." It had seemed to Maddie that the doctor was being petty, trying to punish her for wanting to get Holden out of rehab. She doubted that thought would do much to encourage him, though, so she kept it to herself.

Without giving him opportunity to react further to her I'll-be-sleeping-in-your-room pronouncement, she continued. "The doctor also gave me strict orders not to allow you to bathe on your own." Holden's eyebrows shot up, and he looked ready to choke on the food in his mouth. He swallowed with effort, but she rushed on before he could catch his breath or speak. "I assume you own swim trunks. If not, we'll get you some. Wear them while you shower. I'll be clothed, too. That way I can help, but we can still maintain some professional modesty. It's not perfect, but…"

His eyes still wide, he kept watching her. Her silence filled the awkward void between them with… more awkwardness.

"Is that everything?" More than a decade past the age of breaking voices, and yet his cracked like a pubescent boy caught thumbing through the lingerie pages in his mom's JC Penney catalog.

She nodded, and he took another bite, taking his time to chew and swallow before speaking. "I'm not sure how comfortable I am with this."

"Oh? I hadn't noticed."

He gave his macaroni a stir before changing the subject. "I don't even know your last name. First, you were Nurse Maddie. Then, Maddie. But I never got the rest of it." Holden took a breath and rambled, his voice getting higher with each word. "If I'm going to be sleeping and showering with someone, I ought to at least know her last name."

Her gaze, which had been casually taking in the sights of the room, zeroed in on his face.

"Uh, that didn't quite come out the way I meant. It sounded a lot funnier in my head."

Maddie rolled her eyes. "You're one of those people who always ruins the punch line of the joke you're trying to tell, aren't you?"

"Guilty." The word was accompanied by a cheeky grin, his nervousness of a minute before gone.

She shook her head in resignation. "Smith."

"Smith. Really?"

"Really."

Leaving him to mull over her inordinately boring name, she washed the dishes and put them in the drain rack before collecting blankets from the linen closet and making a pallet for herself on the floor of Holden's bedroom. Sleep wouldn't come easy, but she understood the doctor's point. Besides, in her own room down the hall, she'd spend most of the night straining to listen for her patient. This way she might actually get some rest. After all, sleeping on the cold hard floor was *so much* more delightful than sinking into a welcoming mattress. Ha!

With no good reason to postpone the inevitable, Maddie gathered the various pill bottles and took a seat on the coffee table opposite the couch. This way, she could face him while they went over his prescriptions.

"Everything is twice daily except for the PRN pain meds." Handing them to him one at a time, she explained. "This is your steroid." She gave him the next. "This is the anti-inflammatory."

"I thought the steroid was anti-inflammatory."

"It is. Once you visit your PCP, these should change. The basic anti-inflammatory is just that — basic. The steroid is for extra short-term help in case your increased mobility initially leads to more swelling and discomfort in your spinal area."

No other inquiries were forthcoming, and she raised an eyebrow in question.

He waved her on, so she passed him another pill. "This is to prevent blood clots."

"What do I need that for?"

"Didn't you ask any of this at Lakeview?"

"I swallowed what they handed me. I didn't think to ask."

"The likelihood of developing a clot grows whenever you're immobile for long periods of time, such as being bedridden in a hospital." She studied the label. "I'm pretty sure they've already begun decreasing your dose. As you regain motion and start spending more time on your feet each day, you should get to a point where you don't need it at all. Unless you suffer from an underlying issue, but I'm sure if that were the case, the doctor would have said so. At length."

Offering him the next one, she said, "This is a diuretic. It encourages your kidneys to do their job and get excess fluid out of your system. Once you become more mobile, your need for it should also decrease. I'm surprised they didn't give it as a PRN. You'll definitely want to go over all the meds at your doctor appointment."

The last two bottles were in her hand. "These are for pain and are only to be used as needed. Is it bearable right now, or do you need something?" When Holden didn't answer, she launched into her oft-repeated spiel. "On a scale of one to ten, one being the teeniest tiniest bit of discomfort and ten being the most horrific pain you can possibly imagine, tell me what it feels like."

He remained silent.

An exasperated sigh slipped out between her lips. "I'm tired, and I want to go to bed. This isn't a good time for you to be battling with your pride. Will you please be honest with me so I can do my job?"

"I'm bad at this. I know. Be patient." A head shake. "I have difficulty quantifying a sensation that can't be measured."

She waited for him to continue.

"The pain's tolerable, but as soon as I start trying to get up, it's going to get worse. By the time I brush my teeth and climb into bed, I... I'll be hurting."

"Thank you." None of this was easy for him. Maddie knew that. "You're thinking ahead, which is great. It's always easier to arrest the pain before it escalates than it is to bring it under control once you're in agony. So let's get it under control now before you're moving around, changing clothes, brushing your teeth, and taking care of whatever else you need to do."

Most of the patients she dealt with were in severe enough condition that they weren't able to assert their independence. Working with Holden was going to force her to grow beyond the comfort and skill level she'd developed in the ICU. Balance was needed, and she would have to find that place somewhere between bullying him into living his life to the best of his ability and respecting his efforts to do so.

"So the question is, do you want a pain medication that makes you drowsy or not? Is getting to sleep problematic for you? Or sleeping through till morning?"

"I want the one that knocks me out so I get some real rest, but what if I sleep too hard and can't wake up in the morning?"

Improvement took all shapes and sizes. He'd already admitted he'd been swallowing whatever he was given without question or thought. Some might say it was a small thing that Holden cared about the effects of his pain meds, but Maddie took it as a positive sign. He was embracing the rest of his life. "The fentanyl will do the job *and* put you to sleep but should wear off by morning. If you're concerned, we can see how you handle it. Since I'll be here tomorrow, this is as good a night as any to test it."

Maddie swallowed a couple acetaminophen before crawling onto her pallet.

Getting up from the couch had been hard on Holden, especially after a day already more active than any he'd experienced in weeks. By the time he'd brushed his teeth and taken care of nature's call, his

142

ashen face and sweat-beaded brow had told of his agony.

She'd helped him into bed as best she could. He hadn't spoken once throughout the ordeal, but she hadn't missed his sharp intake of breath through tightly clenched teeth. The pain had reached an excruciating level. The coming days needed to bring him some relief. Maddie didn't like to think of him suffering this much on a daily basis with no end in sight.

 # Sixteen

Holden lay in bed staring at the ceiling. The tears he could no longer hold back seeped from the corners of his eyes and ran down his temples until they soaked into the pillow beneath. It was hard not to feel bleak when the pain's intensity stole his will. He'd barely refrained from screaming out as Maddie had assisted him into bed.

Focusing on the positive was a challenge, but he did find something to smile about.

Okay, God, the joke's on me. If this pain is Your way of helping me avoid tempting thoughts of the nurse asleep mere feet away, Your plan is a success. She's the last thing on my mind right now. Almost.

The medication began taking effect, and the jagged edge of the pain fell away. Holden swiped at the moisture on his face and gingerly rolled to his side. He wrapped his arms around a soft pillow and welcomed the medication's relief.

His last thought before sleep claimed him was a question.

Who on earth is Tom?

Seventeen

Maddie came awake with a start. Disoriented, she sat up and got her bearings. The faint snore coming from the bed told her Holden still slept. Hands running roughly over her face, she fought the remnants of her slumber.

Try as she might to pull back wisps of her dream as they floated away, she couldn't grab onto them. Whatever tale her mind had entertained while she'd slumbered, it had been disturbing enough to wake her.

A glance at her watch confirmed what she already knew. The rooster wasn't even thinking about crowing yet. Nonetheless, any hint of sleep escaped her. Bad dreams had a way of doing that — robbing a person of the desire to close their eyes. Oh, well. She might as well go make some coffee.

As soon as Maddie scooped the grounds and turned the pot on, her phone rang.

She answered before the sound could wake Holden. "You're up awfully early, Tom. What's going on?"

"I'm sitting outside, and I saw your light go on. Can I come in?"

"Sure, but if I let you in, are you going to tell me why you're staking out my temporary digs?"

IGHTEEN

Holden woke to the sound of voices. The glowing numbers of the bedside clock told him his drafting assistant would have to be deranged to show up at this hour. He recognized Maddie's voice — not deranged, thankfully — but her words were indistinct. The other voice belonged to a man. Surely rehab wasn't scheduled for so early in the morning. And if it was, someone would have woken him… Right?

His concentration divided between figuring out who was in his home and whether or not he'd be able to get out of bed on his own. Holden leaned up on his elbows and strained to make out the conversation coming from the far side of the house. The voices fell away, though, and the front door opened and closed.

Panic slipped past his guard before Maddie lightly stepped into the bedroom. "Hey, you're awake. Did you sleep okay?"

"The door…" He tried to will his galloping heart into a slower beat. "I thought you'd left."

"You wish." She chuckled. "Let me help you up. Then you're going to brush your teeth, take care of nature, and get into your swim trunks. Like it or not, you're getting a shower this morning. We've got

149

two things going for us. Your stand-alone shower means you won't be climbing over the edge of a tub to get in, which is good. It's a tad bigger than most of the ones I've seen, too, so hopefully there'll be enough room for both of us without too much trouble."

Should he explain that a supplier had given him the shower to test out in the hope that he would love it enough to upsell the item to clients? Or that the original amenities that had come with the house had been puke green?

"Are you sure this is going to work?" He gained his feet with only a little help from her and began the shuffling trek toward the bathroom with the aid of his walker.

"Not at all, but we've got to give it a try, right?"

Before long, they were both ensconced in Holden's shower, him in his swim trunks and her in shorts and a dark t-shirt. She could barely move in their cramped quarters. "I'm not sure how the doctor pictured this working. How big do you think her shower is? I thought yours would give us plenty of room, but even the size it is, this is a tight squeeze."

Holden opted not to tell her about the supplier's exaggerated wink and nudge when he'd mentioned creative uses for the shower. Somehow this didn't seem like an appropriate time to bring that up… Or to tell her how her hazel eyes looked so much greener when he was this close.

With both of them already filling the space, his walker wouldn't fit, but he still needed to hold onto something for support.

"Place your hands on my shoulders to help keep you steady," she told him, "and I'll soap you up."

Maddie worked up a good lather, washed Holden's chest, and reached around to scrub his back, which placed her in much closer proximity than he was ready for.

He swallowed.

She made quick work of the job, though, before dropping her hands to her sides and looking him up and down.

"What's wrong?" His voice broke, triggering another flashback to puberty.

"I need to wash your hair, but you're taller than me. Put your hands on my waist. I'll be able to reach up better that way."

"I'm perfectly capable of washing my own hair." The close confines echoed with his near shout.

"You're not ready to stand without assistance yet. Not on a slick surface like your shower floor, anyway."

"Why don't I keep one hand on your shoulder? You can put the shampoo in my hand, and I'll wash my hair."

Maddie studied him, and he prayed the shower's steam camouflaged the heat in his cheeks.

Their position under the spray of water left a lot to be desired. By the time the hair-washing was over, shampoo ran down his face and into his eyes. Some even made its way into his mouth. He suppressed the urge to spit. Holden's luck being what it was, his sudsy loogie would land right on his nurse.

"Great. Now I'm crippled and blind." His mutter was half-hearted.

Her arm reaching around his ribcage yet again, Maddie turned off the water. "Look on the bright side. You won't be able to see how much shampoo is still in your hair."

The tiled floor was covered with towels, and Holden's walker rested in the midst of the terry-covered expanse. She helped him over to it, and he sat down with a sigh. "That's the longest I've been on my feet since I first went into the hospital."

"How are you feeling?"

"The muscles in my legs are good and strong. Compared to cooked spaghetti, anyway."

"What about your back?"

"It hurts." He forced himself to focus on the question. "But not as much as I expected it to."

Maddie patted her hair with a towel before wrapping one around Holden's shoulders.

His eyes remained shut, but that did nothing to blot out the sounds of her moving around in his space.

She, of course, sounded entirely too oblivious. "I don't know where my head was. I figured I'd get wet, but…" The *plip-plip-plip* of dripping water filled the small space. "Maybe if I wring it out."

The slap of sodden fabric ignited his imagination, and he squeezed his eyes more tightly closed.

"I almost got one of those shower chairs at the equipment place last night, but I'm glad I didn't spend the money. If I have to be in there with you, there's no way the chair would fit. We should ask the occupational therapist how long he — or she — thinks it'll be before you're allowed to bathe on your own."

Her monologue came to an end, and still Holden refused to open his eyes. The last thing he needed was one more soaking wet image of her burned into his mind. What he'd already seen was more than enough to keep him distracted for the next several months.

"Is everything okay?"

Sluggish, his brain processed the words as he tried to pull his concentration away from the squishy sound of her water-logged clothes. "Mm-hm."

"You're not drying off."

Thank goodness it sounded more like a question than an accusation. Holden was eager to get her out of the room before he embarrassed himself. Right now she just thought him a wuss when it came to shampoo in his eyes. Hopefully. "You should go change out of your wet clothes before you get sick." He needed a way to motivate her retreat to the other bathroom.

"Are you going to dry off?"

No such luck. A more direct approach was called for. "As soon as you leave to go get yourself changed into something dry."

"Okay." Her words tickled his left ear. "Your clothes are laid out on your bed. Get dried off and dressed. Yell if you need anything."

"Okee dokee." *Okee dokee?* That was the best he could do? He couldn't use *certainly* or *indubitably*. It had to be *okee dokee*. Then again, *indubitably* wouldn't have been an improvement. Who uses those kinds of words? Better to leave well enough alone.

Holden's skin prickled under what he imagined to be the narrow-eyed stare of Maddie's displeasure before the door clicked behind her. She must not have been a fan of *okee dokee* either.

Finally, peace. Opened at last, his eyes stared blankly at the bathroom door as they waited for his brain to kick into gear.

This shower plan of hers had to go.

He couldn't shake the image of her standing there in her soaking wet clothes, the material clinging to her in all the right places. And he hadn't been able to do anything about it. Not that he *should have* done something. Knowing that hadn't stopped his imagination from taking flight, though. His only defense had been to close his peepers and let her label him a fool who couldn't wipe shampoo out of his eyes.

Why hadn't he realized the shower was such a bad idea? Ah, yes. Preoccupation. Too busy with his embarrassment at the thought of needing help to bathe, he'd not foreseen his reaction to her up-close-and-personal presence. That was the last time he let prudishness get in the way of prudence.

Why couldn't Maddie look like Burt? Everything would be so much simpler then.

A guttural sigh ripped itself from his throat as he yanked at the terry material draped across his shoulders. His hands worked swiftly as he dried his hair and rubbed the towel over his body.

You're laughing at me, God. I can tell. I did something wrong, didn't I? I made fun of my older brothers when they started having crushes on girls. Is that it? There has to be a reason You're putting me through this.

Dressing himself shouldn't be such a slow process. Holden grumbled about missing breakfast as he buckled his belt. With his clothes finally in place, he shuffled his way toward the kitchen.

He sure hoped the coffee was fresh.

Much as he dreaded the thought of sitting on one of those hard wooden dining chairs, he didn't fancy the idea of lounging on the couch, either.

With a shove, he pushed his wandering thoughts aside and asked the first innocuous question that came to mind as he rounded the corner into the kitchen. "How are you at giving haircuts?"

"Lousy," a man's voice answered, "but Maddie here is practically a pro."

His eyes went to the stranger sitting at the table in his kitchen. Black slacks and a blue button-up shirt gave the impression of authority. Holden instinctively looked for a flaw. The man's brown hair had a spattering of grey in it. Genetics had been kind to him. Either that, or he worked hard. He had the kind of physically fit body that said he stayed in shape without wasting time at a gym.

"Holden, this is Tom. Tom, Holden." She stood at the stove and assessed him with an over-the-shoulder glance. "How do you feel?"

"Better than I've felt in ages," he replied.

"And the pain?"

"Bearable."

"Would you admit if it wasn't?"

Too curious about the other man in the room, Holden didn't bother to lie. "Probably not, but you'd know anyway. You have an uncanny ability to read people."

Maddie stared for a moment before nodding. "Your desk chair's out here. The height is adjusted up so you don't have to squat down so far to get into it. Plus it's comfy. I tried it out." She waved her hand in their guest's general direction. "Go hold it still so it can't roll out from under him."

The mysterious Tom did as he was told.

"After a while you'll be able to push it up against a table or desk or whatever to keep it steady, but I want a little more control until I'm comfortable you can get up and down without assistance."

"I don't need a spotter in order to sit."

"Do you see me over there helping you?" Her eyebrow climbed noticeably before she turned her back on him and flipped the bacon in the pan.

Holden lowered himself into the chair and let out a big sigh.

"Like that, do you?" The gruff voice wasn't entirely unkind. Still…

"Feels like heaven."

The aroma coming from where Maddie stood drew his attention away from his comfortable posterior. "Since when do we have bacon?"

"Tom went out and fetched a couple things for us this morning. I know I said we would go grocery shopping, but I changed my mind. No point in overdoing it on your first day out of the joint. So I gave him a list, and he saw to everything for us."

"I just happened to be in the neighborhood." The man's humor was so dry it made Death Valley look like the Amazon River Basin.

"Ignore him. Being a cop broke his funny bone."

"Hey, little missy, don't you go acting too big for your britches."

Tom's hands were loosely clasped together and resting on the table. Was that...? "How'd you get all those scratches?"

The middle-aged man glared, and from somewhere near the laundry room a hiss echoed in return.

"If she values her cat's life, she's never again going to ask me to catch him."

Maddie waved her spatula at Tom. "He thinks I should have equipped him with a gun full of tranquilizer darts. Mr. Fish Breath is one teeny tiny little cat. I figured Tom was big and strong enough to handle him." The smirk on her face told another story, the one where the pet owner was more than relieved she'd been able to foist that task off onto somebody else.

Tom was what — fifteen years older than her? A little more? Close enough that they might be in a romantic relationship. Why else would a man be

158

willing to fight a cat? The way they spoke to one another didn't suggest it, though. At least, *he* couldn't imagine calling someone he was dating *little missy*.

"So, how long have you two known each other?"

"Forever." "More'n twenty years." Their overlapping responses were perfectly timed.

"Tom's my hero." Maddie's words didn't have the taste of sarcasm she sometimes drizzled into her humor.

She would have been a child when they met. Which landed her right smack in the middle of when she was in the foster care system. Foster kids who needed police intervention…

Holden battled to keep his face neutral as every unsavory story he'd ever heard came to mind.

"Arrested for shoplifting, were you?" No need to push for answers now. Better to give her a way out so she didn't feel cornered.

"More like assaulting an officer." Her impish reply carried a note of realism.

Holden tilted his head to the side and scrutinized her. "You're telling the truth, aren't you?"

Maddie glanced up from the stove and caught him in the act of watching her. She shrugged. "I told you my childhood was colorful."

From the corner of his eye, he saw Tom's mouth drop open.

"Maybe you'll tell me about it sometime." Holden kept his words light, but his attention stayed wholly focused on the feminine enigma in his kitchen.

Her deft turn back to the sizzling stovetop was accompanied by a shrug. A few minutes later, she served up three plates of eggs, bacon, and toast.

"This looks and smells delicious. You didn't have to go to all this trouble, but I sure do appreciate it." Holden smiled up at her as she set a plate in front of him.

"Maddie's a fine cook, that's for sure." Tom nodded to the woman in question. "Makes a mean meatloaf and bakes bread lighter than air."

The grocery-shopping hero started to take a bite, but a hand on his arm stilled him. "Holden likes to bless the meal first."

Setting his fork back down, the older man studied the two of them, an unreadable expression on his face. Then, without complaint, he bowed his head, and Maddie followed suit.

"Thank you, Lord, for all your many blessings. I can't tell you how grateful I am to be in my own home again. Although, hm. I guess I did just tell you. Anyway. Thank you for sending people into my life who are willing to help when they have no obligation to do so. Please bless this food and the hands that prepared it. Amen."

Holden picked up a piece of bacon and sniffed it before placing it in his mouth and savoring the taste. "I haven't eaten real bacon since you ordered it for me my last day in the ICU. Why are people so fascinated with turkey bacon these days?" The words made their way out in between his crunching. Moments like these — not to mention crisp-around-the-edges salted perfection — were too good to let proper decorum get in the way.

"Medical facilities are supposed to make people healthier." Maddie gave a mournful shake of her head. "They think that means replacing real bacon with the turkey stuff. Be thankful Lakeview didn't serve tofu bacon."

Both men shuddered as she laughed at them.

Before anybody else had eaten a fraction of their breakfast, the unexpected guest polished off the last of his and pushed his plate away. "Good meal. Thanks."

She nodded toward the kitchen. "Help yourself to some more coffee if you want." Turning to Holden, she waggled her eyebrows. "It's a cop thing. He swallows his food whole so he always has a hand free for his gun, I think."

When the *cop* sat back down at the table with a fresh cup, Holden peered at him. "Why don't you tell me how the two of you met?"

His voice maintained a nice, easy conversational tone. Or so he thought. The way Tom stiffened shouted his failure. Either that, or the subject was even more touchy than he'd assumed.

Added to that, the officer's expression slid from the edge of sardonic all the way into unyielding steel rebar faster than it took a lightning bug to light up.

Every one of Holden's senses went on high alert. With the way the other two stared at one another, being dubbed a third wheel would feel like a promotion at that point. Something was going on, that much was evident. But the question lingered — what?

Maddie continued to be a mystery. Not that all women weren't unfathomable enigmas, but she was different. For the first time in years, Holden wanted to invest the time and energy to pull back the layers. Instinct told him she boasted many layers and that whatever treasure he found at the center would end up being a mind-bending puzzle.

Understanding this woman wouldn't come easy. She was a private person who allowed him access only to the parts of herself she chose to share. Most of the time, anyway.

While he contemplated the many ways to get Maddie to open up to him, the woman in question nodded at Tom, breaking through the pungent silence that enveloped the table. "I'm eating. You tell it."

Holden was so busy picking his jaw up off the floor, he almost missed the flash of vulnerability on her face before her eyes squeezed shut. "Go ahead."

After scooting his chair around, Tom sat back in a deceptively casual manner, but his hawk-like stare in no way matched his pose.

"I'm a detective now, but I was a beat cop back then." His voice held as much emotion as an overworked teacher reciting the alphabet with his class for the umpteenth time. "We got a report about a grade school student who was nowhere to be found. The school's nurse was worried about her living arrangements and reported it to social services, hoping they'd escort the girl home and take a peek inside the house. Seems the kid freaked out when she learned she wouldn't be going home alone. A minor was MIA and social services would be breathing down my neck any minute."

Tom reached for his coffee, but his eyes bored into Holden. "I was the closest on-duty officer when the call came in, and as first on the scene, I'd have the best chance of finding her. I tried to figure out where a girl would try to hide. That's when another call came in about a disturbance at the Schroeder Building not too far away. Sure enough, it was the tallest structure in sight. If I was a kid, and I wanted to escape, I would go deep where no one would think to search. Or I'd go high where I could gain the advantage by seeing anyone who approached, and the Schroeder Building fit that description to a tee."

Maddie ate, but each bite seemed to be taking longer than the one before. All that lingered of Holden's breakfast was his toast, and he took his time with it, afraid the story would end if his plate was empty. Everything about Tom — except his eyes — seemed relaxed, like he was chatting with a passing neighbor from his front porch. He must be good at tricking offenders into feeling at ease when he got them cornered in the interrogation room.

"I eventually found the kid up on the roof. This was back before everyone was required to lock down their rooftop access. Scrawny little thing. She was already frightened. I didn't want to spook her and make it worse. Couldn't risk her going off the edge of the building in a panic. She was huddled down in this little ball, her whole body shaking. I didn't realize she was armed until it was too late."

Holden's eyes went to Maddie. She no longer ate, but she also wouldn't look at him. Her gaze was trained on Tom, who resumed the tale. "She held a hammer in one hand, a box cutter in the other. The kid was resourceful — I had to give her that. She'd found her weapons lying out on the rooftop. You wouldn't think such a tiny little slip of a thing could be so strong, but she was wild with terror and started swinging that hammer around like a madwoman. She mottled me up with bruises and cracked two of my ribs before I decided tackling her to the ground would be the safest choice for both of us. A hit in the face with the claw of that hammer decided it for me. I took her down. Thankfully the box cutter was missing the blade."

His softly spoken words directed at Maddie, Holden interrupted the telling. "What had you so scared?"

"Remember how I told you I woke up one night with a snake wrapped around me?"

He nodded.

"Turns out it wasn't on accident. My foster family was twisted. They put it in my bed on purpose because I'd told them dinner was gross." She gave the kind of shrug meant to seem dismissive even as it dismissed nothing. "Too many kids suffered their special style of discipline — bullied with the giant snake, a lizard longer than I was tall, and other creepy crawlies. One time they held me down and let the tarantula crawl on me."

Holden sighed, his relief mingled with horror. His mind had gone to sex trafficking and those parents who sell — or rent — their children to the highest bidder. Not to mention the pedophiles who worm their way into positions working with minors only to satisfy their own depraved desires. Thank goodness for Maddie's sake…

He shook his head to rid himself of the worry for what hadn't occurred.

What those people did to her was reprehensible. How could they…? The image of

Maddie as a little girl, pinned down and terrorized by faceless people, filled his mind's eye until he choked on his own bile. Where had her case worker been? Someone should have protected her. His eyes swung to Tom, and his grudging respect for the man grew.

"She fell asleep twice at school that day." The older man frowned and stroked his hairless chin. "Even though the nurse was rightly worried about her home life, the kid was convinced the crackpots she'd been fostered to would sic the snake on her again if they learned she was the reason social services was sniffing around."

Tom's eyes remained on him the entire time he spoke, but Holden had little doubt that the man witnessed every single one of Maddie's reactions. "What eight-year-old wouldn't believe a snake could swallow her whole if its owners ordered it to? So she went to the tallest building. She thought she'd be able to see it coming and be able to defend herself. I didn't know any of this at the time. All I knew for certain was that I had this panic-stricken kid in my arms who went ballistic at the mention of social services. I'd never seen a child claw, scratch, and scream so much. So I promised her I wouldn't let the do-gooders take her just yet."

Breakfast turned sour in Holden's stomach. He sat back in his chair and listened.

"By the time I got her downstairs, her case worker was waiting for us." The material of his shirt stretched taut as Tom gave his collar a tug. "I told the old bat that protocol mandated the kid be taken down to HQ. Assaulting an officer and all. I stuffed the kid in the back of my squad car and got out of there before anyone could question my story. First stop was the hospital for stitches and X-rays. They fixed up my face and taped my ribs, told me not to get in any more fights with a hammer."

"Then we went to the pier." Maddie's reminiscent words took the conversation in a new direction, one with less darkness. "It wasn't a real pier, but it was as close as the area had at the time. A manmade lake surrounded by wooden benches. A man selling hot dogs, too."

"Best hot dogs in town." Tom's smile didn't reach his eyes.

How much did the retelling of this story cost him?

"Rain or shine, he was out there hocking his dogs every day. I bought her one and sat her down where she had a view of the lake. Let her eat in peace. Once she gobbled that up, I handed her some cotton candy and started asking questions."

Maddie reached for her last piece of bacon. "He hadn't turned me over to the social worker or put me in handcuffs, so I figured he was one of the good guys."

Tom smiled at her, the fondness in his eyes his first show of emotion since beginning the tale.

"After that, I took her back to HQ. I put her in a seat where she'd be in my line of sight and went in to face the captain's wrath. The do-gooder from social services had beat me... by three hours. My captain was the recipient of her endless and quite vocal frustration. Needless to say, he wasn't happy with me. When the old man — who was younger than I am now — finished yelling at me, he asked, 'What do you have to say for yourself?'"

Maddie gave a whisper of a laugh. "The captain's voice was petrifying. It boomed through the whole precinct. I swear, the windows should've all shattered when he yelled. I would have run away again right then, but Tom winked at me, so I stuck around."

"The captain listened as I explained everything Maddie'd told me about the goings-on in the foster home. The social worker took my... uh... gentle suggestion and made some calls. She had someone back at her office pull records on the family, and right there from our precinct, she began contacting other children who'd previously been placed with them. I had to give her credit. Once she realized who the bad guy was — and that it wasn't me — she went after them with a vengeance." Tom's chuckle held little mirth.

"The captain questioned me about taking so long to bring the girl in, and I pointed to where she sat in a chair outside his office. 'You see how tiny she is, right? She cracked two ribs and did this to my face. Go ahead. Try and tell me she's not terrified. She needed to feel safe before she'd talk.'"

She'd survived — Holden could see that with his own eyes — but the words, pulled from a place deep inside where he still needed reassurance, came anyway. "What happened?" He didn't stop to investigate his roiling emotions too closely. Some things were better left alone.

Maddie smiled, and his stomach muscles clenched in response. She had a beautiful smile already. Watching her now, though, knowing some of the things she'd been through and seeing that spontaneous smile... He took a blow straight to the solar plexus.

"Enough kids came forward that my foster parents were prosecuted."

His original question, vanquished from his mind the moment she'd smiled, came back into sharp focus at her words.

"They were locked up for a long time and never allowed to work with children again. I still bounced around between the system and my biological parents after that, but Tom stopped in to check on me at least once each month, regardless of where I bunked. The places I stayed were mostly good after that, but even the ones that weren't the best still treated me decent. The last thing a foster parent wants is trouble with the police. Tom's been my champion ever since."

Maddie got up, collected the dirty dishes, and carried them to the kitchen sink.

Holden glanced across the table. "What about you?"

The man in question raised an eyebrow.

"Married? Kids?" What Holden really wanted to ask was whether or not the man's feelings for their companion went beyond the kind of kinship she described.

The detective's speculative gaze pinned him to his seat. "Been married twenty years. Got one kid in college and another in high school. Maddie's been a part of my family for a lot of years." *And I don't take kindly to people messing with my family.* The silent message was unmistakable.

"Give me a week or so to get situated. Then maybe you can bring the wife and kids over for dinner one evening." Holden saw a gleam in Tom's eyes. He wasn't entirely sure, but he thought it might have been respect.

Nineteen

Maddie adjusted her deep blue peasant blouse and sleek black skirt before retrieving the walker from her trunk. The therapist wanted Holden using the contraption, something he continued to balk at. He'd not fought her this morning, though. She was no fool. He didn't want to make Mr. Williams' memorial service harder for her than it already was, so he'd been agreeable.

A placard inside the entrance to the funeral home directed them to the correct room. They slipped in quietly and took seats toward the back so the walker could be stored nearby but still be out of the way of other guests.

A short while later, a man in his thirties — not much older than her — stepped up to the podium at the front of the room. "I want to thank everyone who is here today. As many of you are aware, my parents' church is a small one and couldn't accommodate such a large gathering. So it is that we find ourselves here, at Mew's Funeral Home, to mark the passing of my father from this world into the next."

Maddie hadn't met the Williams boys, but she knew there were two. Kind eyes adorned the solemn face of the one standing before them.

"Please pray with me."

She lowered her head automatically, but for the first time since she'd begun attending funerals, she was cognizant of how real prayer was to some people. To her, funeral prayers had always been nothing more than an extension of the eulogy where people told God, instead of each other, how broken up they were over their loss. It wasn't possible to be around Holden for long, though, without realizing how different the reality of prayer was from her perception.

To people who truly believed, prayer was a conversation with a loved one, a dialogue shared with a dear friend. She might not share his faith, but how she thought of and treated the prayers of others was forever transformed. She had Holden to thank for that.

"…You are the God of all creation and the God of our hearts. Those hearts are heavy today as we stand before You and mourn the loss of a wonderful man who touched us all deeply. We ask You to comfort us in our time of sadness…"

Maddie's mind got stuck on that last phrase. This family, who had lost someone precious to them, didn't blame God for taking him. They asked Him for consolation. They didn't demand to know why He'd not intervened and saved their father, husband, and friend. They sought solace from Him instead.

The logic was backwards, but she couldn't deny the peace on the faces of Mr. Williams' family. The service came to an end as she pondered the question and tried to sort out the meaning of it all.

Holden leaned close. "I'll sit here and wait for you if you want to go speak to Mrs. Williams."

She cast a glance at him and nodded before standing and making her way toward the front of the room. The widow and her two sons stood with their spouses and children accepting hugs, handshakes, and words from people offering condolences. The length of the line was a testament to how well loved Mr. Williams had been.

Maddie soon stood before the widow. "I'm terribly sorry for your loss. I know how much he meant to you." She didn't know, of course, not really, but the words fell out of her mouth anyway.

Mrs. Williams pulled her into a hug. "Thank you so much for coming today. And for fighting so hard to save him." Turning to the two middle-school aged boys standing nearby, she said, "This is the nurse who was with Poppa when he went home to be with Jesus."

Both children held out their hands to shake hers. "Thank you for taking care of Poppa."

"Poppa's in heaven, and I'm trying to be happy for him."

Maddie's eyes flooded with tears. She blinked them back and schooled her features. "I'm sure he would be proud of you both and would tell you it's okay to be sad sometimes."

Mrs. Williams' hand on her arm stalled Maddie as she started to leave. "Thank you for making the time to be here. Losing a patient must be hard. I don't take your presence lightly." Then the older woman turned to the next person in line.

Maddie held her composure together until she got in the car. She dashed tears away as she pulled out of the parking lot. "What do you want for lunch?"

Holden took his cue from her, and she was thankful. Not a word was uttered about her crying. "Let's see what's in the fridge at home. I'm sure we can think of something."

TWENTY

Holden was thankful his business had rebounded enough that he'd been able to give Miles the day off. Still, what should he do? Maddie wouldn't thank him for overstepping, but something was definitely wrong.

Partway into the kitchen Maddie stopped, reversed course, and strode into the hallway, her feet dragging on the low shag of the eggshell carpet. The door to the spare room opened and closed. She hadn't said a word since asking about lunch, which wasn't at all like her.

Go to her.

He didn't hear a voice or words exactly, but with a certainty deep inside, he knew God was telling him not to leave her alone. Snapping the laptop shut, he spun his chair around so the back was secured against the table. With the help of his walker, he got up and made his way down the hall to where he gave her door a light tap — loud enough to be heard but not so loud as to disturb.

"Maddie, is everything okay?"

No answer was forthcoming. What should he do? He didn't want to walk in on her while she was changing her clothes. Their shared shower still haunting him, he wasn't prepared for that kind of awkwardness. Silence met him when he rapped his knuckles against the wood for a second time.

Go to her.

Holden gripped the knob and slowly turned it, giving her plenty of opportunity to yell out if she was indecent. He eased the door open and took a step over the threshold. She lay on her side, still in the clothes she'd worn to the funeral, facing the window opposite the door. Gingerly he maneuvered around the double bed to get a better look at her. His alarm grew when he took in her blank expression. It took some effort due to the bed's height, but he got himself seated with some security on its edge.

"Are you all right?" Her eyes didn't even flicker in his direction. "What's wrong, sweetheart?" He reached out and softly brushed the hair away from her face, tucking the strands behind her ear. Her eyes remained fixed on the window. "Maddie?"

No response.

Holden stood back up and shuffled toward the door. He got to the foot of the bed before stopping. Prudishness versus prudence. Hadn't he recently decided not to sacrifice the latter in favor of the former?

He reached a hesitant hand out to the blue-painted expanse of wall. One more glance at the woman in the bed, and he made up his mind. He was now on the side of the bed closest to the door, and

Maddie's back was to him. He proceeded along said wall, the bed inches from him, until he came to the spot he was looking for.

The mattress dipped as he sat. Then, with a strong shove, he pushed himself backward, away from the wall, and twisted his upper body while turning his hips. The maneuver was anything but graceful, and it didn't come without pain, but with the help of willpower and concentration, he landed fairly close to the middle of the bed.

While his ability to navigate the spongy surface of a mattress was improved, it still wasn't stellar. Rather than attempt to scoot closer, he wrapped one arm around her midsection and gave a gentle tug, tacitly asking her to come to him. She still didn't speak, but she moved until her back rested partly against his chest, near enough that the scent of her shampoo filled his nostrils.

Holden was in danger. He would be a fool not to admit it.

He removed his hand from where it still sat at her waist. The idea of breaking all contact, though, didn't sit well with him. Instead, he settled for running his hand up and down her arm in what he hoped was a soothing motion.

A couple minutes passed before she made any sound. Was that...? The noise repeated, and he closed his eyes. The pressure building inside him eased. Her sniffle was music to his ears. He'd never been so relieved to hear a woman cry.

Catatonically staring through a pane of glass wasn't a healthy way to deal with loss. He ought to know. He'd stared out the window often enough while in rehab.

He held her as close as he dared and kept his thoughts to himself. Even if he had some idea what to say, it wouldn't go well. Holden possessed a special gift that presented itself when he comforted people of the female persuasion.

What was his gift? Catastrophic failure.

Growing up, whenever he'd attempted to comfort them, his sisters invariably told him to stop. Sometimes they threw in phrases like, "You're making it worse," "You're trying to ruin my life," or his personal favorite, "God should have made you a mute." Not many years had gone by before silence became his habit anytime he was confronted with an upset woman.

In time, Maddie's tears subsided.

Holden, pinned in place by her head on his shoulder, was halfway between lying on his back and his side. He wouldn't be able to maintain the position much longer without painful consequences.

Was she asleep? Would he be a cad if he woke her so he could move?

He was wrestling with the question — and with the tightening in his muscles — when she rolled from her side to her back. This freed him to do the same, which he promptly did, swallowing a groan in the process.

Mr. Fish Breath chose that exact moment to jump onto the bed. Tail swishing with his steps, he stalked into the space between their bodies and gave them each a haughty glare before lying down, his purr vibrating the air around them.

"I'm sorry." Her hoarse whisper broke the shroud of silence.

"Don't be."

"It upsets me when I lose a patient."

"I gathered. For the record, I'm not very good at cheering up women. My sisters tell me I'm lousy, in fact."

"You did fine." Fishy's tail swished back and forth in the space between them. "Why hasn't anyone from your family come to visit since you've been ill?"

He somehow didn't mind the question, coming from her. "Everyone lives in a small town with small town jobs and families of their own. Spare funds to finance cross-country travel aren't in anybody's budget. I told them I was fine and they should stay home. They would have all pitched their money together to fly the folks out, but even if they managed to get a cab to bring them to my house, they'd have ended up stuck here. Neither of them can drive in the city traffic, and they're not used to public transit. Right or wrong, telling them not to come saved me the stress."

"Do they know how close you came to dying?"

"Not really, and I'd rather keep it that way."

"Why?"

"If I tell them now, my folks will feel guilty for not coming even though I'm the one who insisted they stay home. That guilt will spill over onto me every time I speak with them. Normally I can manage it. It's part of the dynamic of our relationship — kind of like them trying to talk me into moving back home. That's their way of saying they love me. This time, though..." He shook his head. "I didn't have it in me to deflect the questions and comments, so I kept the severity of things to myself. Time passed, and keeping quiet became easier than fessing up."

"You're used to putting others first. You don't know how to let people — including your family — put you first, do you? That's why you deflect."

Holden shrugged as best as he could on the bed, not that she saw. Maddie's eyes hadn't strayed from the ceiling.

"I think we all ought to put God first, but I suppose you're right. I'm uncomfortable being the center of attention. Only now there's this lie-by-omission sitting between me and my parents, and I need to figure out what to do about it."

"Hm." She offered no suggestion. Nor any condemnation. "Did you eat lunch yet?"

"No. You hungry?"

"Not so much."

"None of your comfort movies are here, are they? They're all at your place."

Her sigh held an edge of the forlorn. He could relate. Whenever he needed to recuperate from a day that had beaten him up, he watched a particular movie. Men with swords, war cries, and spectacular victory-against-the-odds. He'd gone without it during his time at the hospital and rehab.

Maddie shifted her weight on the mattress and looked over at him. "I'm going to pop some popcorn and gorge myself on it and chocolate. Do you want to surf the channels for some ridiculous film we can tear apart and make fun of?"

Holden chuckled. "Is that how you cope with stress?"

"Today, yes."

"I'll gladly find us a terrible movie, but I think I'm going to need you to help me up off this bed first."

"It's a deal.

They annihilated the efforts of the moviemakers, and with each critique, her smile came easier. By the end, she laughed freely and the twinkle was back in her eyes.

The credits began to roll. He was loath to bring it up and ruin her improved mood, but Holden couldn't help but think she needed to talk about it. "Losing a patient is obviously hard on you."

"It's a lot harder for the family than for me."

"Don't minimize your own grief."

She regarded him, head tilted to the side, hazel eyes shiny with unshed tears. "I never even heard the sound of his voice." A blonde curl twisted itself around her index finger.

"What do you normally do to cope?"

She picked at her cuticles. "I'm not accustomed to talking about it. I get through it in my own way, in my own time."

"How has that worked for you in the past?"

"Some nurses can go back the next day." One shoulder lifted. "I'd rather not. I need time to process."

"This is the second time I've seen you in tears over a patient. How often does this sort of thing happen?"

She shook her head, but he couldn't tell if regret or denial powered the motion. "Periodically. It's not the norm. We're a good hospital. The doctors and nurses I work with are excellent at what they do.

We've had more than our share of deaths in recent weeks, though. When there hasn't been time to recover from the last one, the new one ends up hurting even worse."

"Do you ever think of changing to a different nursing field? Like in a doctor's office or something?"

"Every time I lose someone."

Holden didn't have any idea where he was going with his questions, but he wanted to keep her talking. Something in his gut told him it was the best thing for her. "Does it ever get so hard you think about leaving the profession altogether?"

An infomercial began, and Holden turned the volume down. The screen flashed with images of some cooking device guaranteed to save everyone loads of time so they could spend more with their children. Of course, the product was showcased by buxom models and a rugged outdoorsy man better suited to hocking lingerie than promoting family unity.

She stared at the television, her cuticles forgotten. "One time. The pediatric ICU was full up when an accident on 95 brought us a slew of patients. Two parents and their child landed in our ICU. The mom passed away the first day. It would have been a miracle if she'd survived. The dad and kid started to pull through, and things looked good for them. I was on a three-day rotation, and I spent all my days assigned to the boy. He did well, improved each day, and wasn't too far away from being released to the floor. His smile was beautiful. One minute I was using funny voices to make him laugh, and the next I held his lifeless body in my arms."

Holden's heart dropped into his stomach. Talking things through suddenly seemed like an abysmal idea. "What happened?"

"He stroked out. There was no head injury to speak of, and the initial scans were clear, so no additional CTs or MRIs had been ordered. Autopsy later revealed he'd developed a subdural hematoma, which led to a massive stroke. None of the normal symptoms presented, though. His BP and heart rate fluctuated every now and then, but they were well within the acceptable range for his age and size. The scans from when he was admitted showed nothing. *Nothing.* It made no sense. This boy had never missed a well-child visit at his pediatrician's. All his immunizations were up to date. It's not like his parents neglected his health or anything. You don't expect deadly strokes in children, especially with no prior indication of a problem."

"What did you do?" The thought of her facing such a tragedy alone tore at him.

"I went home and crawled into bed. The nursing director took me off the schedule and told me to call her when I was ready to go back. She worried, though, and tried reaching me at home. After eight days without a return phone call, she looked up my emergency contact."

"Tom?"

"Yeah. He barged into my apartment, dragged me out of bed, and made me tell him the whole sorry story."

"Did it help?" Holden needed to buy the man a steak.

"He kind of gets it. In his line of work, he sees innocent people die. Tom and I, we both tend to meet people on the worst days of their lives. He ordered me to get cleaned up. I stared at him until he marched me into the bathroom, stuffed me into my shower stall, and turned the water on. Then he walked out and left me. I stood dressed in my pajamas, with ice cold water pounding down on me, and I finally cried. I'm not sure that's what he had in mind, but it's apparently what I needed. I snapped out of it."

"Do you always go to the funerals?"

"Whenever someone dies on my watch, I go. At first, I only managed it occasionally, but I attended one once — maybe four years into my nursing career. The widower gave me a hug and told me how much it comforted him that the person who was with his wife in her last minutes on earth cared about her and her family enough to be there. Since that day, I make a point to go to the funeral of anyone who passes away while in my care. The way I figure, the service isn't about me or even the patient. It's about the ones left behind, about finding a way to help them deal with the loss. Any sadness I experience is a small price to pay if my attendance helps them."

"It sounds like an obligation."

"Sometimes. It's also a privilege, though. Caring for people in their hour of need is a calling, I guess. Being able to do it is an honor. Just because the grieving family isn't laid up in the hospital doesn't mean they're not in need, too."

"Has anyone ever... Has a family ever been unhappy that you went?"

Her hair billowed out from her face as she turned her head. "Not yet. I sometimes wonder, 'Will this be the one where my presence causes a scene?' But it's never happened."

"I don't know how you do it." Holden was in awe. To work as a nurse with high-risk patients, a person required fortitude — emotional brawn, really — something the woman before him had in spades. "You're a much stronger person than I am."

If only he knew. As far as nurses went, she was being a ninny. She was supposed to be stronger. She *used to be* stronger. "Don't knock yourself. You possess more strength than you realize. Not many people cope with illness or recovery as well as you."

Even he could tell his attempted smile fell flat. "I might not be handling things as well as it seems."

"Anything you want to talk about?"

He shrugged. "Nah. Maybe another time."

The next several days zipped by. Holden got tired of being ferried around to his appointments with Dr. Matthews as well as evaluations with physical and occupational therapy. It was paying off, though. The appropriate people all agreed that he was ready for the water, so they embarked on a new adventure.

They found a fitness center with a large walk-in pool attached. A ramp into the pool provided easy access for people in aqua therapy, allowing them to circumvent the stairs and ladders.

The therapist's instructions had been clear, too. "No swimming. No aerobics. No floating. Got it? Walk laps around the pool. Twenty minutes at a time, no more than once each day. If that's too tiring, try fifteen. Or ten. But not over twenty. Understand?"

Of course he'd understood.

"We'll re-evaluate after a week."

Understanding and obeying were two different things. Holden wasn't completely incompetent, though. He knew enough to keep that thought to himself.

Maddie refused to let her charge into the water on his own. He couldn't bring his walker with him — it was against policy, to say nothing of the impracticality.

"I'll walk right along the wall here and keep my hand on the side the entire time. Lifeguards are stationed every five feet." A slight exaggeration, but it made his point... he thought. "I'll be fine."

Hands on her pink-polka-dotted-swim-suit-clad hips, Maddie pursed her lips. "You're stuck with me, so either accept it, or we'll go get back in the car and head home."

"The therapist said I didn't need supervision."

"She meant you could walk in the water without a therapist's supervision, and you know it."

"I'm not two years old." Admittedly, the whine in his voice brought that into question.

"Holden..."

What else could he do? Tell her he still dreamt about the shower they'd shared and that the last thing he needed was more images like that in his mind?

"Fine." Yep. A two-year-old having a brat attack.

Torture. That was the only word for it. Why did she have to stay right next to him? The whole time? In her wet, clinging suit?

Granted, it was modest as swimsuits went, but still, it was Maddie.

Which brought him back to why he'd been so adamant she not get in the pool with him. Everything had been fine until she'd walked out of the ladies' locker room in her swimsuit. That was when he'd realized how long her legs were and how smooth her skin was. He'd been happy living in ignorance. Or had it been denial?

Hence his campaign against her getting in the pool with him. They walked in circles around that pool for twenty minutes. In awkward silence.

He needed to apologize for his surliness, but what should he say?

I'm sorry for being a jerk. You're sexy, and I'm a cripple.

It lacked a certain finesse. A different approach was called for.

I was rotten, and I'm sorry. It's just that I'm a believer, and I don't think you are, and I'm pretty sure I'm not supposed to be as attracted to you as I am.

Yeah, that would work. Let her think Christian men were wound so tight they couldn't control their lust. Definitely a winning explanation.

Silence. Silence would work. Anything else, and he'd end up making a fool of himself.

They returned to the therapy pool the next day, and fueled by the mingled scent of chlorine and dank clothes, Holden prepared himself for the battle. There was no way he could handle having her in the water with him again, and he would do whatever it took to keep her out.

All his preparation ended up being for naught, though. She walked him down the ramp and made sure he was steady on his feet. After that, she retreated to the deep pool where the roped float lines created lanes for people to swim their laps.

And he couldn't have been more relieved.

Ever since the shower incident, he'd done a good job of avoiding as many water-related encounters with Maddie as he could.

He'd refused any further assistance while showering. She, of course, insisted on being on-hand in case he required help. More times than he cared to recall, he'd suffered through having her in his bathroom while he stood in the stall in his swim trunks and tried ineffectually to concentrate on bathing himself. Talk about being under a microscope.

Finally, a week after he'd been home from rehab, the doctor told Maddie she no longer needed to sleep in his room. Then, a week after that, the occupational therapist had said he no longer needed a chaperone to bathe.

Holden shook his head. He had to get those pictures out of his mind or he was doomed.

Lost in thought, he didn't realize Maddie was no longer in her pool until she spoke. "You're off in la-la land."

Her voice jarred him to attention, and his equilibrium abandoned him. Holden's legs slipped out from under him, but he managed to reach for the steadying security of the pool wall in the nick of time. It wasn't his most elegant moment, but he recovered without help, a victory in and of itself. Then his eyes moved to where she stood on the concrete decking. Their difference in elevation forced him to look up in order to see her face. Her legs were even longer than he remembered.

He ground his teeth. "Is it time to go?"

She frowned. "PT said twenty minutes. I gave you thirty even though I know better. Let's not push it."

"Okay. I'll get out. Meet you over on the other side of the locker rooms?" One of these days she might let him walk to the locker room on his own.

"I thought I'd make sure you're all right getting out."

Holden sighed. He struggled with the adjustment from in-water to out-of-water. Whether he liked it or not, she was right. Frustrated, he said, "I should get a cane."

Shadows skittered across her delicate features.

"I didn't mean that the way it sounded. Believe me, I appreciate your help. Needing so much of it, though, frustrates me sometimes. I'm going to have to find a way to do things on my own. Eventually you're going to go back to your own apartment and life. I can't depend on you forever."

She smiled at him. "No worries. I want that for you, too."

The smile didn't touch her eyes, and he blamed himself. He knew her well enough by now to realize she was sensitive in ways that didn't always make sense to him — and that she'd never admit it out loud.

Despite his bravado, the incline out of the water and lack of a nearby railing gave him difficulties. Maddie sloshed into the water and offered a stabilizing arm. By resting his hand on her forearm, he could maintain the balance he needed to navigate his way up the ramp, breaking away from the pull of the water.

The trek to the locker room didn't win them any speed awards, but it was faster than the day before. His confidence — both in himself and in his steps — grew with each day.

When they got to the door, he waved her off and stepped into the masculine domain. The testosterone-rich air filled his lungs as he wended his way toward his locker. Needing constant help ate away at his sense of self, at his notion of what it meant to be a man.

He *could* do things on his own, and everyone around him should stop saying otherwise.

Twenty-One

Maybe the time had come to think about settling down. She didn't date often, mostly because the men she met were all in the medical field, and while she loved her job, she didn't want to live it 24/7. Having someone to spend time with was proving more enjoyable than she'd expected, though. Holden was engaging and entertaining, almost always good company. If only more men in the world were like him, she might be able to think about making a commitment to someone.

A couple days had passed since he'd mentioned it, but Maddie still pondered what Holden had said at the pool that one day. The time would come for her to go back to her apartment and the private, quiet little life she led with Mr. Fish Breath. The thought left her unsettled.

The doorbell put an end to her introspection. Tonight was a sort-of big night. Tom, his wife, and their youngest daughter were joining them for dinner. Haley, the oldest, was away at college. Holden had even sent Miles home early so they could get the table set and ready for company.

Maddie went out of her way to make a meal they'd all like. Meatloaf, baked potatoes, salad, the works. She'd even whipped up a cheesecake for dessert. Holden ushered in their guests as she put the last dish on the table.

Mirabeth, Tom's wife, came over and pulled her into a hug. "It's been too long since we last saw you."

"I'm a little tied down right now, but that's no excuse for not calling. I didn't mean to be so absent."

A chuckle from her friend. "Tom's kept me apprised. I'd rather see someone face to face any day — you know that. Besides, the phone goes both ways. It's not all on you." Mirabeth abhorred talking on the phone and made no secret about it. "I don't care if it's for a mani-pedi. We need to get together and do something. I miss seeing you."

"Mani-pedis, everyone. Mom's buying!" Sasha's mischievous voice rang through the room.

The mom in question lifted an eyebrow. "Nice try, but unless you bribe me first, it's not happening."

Sasha rolled her eyes and gave Maddie a tight squeeze. "Living with them is pure torture. They always think they're so cute."

She returned the girl's warm hug. "I made your favorite."

The girl perked up. "Meatloaf? At least somebody here loves me."

Maddie glanced up in time to catch Holden's eyes on her. She mouthed the word *teenagers*. One thing was certain. Life never had a chance to get boring with Sasha around.

Everyone settled into seats at the table, but nobody reached for the food. Ah. Tom had warned them.

A nod to the other end of the table, and Holden bowed his head. Not that she was ready to tell anyone, but she now looked forward to his prayers.

"We ask you, Lord, to bless this meal we're about to enjoy. Thank you for Tom, Mirabeth, and Sasha being able to join us, and thank you for Maddie, who worked hard to prepare this feast and who takes such good care of me every day, even when I'm irritable. I'm grateful for the work You've allowed me and Miles to accomplish and that You've kept the business solvent. Be with my folks tonight, Lord. Mom's hip is hurting her again, and she's having a rough go of it, and Dad's lost whenever she's laid up. Please comfort and strengthen them. I ask all these things in the name of Your Son Jesus, Amen."

A chorus of *amen* circled the table before the clang and clatter of dishes being passed and food being scooped up took over.

Tom took a bite of his salad before asking, "So when do you return to work?"

Holden winced, but Maddie avoided looking at him. "I took sixty days."

Her friend's eyes narrowed, but Sasha piped up, cutting off her father's words. "Two whole months? What if you forget everything? What about rent? You can't pay it if you're not working. Unless Mr. Jenkins is paying you, I guess." She shifted her eyes to where their host sat. "Are you paying her what she's worth?"

"Now, dear, don't be nosy." Mirabeth's accent was Southern charm with a hint of prim and proper. "It's not polite to ask people whether or not they're taking advantage of someone you love."

The man in question squirmed at his end of the food-laden wooden table but kept his own counsel.

Maddie took a drink of her sweet tea and joined the conversation. "I won't forget anything, but if my supervisor's worried, I'm sure she'll assign me the easy patients." Or throw her into the fray and sit back to watch what happens.

"You work in the ICU. What exactly constitutes an easy patient?" Ah, so Holden's voice hadn't abandoned him.

"In your last few days with us, you were."

He nodded his understanding and reached for a roll. Tom stretched his hand out for one at the same moment.

Maddie expected their hands to play bumper cars as they fought over the bread, but they both retrieved theirs without incident. Going by the expression on Sasha's face, she'd anticipated a little more action, too.

Maddie directed her words to the youngest in the group. "As for rent, I'll be fine. Don't worry about me."

The teen grinned at her. "I suppose if you become homeless you could always stay with us. You can use my trundle bed."

"There you go again, Sash." Tom's voice rumbled across the table. "Always wanting to bring the strays home."

"Pass the meatloaf." Mirabeth nudged her husband, who handed the platter to her. "The meal is excellent, as always, Maddie. Thank you for inviting us over."

"Actually, I didn't invite you. I merely cooked."

"Oh?" A delicate eyebrow arched as the middle-aged woman stared at her spouse.

"Didn't I tell you," he jabbed a fork in Holden's direction, "he invited us?" Tom stuffed a forkful of baked potato into his mouth and gave his wife a look wide-eyed with innocence.

The woman shook her head before giving her attention to the only other man at the table. "So tell me, what do you do for a living?"

"I'm an architect."

She nodded. "And you work out of your home?"

His chin dipped in acknowledgement. "I used to keep an office, but with my illness, downsizing became practical. Bringing the workplace into my home allowed me to remain solvent. It's crowded but cost-effective."

"Since you make houses, why don't you make yourself a bigger one with a fancy office built in?" Sasha's eyebrow climbed.

"I design them. That's different than building them."

"Well, then, get someone to build it for you." She was like her dad — always trying to fix the problem — and not entirely subtle in the process.

"Hiring a builder takes a lot of capital, something I lack at the moment. Necessity dictates that it wait."

Mirabeth gave her daughter a brief stare before commandeering the conversation again. "Did you design this house?"

Holden shook his head. "I bought this house because it was close to my office, less expensive than renting, and because I wasn't so in love that I wouldn't be able to walk away if the day ever came."

The question sat there, begging to be asked, and Maddie complied. "Have you ever been in love with a house before?"

He offered a half-smile and tapped a finger to the side of his head. "My dream house is safely locked away up here. I'll build it someday when finances permit and there's somebody in my life to share it with."

Tom, who'd appeared to be ignoring the banter up to that point, turned and gave Holden one of his slit-eyed gazes.

Aha. Maddie now understood why he'd been so willing to bring his family over for dinner. The women were doing a thorough interrogation. All he had to do was sit back and take it in.

The time had come to turn the tables.

She winked at the teen. "So Tom, I saw in the paper that your old partner is up for a commendation."

The screech of his metal fork missing its intended target — the potato — and scraping along the edge of the plate echoed in the house like a dozen sets of fingernails all on the same chalkboard. Mirabeth cringed, Holden winced, Sasha choked on her water, Fishy gave an answering hiss from wherever he was hiding, and Maddie smiled innocently.

"The day he gets a commendation is the day I turn in my badge and walk away from it all."

She reached for her sweet tea. "Oh? Maybe I misread."

Tom tossed a disgruntled glance at their host. "So, you a Redskins fan?"

"Oh, great." Sasha's words almost covered her mother's groan. "Nobody told me to dress for a bloodbath."

From the other end of the table, Holden gave her a half-smile as the light caught his chestnut hair and gave it a honeyed appearance. Then, his voice dripping innocence, he asked, "The Redskins? That's lacrosse, right?"

"Lacrosse!"

Maddie chuckled. Smart man — he'd diverted attention from himself and given Tom something to rant about at the same time.

"That didn't go so bad, did it?" Holden stood at the closed door.

"You gained a fan for life in Sasha."

"How so?"

"Lacrosse? Really?" Maddie shook her head ruefully. "Anybody who can get him riled up that easily is going to be a winner in her book."

A half-chuckle met her words. "Purely strategic." Holden was at long last allowed to go without his walker in the house. He left it at the door now as he moved into the living room, his steps slow and deliberate but not as labored as in the past. Once he reached the couch, he sank down with a sigh. "You've got a good family."

"Yeah. They may not be blood, but they're mine."

"They care about you."

She laughed outright. "What gave them away? The questions about how much money I make or the offer of a trundle bed should I become homeless?"

"I figured it out somewhere between the accusation that I'm taking advantage of you and the implication that I'm somehow deficient as a human being because my home isn't bigger."

"Ah, I see. Nothing says love like verbal sparring."

A comfortable peace settled around them. Maddie reached for the remote. "Evening news?"

"Sure."

After a story on a board of education scandal and a triple homicide in a neighboring city, she hit the mute button. "I just wanted to see tomorrow's weather."

Holden contemplated her. "Can I ask you something?"

His eyes were somber, and his teeth worried his lower lip. So much for a what's-for-breakfast kind of inquiry. She nodded.

"What do you believe about God?"

Maddie sucked in her breath. The question had been coming for days, if not weeks. He'd even warned her he would ask someday. Even so, she wasn't remotely prepared. "Why do you ask?"

"I want to understand where you come from. You bow your head when I pray, and you seem okay with me talking to God, but you're not as comfortable whenever I say anything *about* Him."

His question was a difficult one. Not because she didn't know the answer, but because she hadn't allowed herself to go there in such a long time.

"I'm not planning on being judgmental or giving you a fire-and-brimstone sermon if I don't like your answer."

"Fire and brimstone isn't your way, is it?"

He tilted his head to the side, a sign that he wasn't quite sure what she meant.

"You don't preach at people. You'd rather discuss."

His head bobbed briefly. "I suppose that's one way of putting it. My brothers would tell you I talk everything to death."

The words came pouring out. "I was in a foster home for a while when I was about nine. This was after the snake incident. The family went to church all the time. Sunday, Wednesday, and sometimes on other days, too. They were good people, kind to me. I felt safe with them. In Sunday School one day, the teacher spoke about how much Jesus loved us, and the way she talked, it seemed like this Jesus person was at least as nice as my foster family. So I prayed and invited Jesus into my heart."

Maddie struggled with what to say next. She hadn't thought about that time in years, and the memories came back in a rush, washing away the carefully constructed levee that had kept them at bay.

"And after that? What changed?"

Trying to project nonchalance, she shrugged. "A couple months later, my parents got their act together, and I was sent back home to live with them. Several weeks after that, I ended up in a new foster home. Those people wanted nothing to do with church. Next, I got placed with a family who attended church but who didn't practice anything that was preached. They dressed up on Sunday and proclaimed their love for God. At home, though, they were different people. I stayed with too many families like that. Eventually, I gave up on the idea of God. I can't point and say, 'That's the moment I lost faith in the Almighty,' but I guess that's kind of what happened."

Maddie fought an unexpected rush of emotion as she tried to get her thoughts out. Why was she on the verge of tears? Nothing about her reaction made sense. She pushed through, though, wanting Holden to hear what she had to say, all the while hoping he was deaf to the roiling turmoil inside of her. "You're a lot like the foster family I lived with when I was nine. You talk about God, but you also live it."

"I'm far from perfect." His eyes searched the room before settling back on her. "I wish I was a better example of faith to you. I fall short more than I should."

"Perfection is overrated. Authenticity matters a whole lot more."

Again with the head tilt. He asked the question she'd been dreading since she'd first offered to help him. "Would you be willing to go to church with me sometime, or am I asking too much?"

Strangely enough, her heart didn't drop with dismay the way she'd expected. She had no burning pit of acid in her stomach at the thought of attending church with Holden, no uncontrollable urge to backpedal her way out of the conversation. Huh.

"We can give it a try. If I decide church isn't for me and that hurts our working relationship, though...what then?" The sentence hung, the words suspended in the air between them. "Are you sure it's a risk worth taking?"

"If I let your opinion hurt our relationship — which I like to think of as a friendship — I'm not being very authentic, am I?" She made no move to respond, and he continued. "I have to consider the fact that, much as I value you and our friendship, God values you even more. I may want us to remain in each other's lives, but your eternity has to matter more to me than the here and now. Anything less on my part would be pure selfishness. It would be me caring more about what I might lose than about what you could gain."

Maddie thought about Holden's words as she prepared for bed that night. Had he tried to talk to her about church when they'd first met, she'd have pegged him as preachy, dismissed him on the spot, and subsequently avoided him at all costs.

Their relationship was unique. Peculiar, even. It had developed in a pressure cooker. They hadn't been acquainted for long, but they lived together, in a manner of speaking. The situation allowed her greater access to the type of person he was when he thought nobody saw.

Holden, it turned out, was a genuinely amiable guy. He cared about people and didn't take his frustration out on others. On the occasions that he used a sharp tone, he was either in pain or battling a sense of helplessness. But he always apologized, and honestly, those instances were rare.

He was the same with Miles, too. He didn't snap, even when something went poorly.

The world was full of people who dated for years without knowing their significant other as well as she knew Holden. Not that dating was even a conversation between them, but still — she knew who he was at his core, not just the bits that floated to the surface.

He'd asked her to tell him what she thought about God, and answering the question — rather than dodging it — had seemed natural. Next, he'd mentioned church, and much to her surprise, she hadn't wanted to run and hide.

Maddie had begun to wonder if there was more to God than she'd considered in a long time. How could she not, being around Holden all the time?

Somewhere along the way, though, she'd passed the wondering stage. Now she hoped that Holden was right, hoped that God was more real than she'd allowed herself to consider in years.

Sighing, Maddie cracked the door open so she'd hear her patient if he needed her during the night.

Then she climbed onto the bed and settled into the soft mattress and pillow. Was there more to life? The answer remained elusive, a fog-induced mist that shifted away from her each time she reached out to grab it.

Maddie was on the cusp of understanding something of magnitude. She sensed it, but the revelation was right beyond her reach.

Twenty-Two

Two Weeks Later

Holden periodically reached over to tap his cane. Not that he'd developed a fetish or anything, but the freedom it gave him felt good. The physical therapist had finally told him he could use the cane whenever he felt strong enough, though she cautioned him to keep the walker in the trunk so he'd have it in case he ever got into trouble when he was away from home.

The smell of clean cotton tickled his nose as Maddie walked into the room with a laundry basket full of clothes that needed folding. She cut a swath through the dancing sunlight and made her way to the table where he sat enjoying a cup of coffee.

"How is work going? Any luck with contracts?"

Holden grinned in satisfaction. The day had been productive. "I have officially spoken to each person who wanted to break the contract they had with me. Most already hired another architect but some agreed to pay the predetermined contract break fee. More than that, though, they each now know I'm not an unreliable flake, which is important in an industry where reputation pays the bills."

"So they're going to pay you even if they found someone else because you were laid up? Should they be compelled to pay?"

He gave a single perfunctory nod. "I only charged the fee on contracts I could have fulfilled, ones where they didn't need their blueprints any time soon. As for those who refused, we came to an understanding that protects their name as well as mine." Maddie nodded, and he continued. "It's strange, but three of the former clients I spoke to said they received bids from another company that were eerily similar to mine but with a much lower price."

"Is that unusual?"

"It happens, but not usually in such a large cluster." Holden couldn't deny the sense of foreboding that revelation had given him, but he didn't want to worry Maddie. "Two of the commercial customers I spoke with haven't hired anyone to replace me yet and are willing to give me another go at it. I think I can salvage one of them. The other is iffy. We also got two new contracts. They're for private homes, and both clients are men."

"Is it important that they're men? I've never thought of you as sexist."

Caught out, he replied. "Men are easier to work with when it comes to home floorplans. Women want to change everything. Constantly. At first, they like the plans you drew up. Then they decide the pantry should be moved. You redraw everything, and next they want the downstairs bathroom relocated. So you do it all again, and then they tell you to add built-in bookshelves. You make the changes, only for them to opt against the shelving."

Holden gave an exaggerated grimace. "Don't get me wrong. Women are important customers. They'll tell everyone when they're happy with the job you've done, which means valuable referrals. Unhappy with the work, and they'll tell every person they meet about that, too. It can become… tedious. Men are straightforward. They tell you what they want up front, and they're almost always pleased with the end result as long as you did what they said."

Maddie gave him a gentle kick under the table. "Be careful there, mister."

"Which are the easier patients? Men or women?"

"You don't want to go there. And anyway, in the ICU, family members are the vocal ones. The patients themselves are usually too ill."

Holden winced. "I'm pretty sure I heard men are worse. Maybe that wasn't the best comparison."

She grinned. "I'd be a breeze to work with. I have simple tastes. As long as you do your job perfectly, we'd get along great." She winked. Three folded pairs of pants later, she went back to the previous topic. "That's wonderful news, by the way.

About the new contracts, I mean. We should celebrate with a special dinner."

"Nah. We're going to have an entire celebration weekend." Was he pushing too hard? It was too late to back down even if he was. Holden wrapped his hands around the smooth ceramic of his still-warm coffee mug. "What do you say to that?"

She gave him a squinty-eyed stare.

He forged ahead. "I'm taking you out for breakfast Saturday. Afterward, we're driving out to the land where the homes are to be built. I want a chance to study the locations. Miles and I worked hard to get the preliminary proposals put together. We followed up on all the zoning, building codes, and easements. I need to lay eyes on the shape and structure of the properties before finalizing, though. Knowing the environment in which the completed project will stand is vital. It takes a little time, but my plans always get positive alterations out of the experience."

"Will Miles be coming along?" She was no longer squinting at him, and that had to be a good sign.

Holden shook his head. "He has plans with his girl this weekend, and I can do this part on my own. I'll need to bring him on a trip like this at some point, though, so he can learn what I'm looking for and why it's important. He's a quick study, and eventually I'd like to be able to send him out on his own."

"So, does this mean Miles is going to stick around? He said he'd give you a month before deciding, right?"

Holden's smile came easy as he released the now-cold mug and sat back in his chair. She wasn't going to question him anymore about the weekend. "Yeah, he's going to stay with me. The work's only part-time, but that's all he wants right now. He's still taking classes toward his degree."

"Good. I'm glad he's staying. Did he ever tell you why he never came to see you in the hospital?"

"He stopped by the hospital twice, but the first time I was in ICU, and that kind of freaked him out, so he left. The next time he came, I'd been discharged to rehab, but all the hospital would tell him was that I was no longer there." Holden shook his head. "It's a miracle he stuck around as long as he did. Anybody else would have taken off. I'm incredibly blessed not to have lost him during that whole fiasco."

"Wow. I can't believe he didn't look for another job." Maddie continued folding. "Most people would have. Are you sure he's not too good to be true?"

"He's a fantastic drafting assistant and an even better person. Can't go wrong with a combination like that."

Maddie tilted her head to the side. "Did he go without a paycheck the entire time you were hospitalized? That's some pretty spectacular loyalty."

"I knew I'd be laid up for a while." Holden felt his smile begin to slip. "Before I went into the hospital, I talked with my bank and made sure Miles and Yvette would continue to get paid for a set number of hours each week until I got out. I explained it to them both and told them if I over- or underpaid, we'd settle up once I was on my feet again."

"Yvette was your admin assistant?"

Holden nodded, enjoying their relaxed conversation even if it was a subject he'd rather not think about at the moment. "According to Miles, she stuck around for a bit before she stopped showing up. Since she was the one who had the access code to check voicemail, once she left, messages never got checked. She'd also changed the password, so I couldn't even get in to listen to messages until I had my wits about me enough to call the phone company and have the password reset."

"She did all that and still got paid?"

Another nod. "I discussed it with my lawyer. The money it would cost me to take her to court would eat up almost all the funds. If the best I can hope to do is recover something so I can hand it all over to the attorney, I'm better off letting it go and focusing my energy on building the business back up."

"So what's different between her and Miles? Why did he stay when she bailed?"

He waggled his eyebrows. "My charm, of course."

Maddie shook her head. "So your charm sucked him in and repelled her? I'm not sure what that says about you…"

"My dad taught me something years ago." Which reminded him, he ought to call his folks again. "You can teach skill, but you can't teach character. He always said it was important to hire people with good integrity and train them to do the job rather than hire people who knew how to do the work and try to train them to be good people. I followed his advice when hiring Miles, but when my business grew to the point that an administrative assistant was necessary, I contacted an agency. I didn't know where to start a search like that and had no idea what to seek in a candidate. I hired her because of her skills, so I suppose I brought it all on myself."

"Not all skilled people are bad people." Humor glinted in Maddie's eyes.

"Of course not. Still, in the future, I'll be hiring people based on who they are. Hopefully I can find some decent ones who are also competent."

"Do you still have the office space?"

Holden laughed. "I let it go as soon as you brought me home. That was my first call." Dealing with the penalty clause for breaking his lease hadn't been pleasant, but it had still been more affordable than keeping the space. "The other night at dinner when Mirabeth asked about my working from home, I told her it was because of my health situation. That's true enough, but what I didn't say is that my health situation led to a financial situation that necessitated I no longer pour money down the drain for rental space. Miles oversaw the whole ordeal. Movers packed everything and put it into storage." He shrugged. "At least, the furniture went into storage. All the files are piled in my office here. Didn't you notice the boxes?"

"I'm observant, not nosy. There's a difference." The last of the clothes folded, she set the basket aside but seemed in no hurry to leave the table. "I remember Miles bringing in boxes, but I thought they were tools of the trade, supplies you needed to be able to work from home."

"We need to talk about money."

Maddie jumped from her chair and began putting the folded kitchen towels away. So much for not being in a hurry to get away from him.

"Listen while I speak, then. You're aware my insurance won't cover home nursing, which is essentially what you're doing."

She nodded.

"We never discussed salary when you offered to assist me. I couldn't afford to pay you, and pride got in the way. Fear, too. In any event, I should have brought it up ages ago."

Pride and fear were each powerful on their own, but when you mixed them together they became an almost unbeatable force. Too bad they weren't a force for good.

"I did some checking to get an understanding of what you ought to earn for your services, and as soon as I'm able, I'll reimburse you for all your time and effort here."

She waved him off. "I don't need to be paid."

He wouldn't be deterred so easily. "You do, and now that work is starting to trickle in again, I can broach the subject without a panic attack. You've taken a chunk of time off from your job, and while I cover the cost of groceries and your gas when you take me places, you still have rent and other bills, I'm sure. I never expected you to go without pay. When you first said you'd help, I had no clue how I would swing the expense, so I let you postpone the conversation. A bit longer than I should've, too."

Maddie carried a stack of clothes into her room, but her voice still carried out to him. "Your dad taught you wisdom. Tom gave me some, too. Never loan out money you can't afford to kiss goodbye. Same principle here. I had ten weeks of paid vacation accumulated."

Both his eyebrows shot up. Ten weeks was a lot of accumulated time off.

"I know, I know." She held up her hands in surrender as she came back down the hall. "I never had anywhere I wanted to go or anyone to visit. So the time built up."

"You're using your vacation time to be here?"

Her shoulders lifted dismissively. "I still get paid while taking a much-needed sabbatical from the job. It's a win-win as far as I'm concerned. Like I said before — if you hadn't needed my help, I never would have taken a break. So, when you consider that, I owe you, not the other way around."

"Right. I'll make a mental note. 'Invoice Maddie for services rendered.'"

"Now you're pushing it." With that, she rose and carried the basket down the hall toward his room. "The thing is, state law about home health care is kind of murky. It might not happen, but there's a chance I could get in trouble if you insist on paying me. I'd like to think of what we have here as a simple informal arrangement between friends."

"You've never..." He stalled out, took a breath, and started again. "I got the impression that you don't trust people easily. Yet you took all this time off work to help me, and I'm not much more than a stranger to you."

She said nothing, and he realized he hadn't even bothered to include a question in his convoluted sentence. It was probably for the best. Much as he wanted to know why she'd trusted him, he wasn't sure the answer would do him much good at present. "Anyway, thank you for explaining about your vacation time. I'm glad I haven't put you in a difficult financial situation."

What he really wanted to tell her was that he'd never broached the subject with her because he'd been terrified that if she couldn't afford the time off, he'd have to tell her to go back to work... and that he'd end up back at Lakeview. How could he say all that when she just revealed that she'd never planned on accepting any kind of payment from him? He'd always thought he was a generous person, but she put him to shame.

"You look worried, my friend." Joshua's words dropped onto the polished patina of the dining table. "How are you feeling? How's the recovery coming?"

"This is about as recovered as I'm going to get. I can walk with a cane. I can feed and bathe myself, and I have control of all my bodily functions. I'm told I should be thrilled to be doing so well."

"Okay, then. How is work? You mentioned some new clients."

Holden nodded and pursed his lips.

"Not work, then?"

Maddie passed by the table on her way to the front door. "I'm going to meet Mirabeth for lunch and stop by the grocery store. I should be back by the time you finish up, but if you need me to hurry, just text." She stepped out the door and then popped her head back in. "And text if you think of anything you need from the store."

"Will do." Holden nodded to her. "Give Mirabeth my best."

The door closed behind Maddie before Joshua spoke again. "So is it that the problem is Maddie or that you didn't want Maddie to hear the problem?"

Holden ran his fingers through his hair. "A little of both, I suppose."

"I've got all afternoon." Joshua's stonewashed denim eyes were a calm in the midst of the storm Holden felt raging around and through him.

Holden reached for the Bible he'd brought to the table for their study. He thumbed through it aimlessly for a moment before pushing it aside. "I think I've done a good job of keeping my emotions in check where Maddie's concerned. The problem is more…"

Joshua pulled the same Bible to him and began flipping through the pages with purposeful intent.

"The problem is more that I'm struggling with my future and whether or not a woman will ever want to saddle herself with me in marriage."

"Marriage has been a concern of yours since long before your illness. Is the problem here that you think your health will change God's mind about whether or not He has a mate for you?"

The question pushed Holden back into his chair. Was that what he thought?

"I suppose you could argue with me, but I kind of assumed your illness wasn't a surprise to God." Joshua raised his hands in question. "What do you think?"

Bible study with Joshua never failed to challenge Holden. Sometimes those challenges left him exhilarated. And sometimes they exhausted him. "No. This didn't come as a surprise to God. So what am I really upset about?" He didn't expect Joshua to have the answer... mostly.

"You had reached a place of peace about your singleness, right?"

A man of faith, someone who relies on God in all things — that's how Holden had always thought of himself. Faith had been easier, though, when everything in life was going well, when his biggest complaint was how he hadn't yet met that special someone. A future bound to a cane, though, or a walker and wheelchair on bad days, cast Holden's faith in a whole new light, and he wasn't entirely confident in what he saw. "I thought so, but maybe not."

A smile lit Joshua's face as he sat back in his chair. "You've gone through something major. You're still going through it. Don't punish yourself too much. The idea of settling down with that special someone has mattered to you for a long time now. It makes sense that, when your life is knocked sideways, an old habit or two would shake loose."

"Like spiders falling from the rafters when an earthquake hits?"

Joshua's shudder was dressed up with a grin.

"And my bad habit is worrying about marriage."

The older man's shoulders lifted. "Some habits are harder to break than others, but we've talked about this one enough that you know exactly what I'm going to say."

Holden had heard it from his mentor a number of times. *Faith isn't what you believe when you're in the pew. It's what you believe when you're chained up in the cell next to Paul.*

The point hit home. "I need to trust more, worry less, and be confident in what I believe."

Joshua's eyes twinkled as he rested his hand on the Bible. "So are we good on this one, or do we need to hash it out some more and go over scripture?"

They'd been over all those verses before. In fact, Holden kept the list of them tucked into the back of his Bible — the one on the table. "We're good."

"Excellent. So tell me, then, what you meant by *all things considered* when you mentioned Maddie…?"

"So how did the new jobs come in?" Maddie's voice was curious, but her main focus was on her plate. "Did you hear about them, or did the people come to you? By the way, these might be the best eggs benedict I've ever had. Good call on the restaurant."

"I take my breakfast foods seriously." Holden grinned as he reached for his coffee. "One project is with someone I talked to more than two years ago. His plans got put on hold when the economy tanked. The other guy asked around, and someone recommended me. At this point, it doesn't matter. I'm just grateful work is coming in." Holden took another bite before continuing. "Architecture is a funny business. People think it's all about designing beautiful homes or building fantastic skyscrapers. It's really a whole lot of in-between. I love drawing out plans for someone's dream home, but that kind of work doesn't come along often enough to pay the bills. I do a lot of strip malls and commercial projects."

"Huh. I guess I never gave it any thought." Maddie took a drink of her orange juice. "So you have today all mapped out. Breakfast, job sites, and all that. What about tomorrow? I believe you promised me an entire celebration weekend."

He hesitated until she looked up at him. He might as well go for it. "I hoped we could go to church on Sunday. Until Dr. Matthews signs off, I can't drive, and it's been ages since I've gone."

"Sure. Can I ask you something, though?"

He nodded in a single smooth motion.

"Why didn't you ask me to take you before now? I kind of expected you to bring it up when you got home from Lakeview."

His hand paused in mid-reach, again on its way to his coffee. "Different reasons."

"Yeah…" She drew the word out. "I'm going to need more than that."

The light reflected off his fork as he twirled it between his thumb and forefinger before resting it on the edge of his plate. "I wasn't sure you'd be willing."

"So it's my fault you haven't gone? I don't buy that."

He couldn't get anything past her. "But that's not all."

Her stare had an edge to it, and he reminded himself that this wasn't a subject she enjoyed talking about.

"Fine, I'll tell you, but this doesn't exactly paint me in the best light."

"Authenticity, remember?"

His sigh caused his napkin, resting precariously on the edge of the table, to flutter. "Part of it was my constant companion of late — pride. I wanted to be moving around better before going back. I didn't want everyone to witness what a struggle each step was. Foolish pride, but there you have it." Pride was a beast, but one to which most people could relate.

"What was the other part?"

How could he explain it without sounding like a spiritual fraud? "I wasn't very happy with God. I've struggled with what happened to me, what the rest of my life is going to be like, and whether or not I'll ever wholly recover. Who am I if I'm not able to walk up and down stairs without assistance? Am I even a man if I can't bathe without supervision? How can I…" His voice trailed off into silence.

"You're human. I'd be more worried about you if you didn't struggle with those kinds of questions."

He bit his bottom lip before continuing. "I didn't turn my back on God, not really. I just wasn't happy with Him for a while and was afraid if I went

225

to church, it would become obvious to everyone. Remember all that stuff I said about how your eternity should matter more to me than your friendship?"

"Of course."

"I used an easy excuse — you — and told myself if you saw me as a hypocrite, it would push you further away from God. That's not the real reason, though. The truth is, I didn't want to face Him, and I didn't want to face all the people who believed I was rock solid in my faith. I wasn't ready yet, for either of those encounters."

"But you're ready now?"

With a steady hand this time, he reached for his mug and took a drink before answering. "Yeah, I am. I won't lie and say I'm thrilled with the new direction my life has taken, but I'm in this for the long haul, and I'll follow where God leads me."

"You make it sound easy."

His grin twisted. "Not easy, no. I need to move forward, though."

"Did you get angry at Him?"

Holden bit his lip again, in a quandary about how to answer. "Have you ever seen those trust-building exercises where one person falls back and another person catches them?"

She nodded.

"For a while, it felt like I fell back and God just let me drop. He didn't bother to catch me. If your brother does that, you might come up swinging. If, however, your parent lets you fall, anger isn't going to be your first reaction."

"Hurt." It was only one word, but it conveyed a past of similar experiences. She understood exactly what he meant, and that scared him a little.

"It's the kind of hurt we take personally. He could have elected to do this differently, but He didn't. He chose to let me fall, and it cut deep."

"But you're over it now?" Her normally warm hazel eyes had taken on the edge of polished steel.

Surrendering itself to his ministrations, Holden's napkin became a carefully creased and multi-folded fan. "It still hurts, but it's been overshadowed. I needed some time and distance to gain perspective."

"How do you get perspective on something like that?"

The fan-napkin fell under his scrutiny until he glanced up at her. "I compare myself to God. What is my life compared to His? How about my attitude? My goodness? My priorities? And, ultimately, my hurt. How does my suffering compare to what Christ went through?"

He abandoned the napkin and linked his hands together, resting them on the table. "It took me a little while, but I remembered to evaluate my emotions in light of the cross. Twenty different people can sketch the exact same house and end up with twenty utterly dissimilar drawings. It's about perspective — the angle from which they view the subject — and I had to change mine." He frowned, examining himself not for the first time since this ordeal had begun. "Maybe a better person wouldn't have needed the distance, wouldn't have been hurt to begin with."

She reached across the table and gave his hand a light squeeze. "Thank you for explaining. I wondered. I mean, you always pray at meals, and it seems like you never wavered, but I wondered. Don't knock yourself, either. You're one of the best people I know."

He didn't quite know how to explain to her that understanding the answer wasn't quite the same thing as finding peace with it. The peace would come, though. He had to believe that.

Twenty-Three

The first stop was in nearby Springfield. Holden made several sketches while Maddie took his camera and clicked away at the property from a variety of angles. April was upon them and spring was making itself known. Those trees that weren't green yet were showing signs of budding, and everything around them smelled of healthy soil and new life.

"I don't think we're too far away from the therapists and your doctor saying you don't need a babysitter anymore."

His eyes briefly met hers before returning to his sketch pad. "I stopped thinking of you as a babysitter a long time ago. Warden. General. Tormenter. Those are all good choices. Babysitter? Nah."

She shook her head and pointed the camera at him. Oblivious to the pictures she took, he remained wholly focused on his work until his phone rang. He stopped mid-swipe with his pencil and furrowed his brow. Sticking the pencil in his mouth, he reached for his phone, but then he couldn't talk because of the pencil in his mouth. Maddie reached out and snatched it from him and tucked it into his pocket as he clicked the green button on his phone. "Hello?"

His eyes widened, and if she hadn't known any better, she'd have said it was panic doing the widening. Holden's gaze shot to her before skittering away as a blush climbed his neck. What an odd reaction...

"Uh, hi, Mom."

Oh, this should be rich. He always said how much he loved his parents, but he made a point of calling them when she wasn't around. She'd resisted the urge to eavesdrop so far, but his blush was going to make that harder. Plus, there were no walls between them this time.

"Working. What are you up to?" He scrunched his shoulder to hold the phone in place and reached back into his pocket for the pencil.

So, he was one of those. A distracted talker.

"Sounds like fun. You've always enjoyed doing your canning... mm-hm... Yeah, I remember her. No, I don't think..."

Holden closed his eyes, rolled his neck from side to side, and tucked the pencil away in his pocket again. "Listen, Mom, I'm out in a field sketching a building site. No, it's fine, but... I'd really rather you not... But I'm not looking... It's been years... I don't even know her..."

He tucked the phone away and rubbed his forehead.

"Everything okay?" Maddie didn't want to pry, but her curiosity was too piqued not to.

His eyes opened, and he stared at her for a minute, those green orbs a million miles away. "Sally Wentworth's husband cheated on her, and she left him."

Um... what was she supposed to say to that? "And your mom wanted you to know?"

He nodded. "Apparently Sally hasn't aged a day, and those would be good genes to pass on to my parents' future grandchildren."

Maddie bit her bottom lip to try to keep the laughter at bay. "Your mom's trying to fix you up with the new divorcee in town?"

"Worse."

Biting her tongue was no longer cutting it. A snort escaped. "Uh, what could be worse? Unless Sally Wentworth lives *here*?"

Holden's eyes crinkled at the corners. "You just gave me my silver lining. I thought it couldn't get any worse, but at least she's still in another..." The ring of his phone interrupted his words. He retrieved it from his pocket again and groaned. "Hello?"

Maddie swooped in and rescued the sketch pad from Holden's tightening grip.

"Sure, Sally, I remember you. Listen, I'm working... I should really get... Well, it's been nice catching up... Is there any way we can do this another..." He mouthed the word *sorry* to her and stood, waving his arms toward the car. Only, he couldn't talk on the phone and use his walker, which required two hands, at the same time.

She could leave him there to figure it out for himself, but it really was too funny. The woman on the other end of the phone was going to hyperventilate soon. She surely wasn't taking enough pauses to breathe properly.

Maddie folded the walker down, picked it up in her left hand, and offered Holden her right arm. He looped his hand through her elbow, and they began making the way back to the car as Sally went on and on. Her husband wasn't the man she'd thought. She really wanted to start a family. Her biological clock was ticking. She was a fabulous homemaker and believed cleanliness was next to godliness. She was a member of a nice conservative church in town.

How many churches could Holden's hometown have, anyway? Wasn't it a small town?

By the time they made it to the car, Holden's eyes had a glazed look to them. She snapped her fingers in front of his face and lifted her eyebrows. She wasn't sure she wanted to be stuck in the car listening to poor Sally. If he let her talk much longer, she was going to start naming their future children.

"Uh, Sally, listen, I need to go. I've got to get in the car, and I'm afraid I'll lose the connection. Bye."

If she wasn't mistaken, Holden was seriously contemplating throwing that phone back into the trees. Maddie reached out and plucked it from his hand before he gave in to the temptation. "You get in. I'll store the walker in the trunk."

A few minutes later, Maddie was clicking her seatbelt into place.

"I'm sorry you had to hear all that."

She quirked an eyebrow at him. "Are you kidding me? People usually pay big bucks for this kind of live entertainment."

Holden shook his head as he buckled his own belt. "Next stop, Mechanicsville. The site is in an undeveloped wooded area. With any luck we can locate it without too much trouble."

They got back into the car and headed south on I-95. Once they arrived at the next site, they repeated the same process. The terrain was a bit more treacherous and not overly friendly to a walker. He would have been fine with his cane — his progress was that profound — but he needed to sit in order to properly sketch, so they forced the walker through the underbrush and limbs and battled vines intent on tangling themselves around its wheels. His smile and relaxed posture told the story, though. Holden enjoyed what he was doing, even if it had been a fight against nature to get there.

With his task complete at the second site, the two settled into the car's front seat before he spoke. "Should we stop for lunch before we head home, or would you rather get back to familiar territory before we get a bite to eat?"

"How often have you driven 95?"

He tipped an imaginary hat to her and chuckled. "Point well made. Let's eat before we get on the freeway. Knowing the traffic, it'll be past dinnertime before we make it back home."

They enjoyed a leisurely lunch at an open-air café. Maddie, curious about the purpose of the day's trip, asked, "So why the sketches and photos? You already turned in blueprints on these jobs, right?"

Holden nodded. "I submitted a preliminary drawing with my bid. Now I need to work on the final plans. I'm not always able to, but when I can, I like to soak in the natural landscape around the building site. It might prompt me to suggest a change to the plan. They can accept or decline any alterations I recommend — I'll complete the job either way — but I want the homes I design to be lasting testaments to quality work, and sometimes those subtle modifications mean the difference between the client being simply satisfied or ready to give my name to all their friends.

"What sorts of changes would you suggest based on what you saw today?"

In the middle of taking a bite, Holden took his time before he answered. "Nothing jumped out at me in Springfield, but the second site is hillier than I realized. He can build the house the way he wants, but the contractor will be required to tear out big chunks of the surrounding terrain to level the ground. The home will end up in a gully, and whoever lives in it will fight flooding every time it rains."

"How do you fix a problem like that?"

Holden shrugged and said, "I'd consider building on stilts and leaving the existing landscape as-is. The current vegetation will help to prevent a lot of flooding that might otherwise occur. When you start bulldozing and tearing out the plants and trees, you produce a situation where the natural landscape can no longer do its job of absorbing and redirecting the flow of water through the area."

"In other words, you create the problem that leads to the flooding."

"Exactly." Holden popped the last bite of his sandwich into his mouth.

Stifling a laugh, Maddie stood and tucked her chair away as far as it would go under the table.

"What are you laughing at?"

"I've never seen anyone eat with as much gusto as you. I don't think we've ever shared a meal I haven't found entertaining."

He got to his feet and began to push his chair in, too. Someone passed behind him and brushed against his back. Maddie wouldn't have given the encounter a second thought, except Holden suddenly white-knuckled the chair's back.

Swiftly, she got around the table and to his side.

"Don't touch me." His mouth barely moved as he bit the words out.

He wasn't in danger of falling, so Maddie took a half step back. His posture was reminiscent of someone suffering a mild tonic seizure. Instinct, though, told her that was a misleading route. "Is it easing up?" Whatever *it* was.

"Yes."

The next instant, he released the back of the chair, reached for his cane, and started moving away from her at half his normal speed. Holden might be avoiding eye contact now, but she'd seen the panic in his eyes when he'd first stiffened and gripped his seat. A call to the doctor was in order. Especially considering he hadn't acted surprised by the event. This wasn't the first time it had happened. Which meant he'd been hiding it from her...

Twenty-Four

"Yuck!"

"W-what is it?" Holden jerked to wakefulness at the yell from his car mate.

Maddie pointed to a man who was throwing up on the side of the road.

"Wonder if he got carsick." He rubbed his eyes and wished he could un-see what he'd just seen.

She snorted. "We're going five miles per hour. How can anyone possibly get car sick? I'll bet it's food poisoning."

"Exhaust fumes from all this traffic."

"Nah." One hand waved in front of her nose while the other remained on the wheel. "A baby in the car produced a lethal diaper."

"They were watching an in-car movie, and a gross autopsy scene came on."

Maddie shook her head. Either she was done coming up with ideas, or she'd conceded the point to him. He preferred to think the latter, but it was unlikely.

A long couple of miles later, Maddie made a choking sound. Holden, awake this time, looked around. Sure enough, a man stood on the side of the freeway. Relieving himself. More than a little embarrassed on behalf of men everywhere, Holden shook his head. "That's just wrong. The trees — and privacy — are fifteen feet away."

"Maybe he was afraid of woodland monsters." Maddie tossed a grin at him.

"What sorts of woodland monsters want to hang around with all this congestion?"

"Um… werewolves." Her fingers tapped the steering wheel in a staccato rhythm. "Vampires?"

"Please tell me you're not going to say zombies next." Her blush made him smile. "I would have believed black bears, you know. Or even rabid vultures. But definitely not vampires."

"Can vultures get rabies?"

The conversation petered into a silence that remained comfortable for the next twenty minutes. Then Maddie asked, "How many accidents have we passed since we saw that guy using the side of the road as a bathroom?"

"Three. Two on the left and one on the right."

"We've only gone ten miles. This is ridiculous, even for 95."

Holden leaned over toward the passenger window and craned his neck. "A lot of cars are veering onto the shoulder to drive around something up ahead. I can't tell what, but something's obstructing traffic up there."

Maddie checked her mirrors and quickly moved left rather than to the emergency lane.

Several minutes later, they drove by an older model motorhome parked in the right lane. Calling it dilapidated would have been a compliment. Holden examined every window as they passed by at a slow crawl. "I think it's abandoned."

"What do you mean?" Her eyes cut over to him before returning to the brake lights ahead.

"I couldn't see anyone. Would someone leave their motorhome in the middle of the freeway and just walk away?"

"They stopped to use their bathroom."

"Wouldn't they pull off to the shoulder for that? Besides, it took us five minutes to pass it. Surely someone would've popped up in one of the windows if anybody was inside."

"The engine died?" Her voice lacked optimism.

"The hood would be up, or their flashers would be, well, flashing."

"Got it." She snapped her fingers. "They were being chased by zombies, and the traffic was going so slow that the zombies started catching up, and they decided their best bet would be to flee on foot."

"So what you're saying here is that zombies, whose bodies are basically rotting away with each step, can move faster than traffic on this freeway?"

Maddie gave him a *well-duh* look, and Holden laughed. "Point taken."

A short time later she let out a whoop of excitement and gave the steering wheel a forceful tap. Even her hair got in on the action, the blonde curls dancing around her head like an enthusiastic halo.

"Please tell me we're finally going fast enough to outrun the zombies."

"Woohoo! Thirty-five miles per hour." Her triumph was contagious.

He rested his head against his seat. "As frequently as I travel this road, I've never noticed this many bizarre happenings before."

"I'll bet you never had quite as much fun, either."

"Indubitably." The drive might be taking forever, but at least he'd discovered a use for that word.

Another fifteen minutes and a meteoric rise to forty-five miles per hour led them to the incline heading into Triangle, Virginia. Maddie pointed. "It's majestic, isn't it? I never get tired of the sight." The National Museum of the Marine Corps rose above the trees to their right.

"It's a beautiful building, a real work of art."

"They modeled the design after the Iwo Jima monument."

Holden nodded. "I make a point to know the history of interesting buildings, but how did you learn that?"

"I was stuck on the freeway because of an accident one day. I made it to an exit, followed the signs to the museum, and spent the next few hours touring the place and reading lots of placards. It was enlightening."

"We should go sometime. Make a day of it."

"Haven't you been?" Her eyebrow quirked up in that endearing way.

He reached his hands above and behind him to stretch in the cramped space of the car. "Of course, but I only went to study the building. I went over every inch of the facility but didn't take in a single exhibit."

A smile lighting her face, she shook her head. "It may be another month before you can convince me to get on this freeway again."

"Perhaps we can find a different route."

Just then the traffic began to open up and Maddie was able to accelerate almost to the speed limit. The last few miles on 95 flew by in comparison to the inhumanly sluggish ones survived thus far.

Holden stared at his image in the mirror. Too much time had slipped past since his last Sunday at church. Listening to the podcasts wasn't the same as being there. He'd been looking forward to it from the moment Maddie had agreed to take him. A part of him dreaded it, though.

The little voice inside wouldn't leave him be. It told him he was far from ready, people would stare, and a misstep would land him flat on his face in front of everyone — and not in a posture-of-prayer kind of way. The voice was relentless, but he was determined not to give in to its pleas and rants.

On top of his own back-to-church anxiety, he had a guest to contend with, and she brought an entire host of her own anxieties. He needed to be at his best for her sake. Holden might not be able to walk without aid yet, but he could still walk tall.

A wave of satisfaction moved through his soul at its very depths, the kind of satisfaction that came from knowing he was precisely where God wanted him.

His eyes shot up to the mirror again as he straightened his tie. *Is this where You want me, God? Right here? In pain and sharing my house with a woman who makes me wish I wasn't in pain?* Stunned, he leaned on the bathroom counter. *You brought me these jobs, and I give You all the glory for that. Did You bring me the illness, too? Was that part of Your plan for me?*

Not sure he was happy with the answer stirring in his heart, he finished with his tie and reached for the mouthwash. The brand was a new one Maddie had purchased. Holden wasn't finicky, but he did like to know what was going into his mouth. He unscrewed the lid and held the bottle close so he could get a whiff of it first.

Without warning, pain sizzled at lightning speed from his mid-back out around his right side. His hand clenched in reaction and a geyser of mouthwash shot out of the bottle and straight up his nose.

He fought panic as the sensation of drowning — in acid, no less — hit him. His muscles were locked, and he could do nothing except wait it out. With excruciating slowness, the pain in his back and side receded. Holden set the mouthwash down with a gurgling thump. At least he hadn't dropped it.

The burning was bearable now, though he was certain his nasal passage and sinuses would never again be the same.

A glance in the mirror told him more than he wanted to know. His face was beet red, and he had a *nouveau riche* design of minty green inkblots across his shirt, tie, and pants.

Holden picked up the mouthwash and flung it with all his might into his shower. As soon as he released the bottle, he regretted the action. Hadn't he left temper tantrums behind with pre-school?

Apparently not. At least the shower's door had been open.

He'd clean up that mess later. At the rate he was going, he'd barely have time to change clothes.

Holden gave directions as Maddie drove. She tensed with each turn that brought them closer to the place of worship, and he'd misplaced all his calming words that morning. His mood had flipped from peaceful to sour with the mouthwash incident. Had he not already talked to her about giving him a ride, he'd have slammed the door on the idea of church and climbed back into bed.

He would muddle through and hope the day didn't end as disastrously as it had started. Not exactly the best frame of mind for someone bringing a visitor into a house of worship. What did his mom always tell him? *Keep an attitude of gratitude.* If gratitude was a destination, his GPS had been hacked, and he'd been sent to the middle of Siberia.

Twenty-Five

The building came into view and Maddie stared.

Holden made a sound that might have been laughter. Or choking. "What did you expect?"

"I was under the impression you went to a large mega-church." She parked the car and got out. "This place couldn't fit more than, what, fifty, maybe sixty people?" It wasn't much more than a double-wide mobile home next to another double-wide with patio tables and chairs in between.

"It's a quirky little place." They approached the front steps. "I'll tell you more about it over lunch afterward. For now, let's go and enjoy."

Maddie surreptitiously inspected her surroundings as they walked into the church and took their seats. The place was packed, but even so, there were at most eighty people in attendance — still more than she'd guessed. She was so busy taking everything in that she didn't realize everyone was standing to sing a song until Holden said her name.

Looking from him to the hymn book he held out toward her, she decided to pay better attention to what was going on around her. They shared the hymnal and sang along with everybody else. She took the lead from him and remained standing for an opening prayer, sat when that was over, listened to some announcements, stood to sing again, and then sat again when they passed a wooden dish into which people put envelopes and money. Some of it was familiar, but other parts were alien to Maddie. When she last went to church, she'd seen it all through the eyes of a child. Today's experience was much different.

Focusing, she gave the pastor's message her attention. Holden would ask her what she thought when they went to lunch later, and she wanted to at least give him a complete answer. He shared his Bible with her, too, so she could follow along. While she didn't understand every point the pastor made, he seemed passionate and sincere.

She would forget most of the sermon by the time she went to bed that night. One line, though, wasn't going to be shaken so easily.

"No matter where you are in your life right now, think about a time when you drew near to Christ. What did it feel like? Were you different because of it? While you go throughout your lives this week, I want you to ponder this one question: Are you as happy now as you were then?"

Maddie's mind immediately went to that time when she'd been nine years old. Were she to peel away the layers of cynicism built up through the years and peer into the heart of the little girl she'd been back then, a simple truth would be undeniable. Those months had been the happiest of her childhood.

Warmth flooded her fingers as she held the hymnal and stared at the plain wooden cross hanging behind the middle-aged man leading the music for the closing song.

Church ended twenty minutes ago, but they were no closer to the exit than when the final *amen* had been uttered. Every person present wanted to speak with Holden and tell him how glad they were to see him. Then they all, of course, insisted on meeting Maddie. The speculative looks told her most of these people had them married off and toting twin babies around within the year. If only they knew. Holden was a lot more likely to carry around a horned toad than he was to marry her.

Her breath caught in her throat at the zigzagging thought. Maddie wanted him to be happy. With his kindness and generosity, he would make some woman a fantastic husband. It wouldn't be her, though, because she had no intention of trusting anyone to get that close to her.

But was it wrong to wish he wanted to get that close to her?

Maddie crushed the thought before it fully formed and forced a smile to her face, the same one she used when being introduced to family members of a patient. She shook hands, nodded politely, and wondered if she dared ask where the nearest restroom was. With her luck, she'd come out with her skirt tucked into her underwear and toilet paper trailing behind her. Better not to ask at all.

Holden had been a bit off this morning, and she'd worried for a bit. Church had wiped away his funk, though. He flourished as person after person stopped to tell him of their prayers on his behalf.

At one point, a group of older women surrounded him. Was she witnessing a senior flash mob of adoring fans? He glanced up from the ladies and winked at her. The word "auxiliary" floated on the air somewhere nearby.

Ah. The originators of white cotton undergarments — socks, t-shirts, and…

Maddie shook her head. The last thing she ought to be doing in church was thinking about Holden's underwear.

The last well-wisher finally slipped through the exit, and not a moment too soon. Not that she was superstitious, but a lightning storm rolling in wouldn't have surprised her. She was pretty sure senior flash mobs and men's underwear were off limits as far as wandering thoughts went in a house of worship. "Are you ready to go?"

He smiled and nodded. "Yes, I am. Thank you for coming today. I needed to be here more than I realized." Following her to the parking lot, he added, "One of these days I'm going to beat you and do the gentlemanly thing."

"What would that be?"

"Why, open the car door for the lady, of course. Don't tell me no one's ever opened the door for you before?"

Maddie shrugged, glancing in the rearview mirror as she did so. "I can't recall, but that doesn't mean it never happened."

Holden *tsked* as she pulled out into traffic.

"Home, or did you want to eat lunch out somewhere?"

He named a restaurant in reply, and she lifted an eyebrow at him. "That's a bit highbrow. Do we need a reservation?"

"It's taken care of."

She shook her head. Men were mysterious creatures. A sandwich shop would have suited her fine.

Maddie ate her words. Their table, with an unobstructed view of the Potomac River, was worth whatever the cost of the meal was going to be.

Seagulls dipped and danced in the air, sandpipers dotted the shore, and the occasional pelican swooped in for a meal. The gurgling whoosh of the river accompanied by the crisp cerulean sky created an ambiance no restaurant could ever hope to artificially duplicate.

"I should take up canoeing."

Holden chuckled. "I see the water and think of inner-tubing."

She laughed. "I always knew you were wild at heart."

"That sounds about right."

"So tell me, have you learned anything more about those former clients who said they got similar bids?"

Holden's mouth dipped down at both corners. "I asked them to send me what they'd gotten. Two of them did. The written bid is almost word-for-word the same as the one I'd submitted to them, and the drawings are too close to be a coincidence."

"Do you have a suspect in mind?"

"It has to be either Yvette or Miles. I'm not sure what to do about it."

"You should talk to Tom."

Holden's eyebrow lifted.

"He didn't make it to detective based on good looks and charm. He's really good at what he does. If nothing else, he can give you some pointers to help you figure out how to narrow it down."

"I really don't want it to be Miles. Not only do I trust the guy, but I can't run the business without him."

"I'm telling you. Talk to Tom."

Maddie pulled into the driveway and parked, then went to retrieve the walker from her trunk. He didn't need it much anymore, but having it handy had become a habit. She set it down and closed the trunk with more force than necessary. In doing so, she caught sight of someone on the front porch.

"Can we help you?" Her call went unanswered.

The form, half hidden in the shadows, moved forward, and she was able to make out a woman. The visitor could be an old girlfriend, a neighbor, a fan, or who-knew-what. Did architects get stalkers?

She reached for her purse — and the pepper spray nestled within — when Holden exclaimed, "Lauren!" Maddie's head snapped up as he pulled himself from the car and embraced the woman. Seeing her in the bright Virginia sunlight, Maddie couldn't miss the dusting of grey in auburn hair so like Holden's or the fine lines in a feminine face that bore a striking resemblance to his.

"Maddie, I'd like you to meet my sister Lauren. Lauren, this is my friend Maddie." The stranger-who-wasn't-a-stranger cast a speculative gaze from Holden to her before reaching out a hand. Given no other choice, Maddie walked back around the car — and away from her pepper-spray-concealing purse — and shook it. Lauren's grip was firm, but the expression in her green eyes fell somewhere between guarded and outright ambivalent.

Maddie offered them both a smile before going to unlock the front door. Fishy was right there to greet them as he always was whenever they went somewhere together. The cat never bothered to greet *her* at the door, just Holden. They could go sit on the front porch together, and Fishy would be right there waiting for them to come back inside. Fishy was his normal Holden-worshipping self until he noticed Lauren. Then he hissed and took off down the hallway.

Silently applauding her cat, Maddie excused herself and escaped down the same path while brother and sister caught up with each other. Once in her room, she took in every detail, trying to memorize it and capture the essence of peace she'd known since arriving there. Not even two months had passed, and she shouldn't think of this place as home, but she did. The realization held no surprise for her.

With robotic movements, she changed into jeans and a t-shirt before yanking her suitcase out from where it was tucked under the bed. Drawer by drawer, she emptied the dresser.

Holden's sister would need the room, and he was doing well enough that the doctor would be okay with Maddie leaving him in Lauren's care. Even so, she made a mental note to call Dr. Matthews the next day and let him know about the change.

She would wait to mention the strange convulsive attack he'd suffered the day before until they were at a regular appointment. Maddie cringed at the thought. Holden's progress had been slow but sure up to that point, with no big surprises along the way.

Part of her dreaded telling the doctor about that encounter in the café. Holden wouldn't thank her for it, but it would have to be done.

 Twenty-Six

Holden could hear Maddie moving around, first in her room, then in the laundry room. He heard the muffled sound of her voice for a bit. Then a series of yowls brought the hair at the nape of his neck to attention. The loud thump that shook a couple of pictures hanging on the wall he faced didn't help, either. The cat's anger eventually confined itself to hisses, but still… He didn't like to think what Maddie was up to. Why couldn't she sit down and visit with them instead?

Lauren had been elected by the family to come check on him. He'd buffaloed them well enough about the seriousness of his illness — and how dire the consequences — but as soon as he'd let it slip that a female nurse was sharing his residence, his parents and siblings had begun pooling their money together for airfare. His mother, gifted with a sense of drama, had declared he was dancing down the road to perdition.

"In truth, they all just want you to move back home."

"That's not where God wants me." He craned his neck to see what Maddie was up to. "This is where He's called me to be."

"Sharing your home with a woman?" Her eyebrow quirked up, but her gaze was serious.

"Things aren't always the way they seem." Lauren, the only one of his siblings to have gone through a divorce, was the most likely of them all to give him a chance to explain. He was surprised she'd been the one designated to come. "How did you get the job of checking up on me, anyway?"

She smiled. "I volunteered. Any of the others, and you may have ended up with a shotgun and a wedding license greeting you today. I figured I was your best bet."

"I'm pretty sure you can't obtain a wedding license unless you know the bride's name."

Just then Maddie walked past the living room, Fishy's carrier in one hand and her wheeled suitcase towed by the other. Alarm shot through him as her intent became clear. Holden tried to jump up from the couch but couldn't find anything to grip for the boost he needed. Too proud to let his sister see his weakness, he'd refused to bring the walker with them to the couch.

"Blast it, Lauren, give me a hand up." He spat the words, certain Maddie would be gone from his home and life before he could even gain his feet. Clearly not sure how to help him, she offered a hand but not the strong support required to get him up from the sunken couch. "Get the walker!" That was an instruction she at least understood. Within seconds, Holden pulled himself up and maneuvered toward the door.

He gained the foyer as Maddie came back in. The suitcase was gone, but Fishy's carrier still sat inside the entrance. Maddie smiled at him and then past his shoulder to where his sister stood. "I stripped the bed and put fresh linens in the guest room." Her gaze returned to his face. "The bedding I removed is in the washer now. You'll want to transfer it to the dryer later when the cycle finishes."

"Maddie—"

His sister had the decency to speak up. "You don't need to leave on my account."

Her professionally detached smile — the one he'd come to loathe — was front and center. "Of course I do. I'm pretty sure one of the perks of being Holden's family is that you're not forced to sleep on the couch." Turning to Holden, she added, "I spoke to Dr. Matthews, and he said it's fine for Lauren to stay with you during her visit. I'll move back in after she's left unless the doctor clears you to live alone before then."

A rock settled in Holden's stomach. "Maddie—"

The woman in question gave him a bright smile before picking up the cat carrier. "If you need anything, you have my number. I assume Lauren can drive you to the pool and other appointments, but if not, just let me know. It's not a problem."

She stepped through the door without giving him a chance to answer. The only sound was Mr. Fish Breath hissing ferociously as Maddie walked toward her car. The feline even gave his sister the evil eye.

"Well, that could have gone better." Lauren's wry voice fell into the quiet room like a stone into a meat grinder — unwelcome and out of place.

Holden turned and glared at her before pushing his walker aside and walking into the kitchen, where he started a pot of coffee and slammed every cupboard he needed to open in order to complete the task. Then he slammed a few more cupboards for good measure. The action didn't improve his mood. He couldn't shake the image of gold, brown, and smoky green woven together in her eyes... or the hurt he thought he'd seen reflected there.

When he turned around, Lauren stood there, her back against the spiced mocha wall, her arms crossed over her chest, concern on her face. "*Are* you dancing down the road to perdition?"

Holden set his coffee cup down on the table and gingerly settled himself into a chair, when what he really wanted to do was throw himself into it in frustration, something he could no longer do without great personal cost. "This might be easier if I were."

Lauren pulled herself away from the wall and poured herself a cup of coffee before joining him. "Why don't you tell me about it. Believe it or not, I am a woman. I might be able to give you some insight here. Who knows? Maybe it'll even be helpful."

Twenty-Seven

"He really believes this God stuff." Maddie kicked a pebble off the patio and glanced over at Tom where he stood by the grill. Mirabeth was inside, slicing tomatoes and whatever else she did to make the most scrumptious burgers known to man. Tom's job was to guard the grill against ravenous guests and turn the tempting meat patties over from time to time. His wife did everything else. It worked for them.

"Maybe the God stuff's not so crazy."

Something was wrong. She'd always been able to count on him to be cynical with her.

"Do you ever wonder about it?" he asked.

"Are you drinking again?" The question was accompanied with a lifted eyebrow, but he didn't wave off her words like usual.

He didn't turn his head, but his eyes cut to the side to see her, his face inscrutable. "I'm not saying I think this guy is all that. I'm just wondering if you should give God some thought."

Maddie couldn't believe her ears. "Where's this coming from? When's the last time *you* gave Him any thought?"

Tom finished flipping the burgers and put the lid back on the grill. He backed a step away from the heat and peered out over the garden, bright with pink and purple tulips. "Haley's doing real well at school."

She bit her tongue and waited. He would get where he wanted the conversation to go when he was good and ready.

"She's happier than I've ever seen her. More centered, too."

Maddie's grunt could hardly be considered conversation.

"Haley went and got herself involved in this group. I guess they're on all the campuses. They're not a church in the traditional sense, but she goes to meetings, studies the Bible, and hangs out with them."

No. It couldn't be. "Are you telling me she got…"

"Saved, yeah."

"What!"

"About a year ago."

"Why didn't you say anything?" Okay, so it wasn't like they were hiding a drug conviction or unexpected pregnancy, but still. Why hadn't Tom told her?

"It's complicated."

"Why?" Maddie's voice demanded answers. She was done letting him take his sweet time to say what was on his mind.

"At first I was embarrassed. Ashamed, even. We didn't invite anyone over when Haley was home from school because we were hoping she'd snap out of it and no one would ever need to know. Then, somewhere along the way, Mirabeth and I reconsidered. I always told you church folk couldn't be trusted. I'd seen too many supposedly good Christian people brought up on murder charges to put much stock in all that stuff. Once I got past being embarrassed by my own daughter, though, I started to see it. She was different. This thing she believed in had changed her from the inside out, and I couldn't deny it."

"She's always been an incredible kid."

Tom nodded. "Yeah, I can't argue that. Spend some time with her, though, and you'll understand what I mean."

"So, Haley changed, and suddenly that means all this God talk is for real?"

"Do you see it in Holden? Is he different?" He had his serious face on, which always included a frown.

"Holden is…" Her words trailed off as she tried to pull her scattered thoughts together. *Holden is hardworking and honest, funny and compassionate, the man whose emerald eyes I'd like to drown in.* Somehow she didn't think Tom would appreciate that answer. "Holden's the best man I've ever met."

The frown deepened.

"Present company excluded, of course."

"Of course." His wink was almost lost in the glare of the sun. "That difference, it's not just in the way he acts. It comes from inside."

He was right. Holden wasn't the same as most people, and while the difference in him was definitely something on the inside, it reflected through the things he said and did on the outside. Other people might be as thoughtful or considerate, but they didn't possess that inner something that made Holden so special. She'd already decided it had to be God, but Tom's pointing it out rankled. "So what are you saying?"

He offered a half-shrug. "Mirabeth and I started attending church."

Maddie almost choked on an ice cube before spitting it out on the grass and gasping for breath. "*Church?*"

"Yeah."

"Were you ever going to tell me?"

"We wanted a decent grasp on what we were talking about before we spoke up. Your experiences with foster families and church were mixed. It seemed like something worth handling delicately."

Mirabeth stepped out onto the patio then and walked over to them. Her arm snaked around her husband's waist, and she tugged him to her side. "Looks like y'all are having a serious chat out here."

Maddie pulled her eyes away from Tom and gaped at the woman who had shown her so much

264

kindness over the years. "You're going to church." Accusation bristled in each syllable.

Instead of wincing at the harsh tone, Mirabeth nodded kindly. "We are, and we like it. Sasha isn't so crazy about it, but we... Well, we both prayed to accept Christ. We plan to get baptized but wanted you to be there, too. We've been trying to find the right time to tell you. Right or wrong, it didn't seem like bringing it up while we were dinner guests in your friend's home was appropriate."

Whirling away from them, she escaped into the house. The entire axis of her world was spinning out of control, and Maddie could no longer tell which way was up. How long had they been attending? Why hadn't they told her?

Never mind that she'd been to church recently, too. Without sending out a worldwide text announcing it, either. Forget that she'd been wondering about God more and — on some level — even hoping. None of that mattered at the moment. She was driven by panic, by the fear of losing yet another family.

Space — that's what she needed. Space between her and the happy *born again* couple in the back yard. Maddie bolted out the front door of the house only to discover Sasha waiting for her. The girl's presence sealed her fate. There would be no mad dash for freedom today.

"So the folks told you about their religious experience, huh?"

She nodded and resisted the urge to fling her hands in the air and demand a do-over.

"You look about as shocked as I felt when my big sis came home from college for a weekend and wouldn't stop preaching to me about Jesus."

"How long has this been going on?"

Sasha shrugged. "Haley started talking about it a year or so ago. At first I thought she'd been taken over by brain-eating aliens. Every time I talked to her, she preached. Eventually I didn't want to talk to her anymore."

Maddie stared. Where was the rancor? "You're okay with it now?"

A teenage flip of the hair. "She got it together after a while and apologized, went on and on about how she was so excited by the change in her that she wanted me to have it, too, and she hadn't realized how obnoxious she was. She backed off and talked to me about regular stuff again. She's almost like the old Haley now."

"Almost?"

Sasha gave a disinterested eye roll. "Oh, you know. She still prays and brings a Bible with her when she comes home to visit, and maybe she's happier with herself than she used to be, but she's still basically the same."

"And your folks?"

"Started going to church a couple months ago. Like out of the blue, you know? Made me go with them. Dad was going to tell you. He drove over to see you, but he bought you bacon instead. Like that makes sense."

It did, but this wasn't the time to say so.

Sasha continued as though she had no need to breathe. "He was all scratched up, too. Maybe he should have given Fishy the bacon instead of you. Anyway, when Mom questioned him, he told her he hadn't said anything to you yet. You remember what Dad always says about interrogation, right?"

"It's all about the timing." Maddie sighed. Tom had never planned to hide it from her, and she couldn't blame him for her absence these past weeks. She'd thrown herself into caring for Holden to the exclusion of all else. Besides, even if he and Mirabeth wanted to keep it a secret, they had the right. "I'm acting like a spoiled brat."

Sasha grinned and flipped her hair back over her shoulders again. "Nah. I got the corner on that. I'm the baby of the family, remember? My entire life is dedicated to being a diva and throwing tantrums."

Silence settled between them for a minute before Maddie asked, "Are they happy?"

"Mom and Dad? Yeah. They're nicer, too. Not that they were mean before or anything, but they're more patient. They don't snap as much. When Dad gets home from work, instead of talking about all the bad things people did that day, he talks about some of the good stuff now. That's new. I kind of like it, but I'll deny ever saying so."

Maddie held up her hand and parted her fingers Vulcan style. "Scout's honor."

The two giggled. "So, you gonna run away or eat lunch?"

A groan escaped. "I suppose I need to apologize for running out."

"Anything to get at Mom's burgers, right?"

The girl was only half wrong.

"By the way, Dad likes Holden."

"Huh?"

"I'm as surprised as you. He's hated every guy you ever dated."

"We're not dating."

Sasha laughed. "That's probably why he likes him, then."

The two linked arms and walked back into the house.

"Oh, gross. They've been doing more of that, too."

Maddie looked up. Tom and Mirabeth were still on the back patio, wound together in a hug. The couple wasn't kissing, but she could think of only one word to describe the embrace: intimate.

As Maddie pulled into the parking lot at her apartment, her cell phone rang. The area code was unfamiliar, but she went ahead and answered it. "Hello?"

"Let's do lunch." Lauren didn't bother with niceties.

Maddie glowered at her phone. A venomous snake might have been more welcome at this point. "L-lunch?"

"I thought we should get together for some girl talk, but you'll need to pick me up."

"Is Holden all right?" What did his sister want with her?

"Oh, he's fine. To be honest, he doesn't know I'm calling. He'd get all brotherly on me and tell me to stay out of his business. You've done so much to help him, though, and I'd like to properly thank you."

"Um, okay. But he's not supposed to be left alone."

"I'll make sure Miles is here. They'll spend the whole day doing architect stuff and won't even know I'm gone."

Maddie searched the recesses of her mind but couldn't come up with a valid excuse to beg off. "Does tomorrow work?"

"Tomorrow is perfect. I look forward to seeing you. Just text me when you're coming, and I'll pop out the door and meet you out front. Otherwise he might try to invite himself along, and girl talk isn't nearly as fun with my baby brother listening to every word."

Lauren hung up before she could say anything else.

What just happened? Knowing the conservative bent of Holden's family, Maddie wondered if she would be facing an inquisition.

Maddie pulled up to the curb and bit her lower lip as Lauren darted across the lawn and dove into her car. "He knows I'm up to something. Hit it." Her voice faded into a mutter. "So much for Miles keeping him busy."

Holden came through the front door, his eyebrows drawn together and a frown marring his face. Her foot on the accelerator weighed down by guilt, Maddie drove away.

Lauren's phone immediately started buzzing, and Maddie couldn't help but wonder if Holden was the only normal person in the family.

"Yes."

Maddie's eyebrows shot up. "I didn't mean to say that out loud."

Her passenger laughed. "You didn't say anything out loud, but the question was on your face, so I thought I could answer it for you. Yes, our family is strange, and yes, I lied to my brother and told him I was going out to check the mail." She paused for just a second before continuing. "Oh, and yes, I'm going to ignore his texts, and he'll be waiting for us with a big frown when you bring me back. It won't hurt my feelings at all if you push me out at the end of the driveway and take off before he can get to the car."

The day kept getting weirder and weirder... "So, uh, where would you like to eat?"

Lauren shook her head. "You pick. I'll be happy with whatever you choose."

Maddie gave half her concentration to her driving. The other half was dedicated to dreading the meal ahead.

Maddie pulled into one of her favorite diners. "They serve the best soul food around."

Lauren quirked an eyebrow. "What's soul food?"

Maddie chucked. "Food that's good for your soul, but not your body. Chitlins, jowl, chicken liver — all the comfort foods from down South." Despite her secret delight at Lauren's waning face, she took pity on the woman. "The fried chicken is melt-in-your mouth delicious, and the pork chops are so good you'd sell your grandmother to get a single bite."

"Is there salad on the menu?"

"The only things green on this menu are the beans and the collards."

"You don't strike me as a Southerner."

Maddie grinned. "When it comes to the food, I'm all in. Come on, you'll like it. You may end up so full you can't eat for another three days, but if you're going to grill me about Holden, then the least you can do is allow me my guilty pleasure."

They walked through the front door, and a waitress and cook behind the counter waved and called out a welcome. A narrow walkway separated the brown Formica front counter from the well-used grill, stove, and oven. Watching the waitress tending the counter and the cook preparing the meals maneuver around each other was a bit like watching a Vaudeville dance act.

Maddie picked a table in the back corner where the light blazing through the front windows didn't reach. She'd never tested her theory, but she couldn't help but wonder if it was the mustard-colored walls that swallowed the light or the airborne haze created by the deep fryer. Either way, taking an out-of-the-way seat in the back corner seemed best. Maddie's gut told her this wouldn't be a quick lunch. As she sat down, she pulled out her phone to check it. She had close to half a dozen texts.

What are you doing with my sister?
She put you up to this, didn't she?
Where are you two?
What's going on?

The last one was longer. *I can't do anything about this, but she's going to question you about my health. I need to warn you, though. Sometimes she asks inappropriate questions.*

Maddie stared at the screen. Inappropriate? What was that supposed to mean? What kinds of things did his sister like to ask?

An apron-clad waiter stopped by, and she ordered on autopilot. "I want a chop, cole slaw, and green beans, and smother that chop with gravy. Oh, and tea."

Then she nodded to Lauren, prompting her to order. "I'll have a fish filet and the greens, please. With tea also."

The waiter wasn't more than two steps away from their table when Holden's sister jumped straight over small talk and dove into the deep end. "My baby brother says that if you hadn't agreed to stay with him, he'd still be in rehab."

"I'm sure he would have gotten out by now."

Lauren shook her head. "Not the way he tells it. Says he pretty much gave up, figured he would die in that place. Did he tell you he blocked us from getting any information?"

Maddie squinted. Being in the middle of a family squabble didn't appeal.

"Those forms where you list who else can talk to the doctor and get information about you? He specifically excluded all of us so he could hide from us how bad things were. Holden says he almost died."

"I'm not allowed to speak with you about your brother's care in the hospital. I could lose my license."

"Then tell me about rehab."

"Hasn't he told you everything?" Or at least everything he wanted her to know.

The woman in question pulled a napkin from the table's dispenser and began folding it. "I just want to know that my brother is going to be okay, that he's not buffaloing me."

The waiter set their drinks down. "Did you want buffalo wings? I can add them to your order."

Lauren averted her eyes and shook her head while Maddie laughed.

"I'm just messin' with you, ma'am. You look about as comfortable as a frog next to a jar of barbecue sauce."

He left, and the brunette whispered, "What was that supposed to mean?"

"You ever had barbecued frog legs?"

The horror on Lauren's face was answer enough. The none-too-delicate shudder that quaked through her frame confirmed it.

Reptile-hating Maddie had never brought herself to try them either, but she wasn't going to let Holden's sister know that. "You don't seem at ease here."

The Midwesterner searched the diner with her eyes. "It's not the restaurant. I've felt out of place since I got off the plane."

"Nobody here is going to bite you. Unless you bathed in grease or gravy this morning. Then all bets are off."

Lauren reached for her tea and took a gulp. Her eyes widened, and her face turned as red as a pickled beet before she forced the drink down. Once she got her breath and regained her composure, she inspected the contents of her glass. "What *is* that?"

"Tea. Mine's okay. Does yours taste funny?"

"Funny? It's flavored sugar!" Holden's sister stuck her tongue out and crossed her eyes in the effort to examine her insulted taste buds. Then she tucked the offended muscle back behind her teeth. "I think my tongue's been crystalized. There was enough sugar in that to turn a slab of bacon into a dessert."

Maddie shook her head. "Around here, when you order tea, that's what you get. If you want it unsweet, you have to say so. Fail to specify, and you'll end up with sweet tea 98% of the time."

Then, as if the whole beverage complaint had been nothing more than a distraction to trick Maddie into letting her guard down, Lauren launched back into her interrogation. "Are you and my brother sleeping together?"

Ah. So that's what inappropriate sounded like. "I thought you were interested in Holden's health?"

"We'll get back to that. For now, answer the question."

"None of your business."

Lauren's eyes turned into saucers, and Maddie relented. She could walk away at the end of lunch without a care, but she didn't need to make a mess for Holden in the process. "My personal life is not your concern, but no, we're not."

"Is he ever going to fully recover from everything?"

That was a question she could handle. "Your brother is strong and healthy. He will continue to improve as long as he does what his doctors and therapists tell him, but the likelihood of his ever reaching the full mobility and pain-free life he had before are slim."

Having unfolded the napkin, Lauren started folding it again in a different direction. "It's difficult to see him so weak. Every move he makes is slow, and I want to jump ahead of him and do things for him. He gets testy when I do, though, so I'm trying not to help him."

"Holden's come a long way and has worked hard every single day to get where he is now. Treat him as though he's crippled, and you strip him of all the sweat and determination he's put into his recovery. You rob him of his success. Every single thing he does for himself is a victory, and you need to allow him that. A lesser man never would have made it out of the wheelchair."

Lauren paled and sat back in her seat. Her voice was a hoarse whisper. "He might have been an invalid?"

A snort of impatience escaped before Maddie could stop it. "A wheelchair doesn't make someone an invalid, but yeah, a third of the people who get what he had never walk again, and many of those people end up needing around-the-clock care the rest of their lives."

Blinking slowly, Holden's sister unfolded the napkin again and began working new creases into it. "I'm not blessed with your medical knowledge, so I may sound insensitive, but this is my brother we're talking about. The next time our family sees him, they're going to be devastated. No matter what I go back and tell them, they won't be prepared for how grueling it is for him to walk or the grimaces when he's in pain. It'll break their hearts."

Worry tried to dig its claws in. "How bad is it? Is he back to using his walker?"

Lauren waved her hand dismissively. "Just a cane, and he tells me it's better than before, but I'm used to playing flag football with him. This is just... hard. What do I tell my family?"

"You tell them it's a wonder he has any mobility below the waist. Standing on his own two feet, regardless of how labored it seems to you, is a miracle to him, and how dare anybody minimize everything he's gone through to get this far."

Lauren's eyes widened. Thankfully, the waiter picked that moment to deliver their meals. The easy cajoling of his previous visit to their table was absent, but the fragrant steam rising from their platters more than filled the void. After Maddie thanked him for their food, he put a finger to his lips and told them in a stage whisper, "You might want to keep it down a bit. I don't know who this guy is y'all are fightin' over, but he's lucky to have two such fine lookin' women arguing about him."

Turning, she caught a glimpse of the other diners before they all averted their eyes. Heat climbed up her neck and into her cheeks. "Swell."

This time it was Lauren's turn to laugh. "We're a pair, huh?"

Maddie's mouth twisted into a wry grin.

"Is it okay if I bless the meal?"

Used to mealtime prayer from her weeks with Holden, she bowed her head.

"Dear Lord, thank you for this chance to spend time with Maddie, and thank you for all she's done to aid my brother. Please help her, protect her, and keep her close to Your heart. Amen."

The woman, a clear fidgeter, abandoned the multi-creased napkin to pick up her knife and fork. After one taste, she groaned. "This might be the best fish I've ever eaten."

Thankful the third degree was over, she sighed and cut into her pork chop. She was about to put the first morsel into her mouth when Lauren spoke again.

"My baby brother likes you more than he should."

Maddie set her silverware down before taking the bite. "Will you please just say what you came here to say and get it over with?"

Her lunch companion brandished a fork that looked like it had been around since the 1970s. "Eat. I'm not lecturing. This is a friendly conversation."

"It doesn't feel friendly."

With a shrug, Lauren said, "You don't know me very well. Trust me, if I'm unhappy about something, you won't be left in doubt."

"Holden is a good man." Maddie picked up her fork again and took the bite.

"Of course he is, and he has feelings for you, so my question is, what are your plans?"

"He has religious convictions, and I'm not going to mess with those."

"My baby brother's not like anyone else in our family."

"How so?"

"Don't get me wrong. I love my family. They're wonderful people, every single one of them. Holden's different, though. He never completely fit in. He looks like us, so we know he wasn't a stray that

Mom and Dad took in, but his ideas were always too big for our small town. From the time he was in kindergarten and told the teacher his favorite color was vermilion, I knew he was destined for something more than the rest of us."

"He doesn't think he's better than anyone else."

Lauren closed her eyes as she took another bite of fish. Once she swallowed, she picked up the conversation. "Of course not. Because he's not any better than us. Just different. Some people march to the beat of their own drum. Holden marches to a dog whistle — an instrument none of the rest of us can hear."

"He seems normal to me." Maddie drained her tea.

"Now you're getting it."

Maddie shook her head in confusion.

"I do want to know — what are your intentions toward my brother?"

"I don't have any. I've been helping him out. That's all."

"Why? What made you decide to help him?"

She'd asked herself that same question more than once until figuring out the answer. "He was vulnerable, and he let me see it."

Lauren leaned back in her seat. "Huh. I always kind of thought of him as invulnerable. He always takes care of others. When he was a boy, he brought home the wounded animals, defended the lunch money of younger kids, that sort of thing."

Maddie couldn't argue. Holden's eyes told the story more often than he realized. He wasn't used to being in need. Asking for help was alien to him. He chaffed at the new direction his life had taken, and the pain wasn't the thing he took issue with the most.

Lauren swallowed her last bite. "Friends?"

The sister was as surprising as the man. Friends? "I think I can manage that." Then, nodding to Lauren's empty plate, she added, "You should try the sweet potato pie here."

The woman smirked. "So good I'll sell my grandfather for a single morsel?"

Maddie pulled up to the end of the driveway to drop off Lauren. Before the other woman got out of the car, she rested a hand on Maddie's arm. "You're right about his religious convictions, but I'm not sure you're right about where you fit in. Do me a favor, and think about who you are to God, because you need to understand that. I don't think Holden's going to let this go, and you should be prepared for when he seeks you out. I want to tell you not to hurt him, but this is real life, and sometimes it bites."

"I'd never hurt him on purpose."

"I figured that part out for myself, which is why we shared such a friendly lunch."

Maddie laughed. "Heaven help me if I ever get on your bad side."

Lauren climbed from the car then. "Well, hello, baby brother. How are you doing?"

Twenty-Eight

His sister hadn't even stood to her full height yet when Holden cut past her and dove awkwardly into the car. The click of his seat belt was punctuated with a single word. "Drive."

"What is it with your family and quick getaways?"

When he didn't answer, she gave a half-smile. "As you wish. Where to?"

"Anywhere." He knew she didn't like single-word answers, but he was still too irritated at his sister to find his way to longer sentences.

She drove to a coffee house they'd stopped at a time or two. "Will this do?"

Holden ran his right hand over his face and sighed. "I forgot my walker and my cane. I'm an idiot."

Maddie's laughter filled the space between them. "You can lean on me for support if you need to. We'll take it slow. You've been doing well at home."

"Home is different. I have counters, chairs, and tables to put a steadying hand on. This is a parking lot. My luck, I'll rest my hand on somebody's trunk, and their car alarm will be wired straight to the nearest S.W.A.T. team."

"Speaking of home, you didn't just leave your drafting assistant at your sister's mercy, did you?"

Holden snorted. "I want to keep my only employee, remember? He wanted to attend a seminar on campus and was already leaving when Lauren bolted."

"So you were home alone?" A chuckle spilled over into her words.

"I won't tell if you don't."

They climbed out of the car, and Holden looped his hand around her right elbow as they walked toward the entrance. Could he manage the walk without his cane? Perhaps, but why take the chance? It had nothing to do with enjoying Maddie's presence so close by his side.

He held his tongue until they sat down with their drinks. "I'm sorry for whatever my sister said."

"Lauren loves you. She's worried about you."

"Did she grill you too much?"

Maddie shook her head, her golden hair swinging with the motion. "Dealing with family members is part of my job, remember? I told her I couldn't discuss anything from the hospital. Then she wanted to know whether or not you'll be making a full recovery."

Holden frowned. "I love my family. They're good, hardworking people who would do anything for me. I enjoy visiting them, and I like the rare times when someone will make the trip out here to stay with me. I've always been the odd man out, though. I suppose in some ways Lauren has always been the odd woman out. That's made us close, especially in recent years."

"Is she a rebel at heart like her baby brother?"

"Not so much a rebel. It's more that she hasn't always been able to live up to other people's expectations of her. She eventually found a way to be okay with that, though, and to realize that the opinions of other people aren't as important as what she thinks of herself and how God sees her."

Maddie took another sip of her coffee. "Your family doesn't have any idea what to expect, and she's afraid they won't know how to handle it the next time they see you."

His frown deepened. "I'm not sure what to do about that."

"Have you considered online chatting? There are free programs that will let you video chat with one another. That won't eliminate the shock when they see you in person, but it might help."

He waved his hand dismissively. "I'll think about it."

Maddie wasn't through. "You should do it while Lauren's here. She leaves in what, three days? Make her use her phone. Then she can video you moving around and doing something — maybe fixing dinner — while keeping a conversation going with your family so you don't have to. You'll be busy, and she'll be talking. It'll give them an idea of how you're managing without as much pressure on you. The not knowing has to be hard on them."

His right hand snaked up and tugged at the hair along his neck. He needed another haircut, but at this point asking Maddie for anything felt like begging. Maybe once Lauren left and she came back home.

"Okay. Fine. I'll talk to her about it."

She sipped her coffee, but even that couldn't hide the pleased-with-herself smile that danced across her lips.

"So what else did you two discuss?"

"Your sister asked if I'm sleeping with you."

Holden winced. "Ouch. I'm sorry. Lauren can be blunt."

"It's all right." Maddie shrugged. "I was a little put out at first, but she's not so bad. She loves you, and that's what matters. A family member of a patient once accused me of trying to steal the patient from his wife because I had the nerve to do my job and bathe him. People say and do strange things when they're under pressure."

He winced again. "Yeah, about that. She's like that normally. Trust me, you don't want to see her when she's stressed about something." After a short pause, Holden asked, "Anything else?"

"I think she mostly wanted to make sure I wasn't taking advantage of you. She doesn't know me from Adam — or Eve — and yet I was living with you, giving you your prescriptions, telling you what to do. Her concern is understandable." Maddie was holding something back, but prying it out of her would be impossible.

"She didn't make you too uncomfortable, did she?"

"Yeah, but we worked through it."

Holden examined the passers-by on the other side of the window. "I never dated much in high school. Lauren scared off every girl I ever tried to bring home. In the end, I gave up. Plus there wasn't anyone in our small town that I cared about enough to be willing to go toe-to-toe with my big sister for. She loves me, but she can be intrusive and bossy, and you're not even close to being as upset as you should be."

He pulled his eyes away from the view outside and looked back at her. "I'm not sure what I'm going to do with you, Maddie Smith. You're unlike anyone I've ever met."

"I'm sorry for running out the way I did when Lauren showed up."

"I wish you'd stayed, but it's all good."

Silence settled around them until Holden spoke into it. "You know she was sent to investigate the rumor that I'm living in sin with a woman?"

Maddie made a sound somewhere between a choke and a dying man's last breath — portrayed by a dreadful actor in an off-off-off-*off*-Broadway play. On the bright side, she didn't have any coffee in her mouth, so there was no danger of her spitting it all over him in her shock.

Holden looked heavenward. "That couldn't have come out more wrong."

The twinkle in her eyes said Maddie was amused rather than offended... and that his revelation didn't surprise her. Rather than take the bait, though, she changed the subject. "Any luck on figuring out what's going on with your proposals? Did you talk to Tom?"

He'd rather have discussed any subject but that one. "One of the new clients — the one from Mechanicsville — called me to say someone submitted a proposal almost identical to mine, but at a fraction of the cost."

"No. You can't be serious. Does that mean it's Miles?"

"I don't want it to be, but that's what it looks like. If it were only old jobs, I could believe it was Yvette, but the new jobs, too? It no longer makes sense to think it's her. She had keys to the office, but she's never had a key to my home, and this is where we keep the files now. I wish I could believe it was her. That would be so much easier."

"Have you confronted him about it?"

Holden shook his head. "The client is sending over everything to me so I can take a closer look at it."

"I'm telling you, call Tom. Something's hinky. I don't think Miles would do this."

"I talked to Tom earlier today. He's not such a bad guy when you're talking to him about crime."

Maddie's brow crinkled. "When is he ever a bad guy?"

Holden chuckled. "Whenever I bring you up. I think he likes me just fine until I mention your name. Then I'm *persona non grata*."

Twenty-Nine

They waved Lauren off as she made her way past security and onto the concourse. "Will you miss having her around?"

Holden, cane in hand, turned back toward the airport's entrance. "You're moving back in. It's not like I'll have a chance to get into too much trouble."

Maddie gave him a playful smack on the arm, but instead of joking with her, he stiffened. "Is everything okay?" she asked.

A strained smile met her question. "Fine." Holden started moving again.

"What was that?"

He shook his head. "I expected it to hurt, I guess, but it didn't really."

Maddie wasn't sure she could believe him. He'd gotten a little too good at masking his pain. She still couldn't shake the incident that had occurred before Lauren arrived. Everything had been progressing at a nice predictable pace until that.

Holden's next doctor's appointment was in three days. Whatever was going on with him, it needed to come out in the open. He wasn't doing himself any favors by acting like everything was just dandy when it wasn't.

"Do you think we could stop by Lakeview on the way home?" he asked.

"What," Maddie teased, "you don't like my cooking anymore?"

A shake of the head was her answer. "Burt told me I should go back someday and let people see how I've improved. Today seems like as good a day as any."

Maddie shrugged. "Sure. I'm not in a hurry to get back home anyway. I'm pretty sure Fishy's busy plotting his retaliation for today's trip in the cat carrier."

"Mr. Jenkins, look at you." The orderly had answered the intercom page and found them in the foyer.

"Heya, Burt. How've you been?"

"Can't complain, no sirree. I've got my family, my health, and a job I love. What about you? You're walking around with a cane now. I told you that wheelchair wasn't forever, didn't I?"

Maddie wasn't sure what Holden had expected, but he seemed at a loss now that they were actually at Lakeview. He hadn't exactly enjoyed his time there, and she was still surprised that he'd wanted to return. Until he'd made her stop at the nursery, that is.

Burt noticed the more than two dozen plants and flower arrangements covering every surface in the foyer. "Did you bring all those?"

The nursery owner was apparently a former client, and when he learned what Holden was going to do with the purchase, he'd given them a great deal on the price.

"I knew you'd be the perfect person to deliver them. Give them out to anybody who's not getting visitors or who's struggling with being here. You know what I mean."

Burt's stare moved from the greenery back to Holden. "I sure am glad you stopped back by, Mr. Jenkins, and not just for all this. You reminded me that there's still good folks in the world."

Holden held out his hand to the orderly. "Turnabout's fair play. You did exactly the same thing for me when I was in here."

A minute later, they were stepping out into the sunshine and leaving the gloom of Lakeview behind. Maddie turned to Holden. "Do you think he'll notice the cards?" He had painstakingly written encouraging messages to go on cards for every single plant and flower arrangement they'd brought. Most of them had Bible references, too.

"The patients are the ones who need them, not Burt. But if I know him, he'll read every single one of those messages to the people he delivers them to."

"How are you today, Mr. Jenkins?" The doctor walked into the antiseptic mint-green room with the rubberized baseboards and greeted them each with handshakes. Holden had only seen the man twice before ending up in the hospital, both times for regular checkups. Since being discharged from rehab, though, he'd seen enough of the man that he told Maddie they ought to be on a first-name basis.

"I'm well."

Maddie was thankful he resisted the urge to call the doctor by his first name.

"Stronger than I've been in a long time. I'm in considerably less pain. I am more mobile, though I sometimes still struggle to stand if I'm seated on a low seat. I haven't fallen out of bed once. I can bathe myself, cook for myself, and oversee my own medications, some of which I no longer think I need to be taking."

Dr. Matthews chuckled. "I'm sensing here that you might want me to understand you are capable of caring for yourself."

"I was going for subtle. Guess I missed the mark?"

The doctor held his hand in the air, thumb and forefinger a short distance apart. "By this much. You were close, though."

After performing a cursory examination, Dr. Matthew went on to ask Maddie some questions about whether or not the patient was doing as well as he claimed. "He is able to do everything he's told you, and I think he's ready to live independently. His physical therapist concurs but wanted him to wait until seeing you today in case your opinion differed. I have only one concern…"

Holden frowned.

Dr. Matthews lifted a brow.

Maddie took a deep breath and began. "Someone touched Mr. Jenkins' back, and he seized up. The way he reacted leads me to believe it wasn't the first time."

A puzzled expression marred the doctor's normally disinterested face as he turned to his patient. "Do you wish to add anything?"

Holden's face could have been carved from bedrock for all the softness it showed. "No."

"Is this different than when you overexert yourself and your muscles seize up?"

"Maybe." Holden accompanied his mumble with arms crossed over his chest.

"Stand up." Dr. Matthews' mouth dipped down into the kind of frown one would expect to see on an attorney prosecuting a capital case.

He complied, and as soon as he did, the doctor said, "This might be uncomfortable," and touched a spot on his back.

Thirty

The doctor's words had done nothing to prepare Holden for what came next.

His entire body tightened in response to the pain. He tried to fight the reaction, but his body took on a life of its own. The doctor's fingers continued a path along one side of his back and then the other. Though some areas didn't respond to the contact, far too many did. Each new brush of fingers felt like fire pouring directly into his veins. The muscles around his middle tightened convulsively, his arms became stiff, and his jaw clenched so tight he feared for the survival of his teeth.

The doctor kept telling him not to fight it and to just let his body do what it would, but he couldn't help it. At one point, the room began to close in on him with darkness.

"Breathe, Holden."

He stole a look at Maddie and forced himself to take a breath before closing his eyes and dropping his head. What was the point in fighting anymore? No woman worth her salt would want to spend her life with a man whose body randomly freaked out when she touched it. No woman should have to, either.

Much as he yearned to, he couldn't yell at the doctor to stop the torture. His voice was locked inside him, and each new touch came too quickly. Try as he might, Holden couldn't regain control of his body before the next convulsion hit. Moisture built in his eyes, and he squeezed them closed even tighter, hoping to keep the tears at bay. *God, at least allow me that dignity.*

The doctor circled around him and began touching his abdomen and chest with similar results. The fire didn't burn quite as hot, and he was able to combat the muscles that wanted to force him to curl in on himself, but each touch still brought a new wave in the ocean engulfing him. Agony. Shame. Anger. Helplessness. Betrayal. Humiliation.

Dr. Matthews clucked his tongue before speaking. "Sit down, Mr. Jenkins."

Holden's clothes stuck to him in a sticky, sweaty mess as he tried to move. Maddie stepped forward to help, and he waved her back, but not before the picture of her ashen face imprinted itself on his brain. The examination table might as well have been five miles high after what the doctor had just put him through. He stumbled over and collapsed into the black plastic chair set against the wall.

Sitting on the wheeled stool, Dr. Matthews fiddled with his tie before resting his hands on his thighs. "I'm sorry. It couldn't be avoided, but still — I'm sorry."

Holden stared at the floor and refused to acknowledge his words.

"Remember how we talked about the signal interruption in your spinal cord?"

"But that cleared up." Maddie's voice came from his left.

"It did, but it appears Mr. Jenkins suffered some nerve damage."

"Why didn't we know this a month ago?" Her nurse-in-charge voice demanded answers.

"If I had to guess, I'd say our patient here has known for a while."

Of course he'd known something was wrong. And yes, whether it made any sense or not, he'd tried to hide it from everyone. Finally lifting his eyes, he glared at the green wall behind Dr. Matthews' right shoulder.

The sincere apology in the doctor's eyes couldn't be denied, even caught in his peripheral vision as it was. "These things aren't always evident right away. He was on some heavy duty steroids in the hospital, and even though they weaned him off in rehab, some of those drugs can have lasting effects."

"Put him back on steroids, then," Maddie demanded.

The corner of Dr. Matthews' mouth tilted up. "You know as well as I do that the side effects of long-term steroid use are not going to work in anyone's favor here. Nerve damage to this extent is almost always permanent. Steroids won't change that. The good news is that a fairly localized area is affected."

"Localized?" Holden snorted. "How was that localized?" His entire body had turned against him. He'd known the doctor was only lightly touching his skin, yet every impulse in his body had said he was being electrocuted with each touch. The sensation had been as real as if someone had stabbed him with a *sai* wired to a car battery. And every single muscle in his body has reacted as if that was exactly what had happened.

"If the damaged nerves came from higher up your spinal column, it would affect the nerves that control your hands and arms. Your ability to hold a cane — or even a walker — would be compromised. If they came from much lower, it would be your lower extremities at risk. It might not yet sound like good news, but to put it in perspective, imagine a world in which someone passing too close to you in the hallway could cause your legs to collapse under you without warning."

Dr. Matthews was right, and Holden would find the time to be thankful later. For now, though, his exhaustion demanded all his energy. None was left for gratitude.

After making several notations in the small computer he carried, the doctor put it aside and gave his full attention to his sullen patient. "This may not seem like a good news day, but I'm clearing you to live without supervision."

Any enthusiasm felt in anticipation of the doctor's pronouncement had already died an excruciating death. Its bloody and beaten corpse lay sprawled on the exam room floor.

"However, I'm not comfortable allowing you to drive just yet. I want to monitor a bit longer and will confer with your physical and occupational therapists. Speaking of, how did you hide the nerve damage from them?"

"Neither of them touch me that much. They tell me what to do, or they show me, and I do it. The few times it happened in therapy, I fought through it."

Dr. Matthews nodded. "I'm going to refer you to a neurologist, someone who's better equipped to explore the full scope of what you're dealing with. I'll have the order printed before you leave today." He scribbled something onto the back of a business card. "I'd like you to see this one. Dr. Carlisle works out of Our Lady Hospital. I've seen him do some amazing things with patients of mine. Not that I want to give you false hope, but if anyone can help, it'll be him. Check with your insurance first to make sure he's covered, of course, but if you can see him, he's the one I recommend."

Fantastic. Another doctor to put him through the same thing? Holden wouldn't be in a hurry to make that appointment.

"You may not believe it yet, but your prognosis is actually quite good."

Dr. Matthews was right. He didn't believe it.

No celebratory mood accompanied them to the car. Holden, even with his cane, leaned on Maddie for support. The exam had taken more out of him than he was used to.

"Let's stop for coffee."

He squinted at her. Was she out of her mind? His bed and privacy — that's what he wanted.

"You need time to gather yourself. Lauren knew you hoped the doctor would clear you to live on your own, and she wanted to schedule a video chat so you could tell your whole family the good news. They're expecting to hear from you in about..." She glanced at her watch. "...three hours."

"Cancel it."

"Holden..."

"Cancel it."

Her lips thinned, and her hazel eyes snapped. "If I recall, you owe me a decadent coffee."

The bite in her voice demanded he obey, at the same time that her words rang a bell somewhere in a shadowed and cobwebbed corner of his memory. His demand to be taken home turned bitter in his mouth.

Holden would play along with whatever game she was playing. The only question that remained was whether he did so because he wanted to please her or because he hoped to avoid a video conference with his family. "You were supposed to tell me what Maddie stands for."

She shrugged, the motion nothing short of nonchalance dipped in dark chocolate. "Maybe. Maybe not."

While she pulled out of the parking lot, Holden broached a painful subject. "I'm still going to need someone to take me grocery shopping, drive me to appointments, and, if you're willing, take me to church."

Any reply was stalled by their arrival at the coffee house. They went inside, and she ordered a Venti Skinny White Chocolate Cappuccino with Crème de Menthe. "Do you want whipped cream on that?" the gal behind the counter inquired.

"Absolutely. Throw some extra on there, too, while you're at it." He appreciated her enthusiasm, even if it sounded forced.

Then it was Holden's turn to order. "I want ordinary hot coffee. Give me whatever the big size is."

Maddie's musical laughter filled the coffee house. One corner of Holden's mouth tugged itself upward just the slightest bit. So she was going to laugh at his choice of beverage, was she? He was too physically exhausted to fully enjoy her humor, but he was thankful for it nonetheless. He didn't want to wear the dark mood that had cloaked him while at the doctor's office. Spending time with Maddie over a cup of coffee and teasing another laugh out of her — that sounded like good medicine for what ailed him.

A table by the window offered the distraction of passers-by in case conversation became too stilted. His drink, strong and bitter, danced across his tongue in a satisfying way. She, on the other hand, sipped delicately at her luxurious beverage.

He took another swallow, closed his eyes, and concentrated on the memory of her laughter. When he began drifting closer to rational sanity, he joined her game — a game designed to calm and distract him. "I believe there's something you need to tell me now."

Maddie's eyes widened in mock surprise. "Oh?"

"Mm-hm," he answered. "You owe me a name. Or did you plan to renege on our agreement?"

"I suppose it's time. If we're going to manage to still be friends, then you might as well learn the awful truth."

Holden stared at her, waiting for the drama to play out.

"It's so bad that no teachers in school could pronounce it correctly. My foster families gave up and started calling me Maddie. My case worker offered to legally change my name when I was sixteen. Tom still gives me a sympathy gift every year on my birthday."

"This horrifying name that causes people to cringe and shudder — what is it?"

She gave a sigh to rival that of the most exaggerated thespian. "Madeline. With an *ine* on the end. Mad. Uh. Line."

Holden laughed. He couldn't help himself. "How could your teachers possibly mispronounce that?"

"They kept calling me Madelyn. With *lyn* on the end. Do people mix up tin and tine? No. One has an *in* and the other an *ine*. You slap those same sounds into the middle of a name, though, and suddenly it's like a pop quiz on a foreign language nobody studied."

"Your foster families?"

"I was with one family already housing a Madelyn and a Madison, so I got named Maddie to cut down on confusion."

"And the legal name change?"

"That might not be exactly what she meant, but the case worker definitely volunteered to change the name on my file to Maddie instead of the other name."

"The sympathy cards?"

"That's completely true." Her eyes sparked with defiance. "He gives me one every year on my birthday."

"Sympathy for what?"

She worked her napkin between her fingers. "For having put up with him for another year."

Holden took a drink of his coffee and enjoyed the laughter dancing in her eyes. "Do you honestly mind it that much?"

A dainty shrug met his words. "Not so much. I've been Maddie for such a long time, though, that I probably wouldn't even answer if someone called me Madeline."

He indicated her drink with the flap of a hand. "The cost of whatever that thing is was worth it to learn your deep, dark secret."

The effort to smile was there — he could see that — but as quiet settled over their table, the luster in Maddie's eyes dimmed. She had to be thinking about the exact topic he was doing everything he could to dodge.

The urge to pretend the exam had never happened was a live, pulsing monster inside him.

Don't talk about it, and it'll go away. Yeah, right. "Listen..."

"I can't be sorry I spoke up." She cut him off. "It was the right thing to do, but I'm angry at myself for what he put you through."

Throat constricting, Holden held his coffee cup in a death grip. At least it was ceramic and not the disposable paper kind.

Maddie dropped her gaze to the table.

Those minutes in the doctor's office had been a horror movie come to life. Trapped in his own body, he'd been incapable of controlling his responses and unable to force the doctor into giving him a reprieve. He had hated every single second of it, and if he could go back in time, he would cancel the appointment and stay home. Holden would rather live the rest of his life with a constant nursemaid than go through that torture again.

He hadn't been the only one stuck in that room, though.

"It will be a while before I see the good that came out of today's visit to the doctor, but one thing is certain. You are a nurse. It's your profession and your calling. You did the right thing. I don't have to like what came out of it to know that."

Living those moments had been grisly enough. He didn't want to imagine what witnessing them had been like. Single-minded in his need to get it said before the embarrassment of it all overcame him again, he reached across the table and took her hand. "Look at me."

She lifted her eyes to meet his, her reluctance evident in the moisture on her lower lids.

"Nothing that happened is your fault. I tried to hide the problem, and you called me out on it. I'm not upset with you. I just wish…"

Holden turned his head and stared blankly at the people passing by the coffee shop window, but he was reluctant to release her hand just yet. What *did* he wish? That he'd never gotten that stupid virus to begin with. That they'd met under different circumstances. That he was stronger… whole.

"If wishes and wants were candies and nuts, we'd all have a bowl full." Maddie's melodic voice penetrated the fog, and he turned back to her.

"Say that again."

"If wishes and wants were candies and nuts, we'd all have a bowl full."

A smile played tug-of-war with the corner of his mouth, and he decided to let it win. "That's a quaint Southern saying if ever I heard one."

"I wish I could fix things for you."

He gave her hand a last squeeze before letting go and sitting back in his chair. "The only fight I ever recall my parents having was about that same subject."

"Oh?"

"I'm sure they fought other times, but that's the only one I remember. One of my brothers, three years older than me, was being bullied at school by a bigger kid, and Mom wanted to meet with the boy's parents. Dad adamantly refused to allow it. He wanted us kids to become adults who take care of our own problems, and he said if she kept fixing everything for us, we wouldn't ever learn how to cope in the real world. She couldn't stand for her boy to be picked on, though."

"So who won the argument?"

"Lauren."

Maddie's eyes widened.

"The next day, she called a Jenkins family powwow on the playground. There were five of us still at that school. The rest had graduated up. She sent Don to go hang out by the merry-go-round, and then we waited. As soon as the other boy started giving him a hard time, we ran out and tackled him to the ground." Holden smiled at the memory. "Lauren gave him a wedgie."

"You know, your sister told me you were the defender of the younger kids at school, that you defended their lunch money and stood up to the bullies."

"Where do you think I learned it from?""

She shook her head. "So what did your parents say about the playground altercation?"

"The bully was too embarrassed to report it, so neither the school nor the folks ever found out. But we all learned something that day. Lauren told my brother that Mom and Dad might not always be there to fix things, but family was family and no Jenkins would ever let a brother or sister go through something alone."

How had he forgotten that lesson so easily?

"Sounds like your sister is pretty special."

Holden sighed. "She is. They all are."

"Yet you've insisted on going through this by yourself."

"You'll want to hold on tight. It's getting a little crowded on the Holden's-an-Idiot bandwagon."

Maddie stood and pushed her chair in. "Bandwagons aren't my thing."

He struggled to his feet and sighed. "Guess I've been selling them short."

She didn't concur or say any of a number of things guaranteed to make him feel small. He'd been living in the big city too long if someone exhibiting basic human decency could surprise him.

Her pace was slow to allow for his as she walked toward the exit.

"What are you going to do with your newfound freedom?" he asked.

"Go back to work. I'm ready. I needed this break, but it's time to jump back in with both feet."

"You've been missing the ICU, haven't you?"

Maddie quirked a brow. "I love the adrenaline rush and the crazy, hectic atmosphere, but I was burning out. You came along at the perfect time. Much longer, and I would have found myself permanently walking away. Taking time off from the ICU to help you is one of the best things I've ever done for my career, let alone my sanity. But I'm ready to go back now."

A short time later, they were approaching Holden's home. Maddie's repeated glances in the rearview mirror prompted him to turn around and take a look. A truck whose tires were taller than Maddie's entire car hovered right off the bumper.

"You could wave him around."

She chuckled. "Coming from anyone else, I'd take that suggestion to mean I should flip him off."

"You know I didn't..."

"Yeah, I know. That's one of the things I like about you. You mean exactly what you say. It makes the job of listening a whole lot easier." She flipped on her turn signal and tapped her brakes. The behemoth backed off and she pulled into Holden's driveway without getting flattened.

The truck zipped by behind them, and Maddie let out a sigh.

Holden's steps were slow and labored, but the coffee shop had been a good idea. He was recovered enough to fool Lauren and the rest of his family into thinking everything was okay... which meant he was strong enough to tell them it wasn't. And strong enough to hear them say it would be.

Thirty-One

One Week Later

"He needs someone who shares his view of the world."

Mr. Fish Breath ignored her and licked his paw. Maddie was settled back in her own apartment with her reluctant feline, but her thoughts continued to stray to Holden.

"I need to do what's best for Holden."

The cat's ears perked up at the name.

Maddie was in trouble. She'd known for a long time but had managed to stuff it into a dark corner of her heart. Watching him in the doctor's office, though... Years of training were the only thing that had held her back from screaming for Dr. Matthews to stop tormenting him.

The image of his face contorted in pain wasn't one she would ever be able to shake. It would haunt her, but not for the obvious reasons. In her line of work, she'd seen worse. But this was Holden, and that changed everything.

So who was she trying to convince — herself or the cat?

"I can't go on pretending that we're going to find our way to a happily-ever-after. Were he to fall for me, it'd be like I threw him into disfavor with God."

Mr. Fish Breath stood, stretched, and resettled himself, backside to Maddie. At least he no longer hissed at her every time she came near.

"If I were on a diet, Holden would be my chocolate."

The feline's tail swished, but the cat made no move to face her.

"You know how when you diet — well, not *you*, exactly — and all you can think about are the foods you're not allowed to eat? I can't have him, so he's all I can think about."

Maddie reached for the pictures scattered on her coffee table. They were some of the shots she'd taken of Holden when they'd gone to look at those building sites. The man was far too handsome for his own good, far too handsome for *her* good. She tried to tell herself that green eyes and brown hair were too ordinary to be attractive, but even she didn't believe it.

The cat stretched out a hind leg, emphasizing his diet-free shape.

Somewhere along the way, she'd fallen in love. She hadn't meant to. Love wasn't part of her life plan, especially not with someone whose faith was so important to him.

Holden was everything good she had ever seen in other people. Only with him, all that goodness was bundled together in one handsome package. He was spectacular… and entirely off limits.

"I need to do what's right for him, Fishy, even if I don't like it. It's for his own good."

She glared at the cat, then picked up her phone and scrolled through her contacts. When Arlene, the nursing director, answered, she spoke. "This is Maddie. Are there any extra shifts I can pick up?"

April slipped into May with Maddie working a frenetic pace at the hospital. Despite that, she couldn't back out of her commitment to drive Holden to his appointments.

Which was how she ended up sitting in the waiting room while the man she couldn't stop thinking about met with the doctor. Alone. He didn't want her to go back with him again, and she didn't fight him on it. She wouldn't survive another doctor's visit if it was anything like the last one. More accurately, Dr. Matthews wouldn't survive.

The drive over had been strained. They hadn't discussed it, but the fact that she'd been avoiding him had tainted the air in the car.

Maddie set her magazine down as Holden exited the inner vestibule.

His defeat was palpable, his grief stark.

She jumped up to go to him, but the friendly companionship once shared between them was gone, a casualty of the distance she'd forced into its place. It was a toss-up which hurt worse — seeing the upset on his face or realizing she was no longer free to comfort or encourage him.

He walked past her and out the door, and she scrambled to catch up. They reached her car, but she refused to unlock it, instead standing by the driver's door and staring at him over the midnight blue roof. "What's wrong?"

"Take me home."

"Tell me."

"Take me home."

She tucked the keys into her pocket.

Why did he insist on being so stubborn?

She walked around to the passenger side and stood facing him, hands on her hips. "Tell me."

"What do you care? Just take me home."

He wasn't getting away with it, even if she did deserve the brush-off. "Not until you talk."

His eyes cut away to the side. His cane was clutched so tightly in his right hand that the only remaining color rested in the shadows between his knuckles.

Ignoring her unspoken demand for eye contact, he stared across the parking lot. "He says I'll never drive again unless something drastic changes.

Should I spasm while I'm driving, I could lose control of the vehicle and put somebody's life in danger. Blah, blah, blah."

Dr. Matthews had fed him a bitter pill, and by the look of things, Holden was choking on it.

The freedom that came with being able to spontaneously hop into a car and go somewhere was forever gone.

Platitudes would be of no use to him, but a plan — that might do him some good.

"It's his job to take care of your health, but he can only fix what he can see. Doctors can be short-sighted like that sometimes. They get so focused on dealing with a specific problem that they don't realize they're dropping a stone into a giant lake and that the ripples they make will go on for a long time — and will run into the ripples created by others just like them."

Resentment molded Holden's features into a malicious caricature.

"Give it six months. Then get yourself a driving instructor to put you through the paces and determine whether or not you're fit to drive. If the instructor says you're safe on the road, the doctor might sign off."

"And if he — or she — says I'm not?"

She ran a hand through her curls and chose her words carefully. "Then maybe that'll give you peace about the doctor's choice."

His eyes widened, and his nostrils flared before he schooled his features and gave a sarcastic snort. "Nobody's going to want that kind of liability unless they're an outright fool."

"Six months. Make it a matter of prayer. If you still believe in that."

The gauntlet was thrown. She'd issued the challenge, and he would either meet it, or...

Holden shook his head. "You're a piece of work." It should have been an insult, yet it had the sound of flattery. "Fine. Six months."

Hopefully she'd given him something to grab onto, a lifeline to keep him afloat in the sea of discouragement.

"And for the record, I've missed your pep talks."

Maddie unlocked the door for him and returned to her side of the car, a smile tugging at her lips.

Five days had passed since the death-to-driving doctor's appointment. Maddie arrived to take Holden to physical therapy but stopped short of pulling into the driveway. Tom's car was in the way.

What on earth was he doing there?

Tightening her shoulders and taking a deep breath, she climbed stiffly out of her car and walked toward the front door. It opened before she could knock. Tom stood in the entrance, wearing good cheer and wet hair. "We were just about to give up on you."

Maddie squinted. "Are you helping Holden figure out who's been trying to sabotage him?"

The older man shrugged. "You've been working a lot of hours. I thought I'd help the guy out by giving him a lift to the pool a couple times a week so he can get some walking laps in."

Guilt exacted its toll. She hadn't thought about aqua therapy since the day Lauren had shown up on his doorstep. How could she have forgotten about such an important part of his recovery?

Holden's voice called from inside the house. "Don't worry about it, Maddie. You're allowed to have a life."

Tom gave her a kiss on the cheek and stepped through the door. "I'm off to work, but you two have fun."

The breeze moved across her skin as emotions she didn't want to acknowledge grappled for a foothold. Her insides were being pulled in so many different directions, she might as well have been at the epicenter of a multi-team tug-of-war.

It was silly to think they'd been sitting around talking about her like a couple of gossiping hens. Yet insecurity tugged at her.

"Ready to go?" Holden stood by, cane in hand.

She soaked in the sight of him like a desert plant drinking in the rain after a long drought.

Her silence fell between them, and he mistook it for disapproval. "I'm okay with the cane. I don't need my walker."

With a nod, Maddie turned and walked back toward her car.

He spoke again as she merged into traffic. "Is everything all right?"

The words *I've missed you* warred with her tongue, determined to get out, but she subdued them and remained silent.

He tried again. "How's Fishy doing?"

"He's angry with me. I thought he'd be over it by now, but no such luck. If I didn't know any better, I'd say you must have been bribing him with treats so he'd like you while we were here."

Holden broke eye contact. "Cats. Does anybody really know what's going on inside their heads? So, uh, work then. How's work?"

Work. That was a subject she could handle. At least he was staying away from the personal stuff. "The unit's been busy but good."

"I wanted to invite you over for dinner a couple times, but every time I thought about it, you were working."

"I picked up some extra shifts."

Holden watched her from the passenger seat. "Are you sure you're all right?"

"Girl trouble." Great. Now she could add liar to her list of friendship infractions. Avoidance. Insecurity. Forgetfulness. Falling in love. Now dishonesty.

He made a strangled noise. "Girl trouble? As in...?"

"Do you want the gory details?"

His face couldn't make up its mind between deathly pale and flaming red as he held up his hands and backed away from her in the close confines of the car. "No, no, that's fine. Unless you need to talk about it, then I'll listen, but don't feel you have to..."

Irritable as she was, she still couldn't stop the small smile that tugged at the corner of her mouth.

Girl trouble. Ha! No doubt his sisters had tortured him with lengthy commentaries on feminine woes while he was growing up.

 Thirty-Two

Tom examined his fingernails. "One of the tech guys just had a baby. He was happy to do a little something extra for me."

Holden squinted out the windshield of the detective's car. "Isn't that against policy or something? Like taking kickbacks?"

"He didn't use department equipment, and he was off the clock."

"Still…"

"Do you want to know who's behind this or not?"

Holden bit his tongue.

Tom's tech guy had traced the hack on the network. Shortly after he'd gone into the hospital, somebody had logged into the cloud where Holden kept his plans stored and had accessed information on all pending jobs. About a month after he got out of the hospital, the network was again breached, and this time the person went after everything new he'd done.

"The legwork will pay off. Don't worry."

Legwork. Holden scowled at Tom's choice of words. Not that his legs were the problem anymore. His muscles were strong enough and his mobility was much improved. He kept the cane with him, but he relied on it less and less. The neurologist wanted to put him through a battery of tests, though, and the memory of that painful visit to Dr. Matthews still hovered like a dark cloud on the horizon, ready to unleash a torrential downpour.

If Holden knew Tom at all, the use of *legwork* hadn't been an accident. They were almost friends now, but the older man liked to needle him.

"You ever think of going to work for someone else?" The nonchalance in Tom's voice didn't fool Holden.

"I like being my own boss."

The older man nodded. "Sure. I can see how any man would. But what happens if you have a setback?"

Holden tugged at his collar. "Then I'll deal with it."

Tom cast a sideways glance at him. "And if you have a family to support, they'll be forced to deal with it, too."

They might be trapped in a car together on a stakeout of sorts, but Tom wasn't the only one with an arsenal. This was their third trip to observe the people coming and going from the apartment building the network access had been traced back to. Holden had learned a thing or two during their previous visits.

Like how to poke back. "Why didn't you ever adopt Maddie?"

The question didn't faze Tom. "I wondered when you'd get around to asking that." Tom took a drink of his coffee before setting the cup into its holder. "Her parents never gave up their rights, and the courts were hesitant to terminate parental rights back then."

"You could have been a foster parent. She would have had at least some stability then."

"It was a different time, a different place back then. I hadn't met Mirabeth yet, and while a single man might have been able to foster boys, there was no way they'd let me foster a girl. On top of that, I was a cop. I worked irregular hours and was often in danger. Mostly, though, it was about me being a man."

"They can't discriminate based on sex, though, can they?"

Tom handed Holden the binoculars as a new group of people exited the building they were watching. "We're talking over twenty years ago. Like I said, a different world."

Holden peered through the lenses. "What about after you and Mirabeth married? Maddie would have been, what — ten, eleven? You could have still fostered her then."

"My wife's a wonderful person. She would have taken Maddie in without hesitation. The case worker told us not to even apply, though."

"Maddie's case worker?" Holden thought he saw someone he recognized. He played with the focus a bit to make sure his eyes weren't deceiving him.

"I learned to play by the rules. I brought flowers to Maddie's case worker on a regular basis and gave her tickets to the opera whenever a new one came to town. In turn, she made sure I stayed in the know about Maddie's case. If there had been a way for me to foster her, I would have. But then Mirabeth... My wife has a criminal record. Again, in today's world, it wouldn't be such a big deal. It was more misunderstanding than anything else, but back then, the case worker told me not to even apply. If we applied and Mirabeth's record became known, the court could potentially block me from ever seeing Maddie again. So instead, we didn't pursue it. I did my best to keep a watch on her from a distance, visited every new family she was placed with, and hounded her from sunup till sundown about getting her college application in, filling out her financial aid forms, taking her SATs."

"You did the best you could."

"There are times I still don't think it was enough, but I see the woman she's turned into, and I couldn't be more proud of her. Despite everything that girl went through, she's overcome."

Holden rested the binoculars in his lap. "She's something else, that's for sure."

Tom cast a sideways glance at him. "Did you see anyone you recognize?"

A nod. "My old secretary Yvette and her boyfriend. I'll have to go through my papers at home to find his name. She tried to get me to hire him, but I didn't need another drafting assistant at the time."

With a flick of the wrist, Tom started the car back up. "I'll drop you at home. Text me with the name when you find it, and I'll see what I can dig up about him." They'd already checked Yvette's and Miles' names against the apartment building and had found no record of either of them ever living there. Yvette's boyfriend had to be the puzzle piece they'd been missing.

Thirty minutes later, Tom pulled up to the curb in front of Holden's house. He turned to his passenger. "You like her, don't you?"

Holden wasn't about to answer that question. He might not be a detective, but he knew a trap when he saw one.

A half-smile shaped Tom's lips, but his sunglasses hid his eyes. "Just remember, I know where to bury the body so it's never found."

What could he say to that? Nothing. He got out of the car and shut the door. Tom sped down the block, and Holden traipsed up the walkway as his phone rang. "Hello?"

"Hi there, son. How you doing today?"

"Hi, Dad. I'm good. Just got back from an errand."

"Your mom wanted to talk to you, but we don't have one of them fancy phones like Lauren."

"We don't need a phone that's smarter than us." His mom's voice came over the line from a distance.

Holden grinned. "We can talk without video chat. We're talking right now, aren't we?" It was a nice day, and he decided not to go in just yet. He settled down onto the top step of his front porch.

His mom rattled some question off in the background, and his dad grunted before repeating it. "Your mom wants to know if you'll be able to make it home for a visit anytime soon."

"Uh..." He hadn't given that even a tiny bit of thought yet. "Well, the doctor would probably let me go if I had a direct flight, but business is still slow."

"We were thinking we might buy your ticket and make that a birthday gift from the whole family."

"Oh, that's..." Really nice. That's what it was. Nicer than he probably deserved. "Let me ask the doctor at my next appointment. I can't see why he'd say no, but I want to make sure I don't have any travel restrictions. I didn't think to ask last time."

His mom's voice came over the line again. "Tell him about the wheelchair. Don't forget that part."

"Airports can have wheelchairs available for them that need 'em. We could make sure there's one for you if you'll be needing it." The whispered thickness of his dad's voice spoke to the difficulty of the question.

"Let me talk to my doctor first and see what I can do, okay?"

"You sure you don't mind coming for a visit? You weren't too keen on having us out there."

Holden rubbed his forehead. "It was bad timing, that's all. Honestly, I'd rather come back there for a visit. Then I get to see everyone. I have nieces and nephews to spoil. If you guys come out here, as great as it would be, it would only make me miss everybody else more."

The chattering commenced in the background before his dad came back on the line. "Your mom wants to know if the lady friend Lauren told us about might be accompanying you."

Holden ran his fingers through his hair and contemplated going inside. The cement step was starting to get uncomfortable. "I don't think so."

"Well, you know God's still in the miracle business, right?"

Laughter choked him. So now his ever having a serious relationship was going to take an act of

God? Even if his parents were right, they didn't need to say it out loud...

"Lauren made it sound like you really care about this woman. What's her name? Mandy or something?"

"Maddie, and Lauren should keep her mouth closed more."

Dad's laughter rumbled over the line. "That's the same thing you said when she tattled on you for using the tractor to excavate a piece of land because you wanted to build your own playhouse."

His parents remembered everything. He'd been eight when he'd had that grand plan...

"I hate to cut it short, but I should get going, Dad. I'll talk to my doctor the next time I see him, and we'll see if we can get something on the calendar for me to come home for a visit, okay?"

"As long as it won't be an inconvenience. A man's got to make a living."

"One of the perks of being my own boss is that I usually know my schedule in advance. Give Mom my love. I'll talk to you later."

The call disconnected, and Holden's mind drifted back to the conversation Tom had tried to have with him earlier. Was he right to fight so hard to keep his own business? Did it make sense when he still couldn't access some of the sites he might get contracted to work on? Miles was great, but he wouldn't be around forever. Working for another company, though… The idea of punching a clock for someone else held no appeal.

With no answer immediately forthcoming, Holden used the railing to leverage himself onto his feet. Then he turned toward the door and reached into his pocket for his keys.

"No. No, no, no, no."

He leaned his forehead against the front door as he punched in the name and dialed. "Maddie? It's Holden. I, uh, locked myself out. Do you still have my spare key?"

Thirty-Three

Two days later Maddie got called into the office of Arlene, the nursing director. The older woman with the honeyed ginger hair sat her down, smiling kindly. "Do you require more time off?"

Maddie gave a swift shake of the head, denying the concern in the other woman's eyes. "Why do you ask?"

"You asked about picking up some extra hours, and I was fine with that. Happy to have you back, in fact. But then you started picking up shifts directly from other nurses, and you took on more than I ever would have cleared you for. I don't mind when people trade shifts occasionally, but the hospital frowns on it when nurses work too many days without a real break. A tired nurse is a careless nurse."

"Did I do something wrong?"

Arlene frowned. "Not to my knowledge. I'm just worried about you. You seem to have lost your balance. What's going on?"

"I don't have to answer that." Maddie winced at the vinegar in her own voice. "I'm sorry. That didn't come out right."

Sadness tugged at the corners of Arlene's eyes. "You're off for the next two days. I suggest you get some rest and sort out what's bothering you."

Maddie jumped from her chair. "I'm on the schedule to work."

A shake of the head met her defiance. "I gave your shifts to one of the nurses you covered for last week. You're not required to tell me what has you at sixes and sevens, but you do need to figure it out for yourself. I can't force you to deal with it, but I will do my part to make sure you don't crash and burn."

Shoulders drooping with the weight of problems she didn't want to identify, Maddie left Arlene's office. At least the talk had been kept till the end of her shift. When she got to the parking garage, she stopped and looked back at the building, wondering if it was time to walk away. The name glowed in white neon. Ferito Technology Memorial Hospital. With a shake of her head, Maddie turned back to the garage and started climbing the stairs to level D.

Years ago, before she'd worked there, it had been a Catholic hospital. Financial trouble and a shifting political climate had prompted the buyout by a technology conglomerate. What business a bunch of tech heads had running a healthcare facility was anyone's guess. The place flourished under their ownership, though, so the complaints had died out a decade or so ago. Most of them, anyway.

Locals continued to commemorate the hospital's storied history by referring to it as Our Lady Hospital — an abbreviated version of its previous name. The hospital's name had become a bit of a game to the staff. They called it everything from Our Lady of the Underpaid to Our Lady of the Accident Prone. Whatever fit at the time. Today, as Maddie reached her car, she wondered what a fitting name would be. Our Lady of Disillusionment? Not really. It was her own doing, after all. Our Lady of Burying Yourself in Your Work and Avoiding Your Problems? Maybe, but it was too long. Our Lady of Faking Your Way Through Life? Also too long.

With the flip of her key, the ignition came to life.

Ah, she had it.

Our Lady of the Runaways. That was what she'd been doing, wasn't it? Running away from her problems, running away from her fears, running away from a man she'd come to care about, and even running away from God.

Maddie drove aimlessly, avoiding home. Just because she'd figured out that she was running away from everything didn't mean she was ready yet to face any of it. Besides, Mr. Fish Breath hadn't been happy with her since leaving Holden's, and no amount of human contraband or decadent feline treats had changed his mind. He'd even stopped trying to trip her as she walked. Instead, he stared out the window all day. Near as she could guess, he was searching for his beloved house in the maze of structures below.

Her small car took turn after turn until Maddie pulled into a parking lot she hadn't seen since the day Lauren arrived. Another of her broken promises.

It was going on eleven at night, and the lights of Holden's church shone brightly.

Not giving herself an opportunity to change her mind, she climbed from her car and walked toward the entrance. The sanctuary itself wasn't much more than a modular structure. Another building off to the left housed offices and classrooms, but it held no lure.

She pulled the door open a slit, an inch at most, and peered inside. People sat, heads bowed. A soft murmur came from the front. Maddie widened the opening and slipped through, settling in a back pew.

Why had she gone in? What was she even doing there?

The prayer closed with a whispered *amen* from the small crowd, and the pastor's head lifted before she could slip back out the door. She couldn't leave now without being rude. There were 20 people in the pews — give or take — and the closest was more than six rows in front of her. Sitting in the last pew might have been a bit too obvious. Even though people's backs were to her, she felt as though everyone's eyes were on her.

The pastor stood at the pulpit, and his gaze roamed over the room. Even from where she sat, Maddie could feel the penetrating intensity of his brown eyes. He was different from the pastor she'd met that one Sunday with Holden.

With a nod to his congregation, the pastor spoke. "Ladies and gentlemen, thank you for coming tonight. You may be aware that we hold a variety of services here to reach different audiences. Tonight's service is being recorded as part of our podcast ministry to our friends in Brazil and other parts of the world. *Bem-vindo à casa de Deus esta noite.*"

Say what? Maddie finally realized she was the only Anglo present. She sat, stunned. A couple words here and there made sense from her days studying Spanish, but this wasn't like any Spanish she'd ever heard.

What did people speak in Brazil, anyway?

Could she make her escape without disturbing the service? Surely everyone would understand.

Before she made her getaway, someone touched her arm. An older man with the kind of dark leathery skin that spoke of a lifetime spent outdoors stood behind her. He had a head full of wavy salt and pepper hair and eyes that twinkled with humor. A finger to his lips in the international symbol for quiet — something she could understand — and a tilt of his head indicated she should follow. She rose and gratefully stepped behind him through the exit.

A mishmash of tables and benches adorned the comfortable space between the sanctuary and other building. Fireflies silently faded in and out over a nearby patch of greenery. The man held out a chair for her at a wrought iron table with two delicately scrolled matching chairs. The cool metal raised gooseflesh along her skin.

He sank into the seat opposite her. "My name is Pablo Cardoso. You seemed a bit lost in the service. Do you speak Portuguese?" His accent lent his words the cadence of a lullaby. It worked like magic on her, making her want to relax and trust him.

Maddie shook her head. "I wasn't planning to come here, but then I ended up in the parking lot and figured I might as well go in."

Pablo's grin was infectious. "When that happens to me, I usually end up in the candy aisle of a convenience store, not at church. You're already a step ahead."

She smiled at the warmth in his eyes and felt at ease for the first time since deciding to stay away from Holden. "I was driving around and thinking through some things." Her hands fluttered nervously before she clasped them together to keep them in her lap.

"Sometimes life demands time and thought." Pablo dipped his chin in a half-nod. "Tell me, have you ever been here before?"

"Once, with a friend. I gave him a ride. I was supposed to do that again, but my schedule has been in knots."

It was as if he could see right through her. His eyes glowed, and the wisdom in their depths reached out to her, touched her gently, and coaxed her to open up.

"I stopped believing in God a long time ago. He didn't ever seem to be around when I needed Him, so eventually I figured the whole thing must be a hoax. I have this friend, though..." Maddie swallowed the dry lump in her throat. "He believes, and he lives out his beliefs, too, you know?"

"It's a beautiful thing when a man — or woman — shines like that."

She nodded her agreement. "I like him." The words were out before she could stop them. What about this man made her want to blurt out all her deepest, darkest thoughts?

Pablo steepled his fingers. "But this is a problem for you."

"I don't think I believe the way he does, and I don't even know if he feels the same way about me."

The older man grinned, and his eyes danced with mirth. "When a man likes a woman the way men like women, he's not very good about hiding it. If this man has those sorts of feelings for you, it'll be obvious."

Maddie blushed. "I suppose. My lack of faith holds him back."

"It seems to me that people often say they have no faith, when in truth, they simply possess a damaged faith."

He spoke directly to her heart, which thumped out a rapid *tat-a-tat-tat* in her chest.

"You say you once believed in God. What happened to change that?"

"I grew up in foster care. Too many kids — they didn't get their happy ending. They wanted it, wished it, and prayed for it, only to be disappointed time and time again. Even the ones that got adopted sometimes ended up back in the system, rejected by the new families that had sworn to love and protect them."

"Were you like these other kids? Did you long for a home filled with love?"

Maddie shook her head. "I think I got broken somewhere along the way. I wanted to be left alone."

"Was it always that way, or did rejection shape you?"

She gazed off into the dark. That was too soul-searing a conversation to share with a stranger sitting at a table under the city-hidden stars.

"This man," Pablo continued, "he means a lot to you."

"More than I want him to."

"He makes you want to believe in things you gave up on. Love, family, happy endings, and... God."

Her gaze shot to his, and something she didn't understand pulsed between them. "Who are you?"

His fingers, still steepled, began to tap softly together. "I see to the grounds here at the church."

"You don't seem like a groundskeeper." Not even close.

"I haven't always been one, but today I am. You?"

Maddie pointed at her scrubs. "Nurse."

"And this man you're not sure you want to care for — what does he do?"

"He's an architect."

Pablo's fingers stilled. "A noble profession. He is a man who depends on his ability to build things up rather than tear them down."

The metal of the chair now fed back the warmth with which her body had infused it, battling the slight chill in the air. She didn't know what to say to the man who sat across from her, but she didn't want to leave. Something about him soothed the chaos inside her.

"You're not marrying the man today, no?"

Maddie's sharp intake of breath was loud in the night despite the nearness of the traffic that should have drowned it out.

"Take time to decide if this is what's right for you." He chuckled and waved his hand airily. "Take that time. Enjoy it. Savor it. Figure out if you want to cultivate a relationship with God, or with this man. In my youth we called it courtship. There are different names now, but the concept remains. Spend time with the man and explore your friendship with him."

"What if I never share his belief about God?"

"Can you not also enter a courtship with God? Spend time with and get to know Him, explore that relationship, and see how He handles the ups and downs."

"Holden can't date me if we don't have the same beliefs."

"Some people learn by reading. Others by hearing. Then there are those who come to a better understanding by doing. What if you're the latter? Watch God at work in the day-to-day part of your life. Then you can better understand what you think of Him."

"What if I learn something I don't like?"

"You may end up hurt and alone, but how different is that than where you are now?"

Maddie pondered his question. Was she hurt and alone?

A short time later, people began streaming out from the sanctuary. Pablo rose and shook her hand. "I have to leave now, but I'm here every Tuesday night. Stop by sometime and tell me what you decide and how it works out. In the meantime, I'll be praying for you to find your way in both relationships — with God and with this man who has you driving around in the middle of the night."

He vanished into the meandering people before she could gain her feet or respond to his words. It was a skeletal crowd. Disappearing shouldn't have been so easy, yet there she was, alone at a table, with Pablo nowhere to be seen. The entire encounter had been surreal.

Maddie woke slowly the next morning. Her late night drive meant she'd greeted sleep much later than usual, but her internal alarm still roused her bright and early — and it didn't have a snooze button. The sky was barely starting to lighten in the east. The vibrant streaks of sunrise she normally enjoyed hadn't even deigned to put in an appearance yet.

She walked into the kitchen to start her coffee and discovered that Fishy, who as a rule stayed out of trouble, had been up to mischief. The plastic on a six-pack of paper towels had been ripped open, and the towels themselves were shredded. The mutilated remains mocked her from the linoleum. The cat was markedly absent as Maddie crept through the rest of the apartment to search for more damage.

What on earth?

Bras and panties lay scattered across her living room furniture. There were clothes, too, but the underwear was what drew her attention.

Shouldn't those be…?

A shudder shook her frame at the thought of Mr. Fish Breath carrying her dirty laundry everywhere.

That was what she got for keeping the litter box and hamper in the laundry room together.

Maddie gingerly picked up all the dirty clothes and returned them to their rightful place. Once the living room no longer looked like a bachelor party gone bad, she continued her investigation.

The faint trace of brown on her carpet caused her to gag. Dealing with these sorts of things on the job was one thing, but in her own home? Fishy wasn't the type to do his business anywhere other than his litter box. Maddie had listened to stories, though, of cats whose proclivity for venting ire through misplaced feces was a bane to their owners. He'd certainly been upset with her lately, but he would never… She shuddered.

Careful not to step on it, she followed the brown markings. They led her to the guest bathroom. She pushed the door open and took a quick peek inside.

Who would have ever thought she'd be relieved to find the place full of mud?

The fern Tom and Mirabeth had given her as an apartment-warming gift lay on its side. That hadn't been enough, though. Muddy paw prints all over the seat of the toilet told the tale. Fishy had splashed water from the toilet bowl onto the floor until he turned the potting soil into a viscous sludge – now half-dried.

Maddie went back to the kitchen and plucked up a fistful of shredded paper towels to wipe down the seat and scoop up most of the mud.

She would clean it better later. With disinfectant.

Next, she followed the faint trace of mud back out of the bathroom and across the living room floor to...

"Really, Fishy?"

All the paper in her printer had been removed and scattered hither and yon on the carpet of her small office. Irritation pulsed through her veins in rhythm with the beat of her heart.

Maddie picked up all the papers and tossed them into her recycling bin, then returned to the kitchen. With a sigh, she started the coffee and then reached under the sink for her handheld broom and dustpan.

"Fishy, Fishy, Fishy," she muttered as she put it back and decided to just use her hands to pick up the scattered paper towel shreds. She'd never had a reason to get a bigger broom. When she cleaned, she ran the vacuum over the kitchen floor. Of course, she'd never encountered a mess quite like that one. Even as a kitten, Mr. Fish Breath hadn't been this destructive.

He was still mad at her for taking him away from Holden. That had to be the problem. The cat was obsessed.

After the remainder of the wreckage was cleaned up, Maddie savored a cup of coffee before showering and getting dressed for the day. She kept an eye out for Fishy, who, when he deigned to put in an appearance, watched her warily. With an exasperated shake of her head, she pulled her purse from its hook and headed out the front door.

There was no guarantee he'd be there. Between Miles and Tom, Holden didn't even need her to drive him around anymore if he planned well. For all she knew, he could be meeting with a client or examining a property. She had to try, though. The need to see him had grown so insistent she could no longer deny it.

Thirty-Four

Holden, who had kept his office computer set up at his dining table even after Maddie moved out, was scanning his email and taking a drink of coffee when a glint of light outside his front window caught his eye. He craned his neck to see around a shrub and sucked in his breath when he recognized the car of the woman who hadn't been far from his mind since she'd walked out of his home.

Who was he kidding? She was on his mind prior to her ever walking *into* his home.

Using his arms to push up from the table, he rose and haltingly made his way to the door, opening it before she rang the bell.

She eyed him speculatively, but oh, what beautiful eyes they were. Their gold in them stood out the most today. "You don't look so hot. Are you okay?" she asked.

With a noncommittal shrug, he turned back toward his chair. "I overdid it yesterday. I'm sore." A wave of his hand indicated his clothes. "Pardon my slept-in appearance."

Holden still wore pajamas and hadn't bothered to comb his hair yet. The time standing in the bathroom to brush his teeth had hurt enough.

Irony had become his way of life. He was a healthy thirty-something man trapped in what felt like an old man's body, and his old-man body was reacting to the sight of Maddie as though he were a hormonal teen. His heart raced, his palms got slick with sweat, and his breath hitched in his lungs as he drank in the sight of her. Then his back twinged, and pain shot down his legs and straight up to his skull. Yep, irony. Maybe if he averaged his old-man age with his lovesick-teenager age, he'd end up somewhere close to his actual age...

"Did we make plans for today? I don't have an appointment. Or do I?"

She offered a delicate shrug. The black and aqua colors in her blouse shimmered with the movement and set off the highlights in her fair hair. "I thought I'd see if you wanted to go to the pool."

The pool sounded heavenly. Walking in the water would do wonders for the stiffness in his back. He had to work through the discomfort, keep moving even when he was tempted to give up, or the pain would grow until it took over his mind and became the only thing he could think about. He'd learned that lesson the same way he seemed to learn everything these days — the hard way. "I don't know."

Maddie's smile faded the smallest bit.

"It's not that I don't want to. It's just..." His words trailed off as he lost the thread of what he'd planned to say. The pain had to be worse than he realized. Either that, or she was more distracting than he remembered.

"You need a reason to get out of the house. So you don't want to go to the pool. Fine. What about coffee?"

Holden held the back of his office chair as he stood by the table. He stared at his hands. The knuckles were white with the strain of his grip. Yeah, he was definitely in more pain than he was willing to admit. "The pool sounds good. Miles put in a lot of extra hours the last two days, so I gave him today off. I intended to catch up on correspondence."

Her eyes didn't leave his face. Could he have felt any more like a patient? Not with the way she assessed him. In his current frame of mind, he would rebel if she turned into Nurse Maddie on him.

Her voice was even as she spoke. "Why don't you change into your trunks and comb your hair. Throw whatever you'll need into a bag and bring it. No point in getting into street clothes here and then having to switch to your swim trunks in the locker room."

He nodded and turned silently toward the hallway leading to his room. She'd nursed him, all right, making sure he didn't struggle through changing his clothes twice while in so much pain. She'd done it without drawing any attention to it, though. Hm. He'd forgotten that being nursed by Maddie wasn't so bad.

In fact, he liked it.

The place was crowded with screaming preschoolers. Apparently swim lessons were upon them. Holden concentrated to block out the commotion around him. He made slow progress while Maddie swam laps over in the competitive pool. Each step needed his full focus, leaving him with little time to enjoy her graceful strokes.

The back pain had eased as soon as he'd gotten into the water, and he took advantage of the relief to tighten and release different muscle groups as he walked. His physical therapist had been teaching him to do that as a way to keep limber when he wasn't active, but he hoped that doing it today would help ease the discomfort he was sure to feel later when he was out of the pool and missing the added buoyancy the water gave him.

In no time at all, Maddie stood on the wet cement near his left shoulder. "It's been forty-five minutes. We can keep going if you want, but since you mentioned overdoing it yesterday, I thought this might be a good time to stop."

Holden absorbed the sight of her long tanned legs. He wouldn't have minded getting shots so much as a kid if the nurse then had been nearly as striking as the one standing beside the pool.

"Let me finish this lap. I'll get out after that."

She moved with ease toward the ramp to wait for him. A lifeguard approached and talked to her. All wrapped up in smile and swagger, he gifted her with his charm. Then, all the sudden, Maddie clapped her hands and gave the guy a face-splitting grin. Holden swallowed down the bile that rose at the back of his throat.

Perfect teeth. Tan and toned body. No cane. Jerk.

Holden ground his teeth together as he climbed into Maddie's car. "That lifeguard seemed awfully familiar with you." Familiar? What was he, ninety years old?

She didn't even spare him a look as she answered. "Zach's a good guy. He had a hard time choosing where to go for college, but when I told him about my alma mater, that's where he decided to go."

"So he selected a school. Why is that such a big deal?"

"He got accepted. Their nursing program is competitive, and Zach wasn't sure he'd make the cut.

The letter came yesterday, though, and he wanted to tell me."

"He's going to be a nurse?" The lifeguard could make a killing as a model, and he sought the education to be a nurse?

"You're testy today. Do you have something against male nurses?"

Only when they talked to her. Heat climbed up Holden's neck. The irrationality of his reaction wasn't lost on him.

His mother's voice echoed in his head. She'd always advised him that if he didn't have anything nice to say, he should keep his mouth closed.

He ground his teeth some more.

Joshua settled into his chair at the table, two cups of hot coffee in-hand. After handing one across to Holden, he took a long draw on his. "I thought we'd take a look at Mordecai today, unless there's something else you'd like to study?"

"Mordecai?" Holden had heard of him, sure, but wasn't Esther the star of that story?

"He tends to get overlooked in everybody's hurry to honor one of the few women who has a book of the Bible named after her, but Mordecai was an interesting fellow. He was put in a terrible position, yet he stayed true to himself. I'm partial to the story myself. I mean, what would you do if you were ordered to bow to someone, to grovel at their feet, when they had no right to demand it of you?"

The words were hot on Holden's lips. *I'd deck him.* He wasn't picturing Haman of the Bible, though — the man who'd persecuted Mordecai. *That is, unless Haman makes a habit of wearing swim trunks...*

Joshua's eyebrow lifted. "Anything you want to talk about?"

Holden's shoulders slumped. "Remember how I told you I was keeping my feelings for Maddie under control?"

His friend nodded.

"That might not be the case anymore."

"What makes you say that?"

"She, uh, took me to the pool yesterday, and a lifeguard stopped to talk to her, and I could picture myself pulling his spleen out. Through his nose."

Joshua sat back in his chair. "I see."

"I know, I know. Violence is never the answer."

The chuckle that floated across the table did little to make Holden feel better.

"And now you're going to laugh at me?"

"I'm just glad to know you're still alive. You've been like a monk with a beautiful woman sharing your home, and frankly I was beginning to worry that your illness had done more damage than you were telling me. I don't care how focused on God you are, you're still a man."

It hit him then. Like a ton of giant cinder blocks falling on his head. The question he'd been too afraid to acknowledge stared him down and spit in his face. "Am I?"

Joshua leaned forward again, resting his elbows on the table, the laughter gone from his eyes. "Are you what, a man?"

Tears burned at the backs of Holden's eyes. Was he? He didn't know any more. "I thought I'd recover, that everything would go back to the way it was. God chose not to make me whole again, though, and if I'm not whole, am I still a man?"

"Maybe you have the wrong idea of what it means to be a man. What do you think manhood is? Where do you see yourself falling short?"

Holden lifted his hands. "If a man breaks into my house, I'll be struggling to get out of bed. I have no chance of defending my family. If I'm walking down the street with a woman and a mugger attacks us, what can I do? Poke him with my cane? One punch from the guy, and I'll be stranded on the sidewalk like a turtle on its back. And sex? Come on. Half the time that someone touches me, I tense up and can't react the way I want to. No woman is going to want to deal with that."

Joshua's blue eyes were solemn pools of understanding. "Is this how we determine manhood now? Muscles, might, and sexual prowess?"

It sounded foolish on his mentor's lips, but yeah, that was exactly how he saw it.

"Are you willing to take a look at some Bible verses with me that talk about what God thinks it means for a man to really be a man?"

Like he could say no. He wanted to... but he couldn't. "Fine." Holden hadn't done a good job of keeping the resignation out of his voice.

Joshua reached for the Bible that sat between them. "Let's start with 1 Timothy chapter four." He pushed the Bible back across to Holden. "Read verse eight, if you don't mind."

"'...for the training of the body has a limited benefit, but godliness is beneficial in every way, since it holds promise for the present life and also for the life to come.'" Holden rolled his eyes. "Isn't this the verse people use to get out of dieting?"

A smile lifted one side of Joshua's mouth. "Maybe, but I wanted to remind you that your physical body isn't the most important part of who you are. Can you agree to that?"

Holden scanned the verse again. "It's not unimportant. It's just not as important."

"Agreed." Joshua reached for the Bible and pulled it back to his side of the table.

"Let's go to the book of Micah, chapter six. Micah is having this conversation with God, if you will, about what He has done for the people of Judah and how they have scorned Him or turned their backs on him. So then we come to verses six and seven, and Micah is asking God what the people of Judah should do, what offerings could they possibly give to make up for all they've done. Now read verse eight. That's God's answer."

After Holden read the verse, Joshua prodded him. "What, then, are the key things God wants from His people here?"

"They should act justly, love faithfulness, and walk humbly with God."

"Right. Are you unable to do any of those things since your illness?"

Holden shook his head. "I'm not sure you're understanding me."

"I'm taking the scenic route, but I am going somewhere with this. I give you my word."

A frown tugged at Holden's lips. "All right. What's the next stop on our circuitous journey?"

Joshua gave him a smile as he slid the Bible closer. "First Timothy."

Holden had never met anyone who could get as excited about God's word as Joshua. He used to come close before everything in his life went sideways. Tracing the thread backward, it seemed like he'd been in rehab when he'd first started struggling.

If he'd faced it and admitted it then, maybe he could have dealt with it before it burrowed into his soul. He hadn't, though, and it had been eating away at his armor bit by bit ever since.

"We're in chapter six. Verses four and five name all sorts of terrible things people shouldn't do. Then verse six jumps off the page. It says, 'But godliness with contentment is great gain.' Then verses seven through ten list more bad stuff people shouldn't do. Here." He pushed the Bible back over to Holden. "Now read verse eight."

Holden did as he was told.

"We haven't made it to the destination yet, but let's take a pit stop here for a minute, okay?"

Holden shrugged. "Sure."

"If you are a man of God, you should be someone who pursues righteousness. So what about it? Do you pursue righteousness?"

"I try."

"I know you try. Do you succeed more or fail more?"

The shower and every other tempting thought he'd had of Maddie jumped to the front of his mind. "I'm not sure."

"Are you thinking about Maddie?"

Holden nodded.

"Like I said, you're a man. I'd be worried if you didn't have any thoughts about her. What did you do with them?"

This one he could answer. "My thoughts weren't always righteous, but I've treated her well. Aside from snapping occasionally when I needed to put distance between us, I believe I've done right by her."

"Okay, so what about this one — godliness. Are you living in godliness?"

How could Holden answer that? "If I say yes, I'm egotistical. If I say no, I'm a sinner. It's lose-lose."

Joshua tilted his head to the side. "Well, since we're all sinners, I suppose that puts you in good company. What's the first answer your gut gives you? Are you living in godliness?"

"Not as much as I used to. I think so, yeah, but not like before."

"Honesty's good. We can work with that." Joshua pointed back to the verse. "What about faith?"

Holden's right shoulder lifted. "I'm struggling. I keep thinking I've got it licked, but then something comes up, and I realize…"

Joshua waited.

The lump in Holden's throat had grown to gargantuan proportion. "I realize I haven't quite forgiven God for doing this to me."

Sitting back in his chair and crossing his arms in that fatherly way of his, Joshua asked, "Does He need your forgiveness?"

"No, but I need to give it. Does that make sense?"

"Perfectly. I'm not going to sit here and tell you that your faith isn't strong enough, that you have no right to question why God allowed this, or that if you were a better man God would heal you. As far as I'm concerned, that's all poppycock. Life happens, and sometimes it makes our blood curdle with how bad it is, and we have to find a way to deal with it, and sometimes that dealing takes time. As long as you keep asking the questions, I believe you'll find the answers you seek. I also think — and maybe this is just me — but I think part of the reason you're struggling with God right now comes back to your view of manhood. You've got a worldly idea of what it means to be a man. Provider, big, brawny, battle-ready. If you realign your idea of manhood so that it's more in line with God's idea, I think you might find some peace."

"Is the world's idea of manhood all that wrong?"

Joshua gave him a sad smile. "I volunteer twice a month up at Bethesda as a chaplain. Do you know how many soldiers get sent back home every day with missing limbs? Or injuries that will prevent them from ever working a full day again in their lives?"

He'd known Joshua volunteered, but he'd never given it much thought.

His friend and mentor continued. "Are those men who sacrificed to serve their country — are they no longer men now? Is that what I should tell them the next time I go there?"

Holden felt lower than a worm.

"At some point, you're going to have to stop looking in the mirror so much. There are people in this world who are far worse off than you are, and they're still contributing, productive members of society. They're still men and women of valor. They aren't less because of what they've suffered — whether their injuries came in the military, from elsewhere, or were something they were born with. In a lot of ways, they're more. If you'd stop feeling so sorry for yourself, you might learn a thing or two from them."

Not even a worm. Maybe an amoeba. He was officially lower than an amoeba.

"Lecture over. I want to get you to our destination before you kick me out. Take us to Titus chapter two."

Holden flipped through the pages.

"Read verses two and then six through eight."

"'Older men are to be level-headed, worthy of respect, sensible, and sound in faith, love, and endurance... In the same way, encourage the young men to be self-controlled in everything. Make yourself an example of good works with integrity and dignity in your teaching. Your message is to be sound beyond reproach, so that the opponent will be ashamed, having nothing bad to say about us.'"

"Listen to me, Holden. This is God's instruction as to what it means to be a man. Every man should aspire to be level-headed, worthy of respect, sensible, and sound in their faith, love, and endurance. You are all of those things. You might be struggling a bit in the faith department right now, but you've got this. These words right here are who you are. Then, on top of that, you're supposed to set an example for the next generation. You're to show them integrity and dignity and live in a way that nobody can find anything bad to say about you. That's you right there. As far as God's word is concerned, you are one hundred percent man because it's a whole lot more about how you treat the people around you than it is about what you can do for them." Joshua reached out and tapped the pages of the Bible. "And I believe that once you come to terms with this, you'll be a whole lot closer to that forgiveness you're doing battle with."

Holden sat back in his chair. Was it really that simple? How could his idea of manhood be so skewed? It wasn't like he'd grown up watching TV all the time. His family hadn't allowed it. His family... He was the youngest of eight and the only boy who hadn't played football, the only boy who hadn't taken his future wife to homecoming or prom at some point, the only boy who hadn't gone into the backbreaking labor of farming.

He looked up to his brothers, every single one of them, and the men that his sisters were married to. They were good, hard-working, honest men. They set the bar high, though, and there was a part of Holden that had always known he'd never reach it. Would he have felt this inadequate without his illness? Would he have still felt that he was always going to fall short of what it meant to be a man? He wasn't ready to tackle that question just yet, but one thing was clear. He needed to figure out where God wanted him to set the bar, and that was the only one he needed to strive toward reaching.

"All right, I think I get it."

Joshua patted his pockets until he found a piece of paper. He pulled it out and jotted down the verses they'd looked at. "I'm going to leave you be now. I think I've given you enough to chew on. Call or text if you need anything, though. I can come back over, or we can talk on the phone."

Holden reached for the paper and nodded. He was already thumbing back through to 1 Timothy when Joshua let himself out the front door. Every man needed a friend who understood when to speak up and when to be silent, and every man needed someone who didn't pull their punches and said it like it was without all the dancing around and being politically correct. Joshua was better at it than most. He hadn't told Holden he was being a selfish swine with all his whining, but he'd made the point anyway.

Sometimes it took a hard hit to get a man's attention, especially his.

 Thirty-Five

Pablo had been right about her feelings.

The mature approach would have been to sit and talk it over with Holden. Unfortunately, she'd chickened out yesterday after the pool. Maturity didn't seem to hold much appeal for her at the moment.

She'd made a mess of everything. Her job. Her relationship with Tom and Mirabeth. And Holden.

Maddie wandered through the mall — a place she normally hated to go — and wondered if everything was beyond repair. Would she be able to salvage any part of her life?

Her stomach finally growled late in the day, and she decided to head home and stop at her favorite deli along the way. Maybe if she played her cards right — and gave Fishy some roast beef — she could finally convince her housemate that she wasn't evil and that they were better off without Holden in their lives. If bribery was what it took, then so be it.

Maddie pulled into the police station parking lot with two sandwiches. How she ended up there instead of at her apartment with her cat's bribe was anyone's guess.

She put the car in park and stared out the front window at the red brick and glass facade. This was a mistake. In all probability, Tom wasn't even in-house.

Her phone chirped, and she answered it with a sigh.

"You coming up, or am I coming down?" Tom's grave voice came through clearly, but the answer — even to his simple question — hid from her in a cloud of bewilderment.

"I'll be down in two, then." The line went dead.

Maddie was still staring at her phone when he opened her door. "Move over. Let me drive."

She climbed clumsily across the center console and buckled in to the passenger seat.

"Smells good in here."

"I brought you a sandwich."

With her eyes closed, the cityscape passed unnoticed. Her friend, protector, and confidant allowed her the silence.

Once the engine finally fell silent, she opened her eyes and smiled. The pier. The lake was almost dried up, the landscape was neglected, and fat carpenter bees buzzed around the benches. The hot dog man had long since abandoned the site that was now surrounded by one of the less favorable parts of town, but the sight of the old pier caused Maddie to blink back tears.

Abandoning the wooden benches to the bees, she and Tom took a seat on a retaining wall made of crumbling stone. They each pulled out a sandwich, but she didn't eat. "Go ahead and pray if you want."

"Thank you, Lord, for this amazing woman sitting next to me, a woman who has overcome so much and who gives of herself to others so freely. Bless Maddie, Lord, and give her the words to say what's on her heart. Amen."

She bit into her lunch, but not because she was hungry. She felt naked, and the only thing available behind which she could conceal herself was fresh-baked bread piled high with savory roast beef and coleslaw. Her sandwich was the closest thing she had to armor, hiding her face at a time when her face could hide nothing.

"I never meant… to spring it on you." Tom's words came out between bites.

"I know."

Silence fell again. She had too much to say, enough that her jumbled thoughts got in the way and choked off anything she might have said.

"Sasha was real upset at her sister at first. We weren't too thrilled either."

"How come?"

"She changed. She stopped being Haley. Things were... stressful whenever she was around."

Maddie took another bite and chewed. Tom continued talking, and the stress bled away. Order returned to her thoughts, and she was reminded of what a solid man he'd always been, a consistent influence for good and right in her life.

"Mirabeth and I made a promise to Sasha, and we're making the same one to you. We won't become different people."

"What will you become?"

"Better versions of ourselves, hopefully."

"God transforms, doesn't he?"

Tom nodded. "Sure as I'm sitting here. That doesn't mean I'm going to shove the Bible at you every time you walk through my front door, though."

"A man told me I should let God court me."

"Holden?"

She shook her head, and his eyebrows lifted.

"This man — he told me to spend time with God and get to know Him."

He swallowed the last bite of his sandwich. "Sounds like a good plan. You gonna eat your pickle?"

"You can have it."

The pickle disappeared in two bites.

"I'd like to see you and Mirabeth baptized. If I haven't missed it, that is."

Tom was the only person she'd met whose eyes could smile while his mouth remained unaffected. "This Sunday. We'd love for you to be there."

"Okay. Text me the details?"

He nodded. She half expected him to tell her to invite Holden, but maybe not. Seeing as how they were pool buddies now, Tom had probably already told him about it.

They drove back to the station in companionable silence. After he climbed out of the car, though, Tom stooped down and met her eyes. "Sometimes God shows up in unexpected places. I don't have any other wisdom to offer you. Except that you should know you're part of our family. Difference of opinion has never gotten in our way before, and it won't now."

Tom and Mirabeth's church was grand compared to Holden's. She didn't mean to compare them, but Maddie couldn't help it as she took in the vaulted ceiling adorned with shining wood crossbeams against ivory plaster. Plush carpet the color of coffee-vanilla ice cream was offset by chairs — rather than pews — upholstered with a deep plum fabric. The seating gave the sanctuary a splash of color that kept it lively. All in all, where Holden's church felt like a comfortable hodgepodge of put-together pieces, Tom and Mirabeth's felt graceful and elegant. So different, and yet both were somehow surprisingly inviting.

Baptism was a big deal. Maddie had always known it, but seeing it made it even more obvious. Haley had come home from college for the weekend so she could be there. Sasha was in attendance — and wearing a dress. Someone from the church was videotaping the whole thing, and random people throughout the congregation were holding up their phones to take pictures.

She'd seen baptisms before, but it had been years ago. This had a very different feel to it than she remembered.

"In the name of the Father, Son, and Holy Spirit…" The pastor's voice rang across the sanctuary as Tom went under the water and came back up.

Mirabeth was next, and when she came up out of the water, the pastor declared her his sister in Christ. "Welcome to the family."

Had it been anybody else up there, she would have found the whole thing hokey. This was Tom and Mirabeth, though, and they had held off on getting baptized especially for her, because they'd wanted her to be there. This mattered to them, and they mattered to her.

As for God, she wanted Him to be real. For their sake, for Holden's, and for her own.

She'd been reading a Bible she'd picked up at the bookstore. The sales associate had trailed her the whole time she'd been there. He had to have been afraid she'd knock over another display. She couldn't blame him, not after the debacle with the display of cat books. Sure, she'd dramatized the story when she'd told it to Holden and Joshua, but every good drama holds a kernel of truth, embellished though it may be.

When she'd found her way to the Bibles — giving the animal section a wide berth — she'd been stunned. Who knew there could be so many versions or varieties of God's word? The hovering sales associate had been no help, so she'd closed her eyes and picked one.

Sometimes what she read made sense to her, but more often it did not.

Maddie let out a sigh as Tom and Mirabeth slid into their seats, hair wet and faces shining. Then the pastor took to the pulpit, and she gripped the Bible in her hand, ready to try to find whatever passage he called out. Meanwhile, she tried not to think of Holden or miss the way he'd shared his Bible with her when she'd taken him to church.

After opening in prayer, the pastor launched into his sermon. "I'm going to tell you today about some literary terms — static and dynamic. Most of you have read a novel at some point in your life, so you should be able to relate to this." A light chuckle worked its way through the crowd. "A static character is one that never changes. The action of the book goes on around them, but nothing happens to alter their character. They don't grow, learn new things, or develop. They're simply there to add to the scenery. A dynamic character, though, is one that changes as you read the book. They deal with conflict, either internal or external, and they grow from that experience. Whether it's a physical, spiritual, or emotional trial, they overcome it and are better for the experience. Have you ever read a book like that? Where the hero's journey is so profound that you can't help but root for them, relate to them, and feel like you know them long after you've turned the last page?"

What was the pastor getting at? She was pretty sure they were supposed to believe the Bible was the living word of God, not a piece of fiction to be analyzed and assessed.

"Turn with me, if you will, to First Peter chapter one. Follow along as I read verses three and four."

As he read about new birth and living hope, the pastor's voice caught Maddie and pulled her in, made her want to understand what he was trying to convey.

"There it is, folks. The hope we have in Jesus is alive. It is a living, breathing, *dynamic* entity. Our hope isn't some static character that sits in the background and never changes. It's a hope that meets us in our darkest hour, comes to us when we need it most, and never shies away from the challenges we face. It's living hope. Don't you want your hope to be alive? Isn't that so much better than a dead, dried up, rejected hope that can do nothing for you?"

The pastor's voice faded into the background as Maddie turned once again to her Bible. *You rejoice in this, though now for a short time you have had to struggle in various trials... You love Him, though you have not seen Him. And though not seeing Him now, you believe in Him and rejoice with inexpressible and glorious joy... the goal of your faith, the salvation of your souls.*

Maddie looked around, but nobody was watching her. She wanted to catch Tom's eye, but Sasha and Mirabeth sat between then, and he was facing straight ahead at the pastor anyway. A glance to her right told her Haley knew she was agitated, but she couldn't very well ask the girl to explain a Bible verse in the middle of the pastor's preaching.

A cool hand on her arm drew her attention. Haley leaned close and whispered, "Do you have questions?" Maddie nodded, relieved by the request. "After service, okay?"

Maddie made herself settle back into the pew, but she heard nothing else of what the pastor said. Her eyes kept wandering to the open Bible in her lap. *...living hope...struggle in various trials...genuineness of your* *faith...You love Him, though you have not seen Him. You love Him, though you have not seen Him.* Could she love someone she hadn't seen?

Yes.

The answer resonated in her soul. Everything Holden had said over the past months, the words from Pablo about getting to know God, and everything Tom had said to her finally came together into a solid picture she could make sense of. Could she put her faith and love in something she would never lay eyes on? Yes, she could. Not only could she, but she wanted to.

Closing her eyes, Maddie began to pray. *Lord, it's me. I'm here, and I'm ready. I submit to You, and I acknowledge Christ as Savior. Forgive me of my sins. Forgive me of my pride and confusion. Save me from myself. I want what Tom and Mirabeth have. I want what Holden has. I don't know what else to say except thank you for bringing these people into my life, and I'll try to get better at knowing what to say to You. Amen.*

She hoped it wasn't sacrilegious that she hadn't bowed her head. She hadn't wanted to draw any more attention to herself than she already had. Haley would understand. A turn to her right revealed the college sophomore praying, eyes closed and fingers clasped in her lap. Maddie reached over and rested her own hand on top of Haley's, and the girl opened her shining eyes.

One look at Maddie's face and Haley clutched her hand and gave it a squeeze as a tear traced down her cheek.

Maddie swallowed down a snort of laughter as she recalled what Tom had said about them being ashamed of their eldest daughter and trying to make sure nobody came by the house whenever she was home from school because they didn't want people to know she'd gotten religious. This wasn't a good time to laugh, though. Today was a day for celebration. She couldn't wait for the service to end so she could talk to Tom and Mirabeth.

Thirty-Six

Tom picked Holden up. They were heading to The Brighton Architecture Group. The detective's research had led to some solid answers, and it was time to confront the problem. They had a meeting with the Vice President of Public Relations. Holden couldn't help the bounce in his step as he swung his cane. He was going to be glad to get some resolution.

"Gentlemen, right this way." The auburn-haired secretary saw them into a conference room. "Mr. Brighton will be right with you."

Tom's lifted eyebrow reflected the same surprise Holden felt.

The two didn't have a chance to discuss the change before the wide mahogany door opened, and Mr. Brighton walked in. Anybody who was anybody in architecture along the eastern seaboard knew who Alec Brighton was. His fame was well-known, as were his business ethics, which was why Holden had been hopeful the company would take action against Lance McElroy, Yvette's boyfriend.

"Gentlemen, thank you for coming in today." Mr. Brighton shook both their hands before sitting down at the conference table.

"We called your company and made an appointment. Why wouldn't we be here?"

The architect smiled. "Good point. I guess what I should say is thank you for coming to me with your problem rather than going to the police."

Tom held a hand up to silence Holden. "What do you know about our problem?"

"I've had an investigator looking into one of our junior architects. His superior felt something was off with the young man's work and passed the concern up the chain. In talking with the clients McElroy signed, the investigator stumbled across your name, Mr. Jenkins. A couple of those clients compared McElroy's work to yours. It made the investigator's job a lot easier. We'd determined McElroy was stealing material, but we didn't know from whom."

This time Tom didn't try to stop him from speaking. "So you're aware of what Lance McElroy's been up to?"

Mr. Brighton nodded. "He brought in a lot of work very quickly, and he bid the jobs well below what we would normally allow. He turned in the blueprints in record time, though, so each job stayed within budget. No red flags were raised at first. As one of the jobs got further along, though, a discrepancy was noticed on the blueprint, and the head architect on the job began looking into the work that young Mr. McElroy had turned in. He became suspicious. Eventually the ethics team decided to dangle some bait and see what would happen."

Holden leaned forward in his seat. "Bait?"

Mr. Brighton waved a dismissive hand. "He may have been told he would be submitted early for an associate position if he could keep bringing in jobs as quickly as he had been."

"And when was this bait dangled?" Tom asked the question, his voice loud in the still room.

"A month ago, give or take."

That was when the plans for the Mechanicsville job had been taken.

"It turns out my junior architect was dating your former administrative assistant, and she still had password access to your network. I would lecture you on the necessity of changing passwords whenever an employee is let go, but I realize you've been in the midst of some unusual circumstances of your own recently."

Mr. Brighton tilted his head to the side, and his eyes showed warmth. "You may not remember me, but I guest-lectured in a college class you attended."

Holden smiled. "I would expect you to forget me, not the other way around."

"I was sorry to learn of your illness. How are you doing?"

"As well as can be expected."

"You still have your own firm?"

Holden nodded. "I enjoy the freedom it gives me."

Mr. Brighton poured himself some coffee from the carafe on the table. "Mr. McElroy has been terminated. The Architectural Licensing Board has been notified, as well, of the termination and cause thereof. It will be a permanent mark on the young man's record. He may still find work in the field, but it won't come easily for him. He'll have to prove himself before anyone trusts him."

Holden was about to thank him when the older architect continued. "You have legal grounds to sue us for recompense, but I'd like to offer you a trade instead."

Tom leaned forward. "Go on."

"I won't bore you with the details of how my company is structured or what makes us so successful, but I will tell you that I have one architectural team where everyone but the head architect telecommutes." Another dismissive wave of his hand. "One member is, I'm told, a genius who doesn't work well with others. Another is caring for an ailing parent, that sort of thing. Each person on this team has proven their worth to this company. One of the part-time design architects on the team is going to be taking the next several months off. She and her husband are expecting triplets, and the doctor has placed her on strict bed rest. No stress, no work. She'll be out for eight months or so. You can have her spot during that time. If the head architect thinks you mesh well with the team, he may decide to extend the offer."

Holden took a deep breath. Where to start? Too many thoughts swirled through his head.

Mr. Brighton continued on as if the other two weren't even in the room. "You'll have to sign a non-compete agreement, of course. You can still do your own architectural work on the side. You just can't bid for jobs that Brighton has already bid on."

"How will I know if you've already bid on something?"

"If you're designated freelance with Brighton, you'll get an email each morning listing the previous day's bids. There are times when Brighton bids on something after you have. As long as you have the documentation to prove your bid was submitted prior to the daily email, you'll be fine. Just alert your head architect so that it can be noted. The goal of the noncompete isn't to cripple you." The older man winced. "Poor choice of words."

Holden stood. "What's in the fine print that you're not telling me?"

"Do you remember the lecture I gave to your class?"

Of course he did. "Ethics in Architecture." The Brighton Group was a force to be reckoned with when it came to maintaining honest work practices in their chosen field.

The older man nodded. "Someone working for my company wronged you. Your former employee was complicit, but still, I take responsibility for what my people do. I wish to make amends. After looking over all the plans, I also happen to think you have a skill that would benefit this company, even if you only work freelance and decide to pick and choose which jobs to take on. I see this as an opportunity to take something negative and turn it into a positive."

Holden could join him or not. The truth was, The Brighton Group would still be standing tomorrow with or without his help. His company, though, his ability to make a future for himself, was still in jeopardy. He needed The Brighton Group a lot more than they needed him. "I have a drafting assistant."

"He's already been vetted. He'd work as a subcontractor under you, but he'd still have to sign all the same noncompete and nondisclosure documents."

He would get to keep his independence while also being assured of steady work and the paycheck that went with it. The whole thing was too good to be true. Wasn't it? Then again, hadn't his dad recently reminded him that God was in the miracle business?

Holden held out his hand. "I accept your offer."

Mr. Brighton's grip was firm. Ready-made laugh lines appeared around his eyes as he smiled, too.

Tom snorted. "And you wanted to do this over the phone. I told you coming in would make a stronger impression."

Holden was still stunned as he sat down to lunch with Tom.

"You're buyin', you know. Great new job, you can afford it." The detective smirked at him.

"God was looking out for me even when I didn't know to ask Him."

Tom nodded. "Sometimes cops get so busy looking at who they think the suspect is that they miss out on all the clues telling them what really happened. It's the same with people. We're so busy staring at where we expect God to show up that we don't see His approach."

"So how's Maddie doing?" His chest weighed down with the question. She didn't come by to see him anymore, and with his doctor's visits coming less frequently, he had little need to call on her for help. The last time they'd really spent any time together was when she'd shown up unexpectedly to take him to the pool, but when she'd dropped him off afterward, she'd quickly gone on her way.

"She's vulnerable."

Eyes on his menu, Holden said, "I've been praying for her."

"What have you been praying where my girl's concerned? If you don't mind a nosy old man asking."

Nosy old man. Right. Tom was trying to act feeble to get him to let down his defenses. Holden was onto his tricks, not that he could get out of answering. "I've been asking God to bring people into her life that would encourage her to seek Him."

"Huh." Tom's eyes never left his menu. "And that's all?"

Holden set his menu aside and stared at the man sitting across from him. "I've been asking God to help me understand the feelings I have for her and to make the way clear if He wants me to pursue those feelings."

"Hm. What exactly does a clear way look like?"

The waitress approached and Holden waved her away. He didn't know about Tom, but he wasn't ready to order yet. "Salvation's the easy answer, but there's more to it than that. I'm not sure what that more is supposed to look like, though. Hence the praying about it."

Tom tipped his menu down far enough to glare over the top of it. "You should have come to our baptism."

"I was there."

A grunt. "You were there?"

Holden nodded.

Tom tossed his menu onto the tabletop. "We didn't see you."

"I didn't want to make Maddie uncomfortable. I left right before the service closed so she wouldn't see me."

"What went wrong between you two anyway?"

"I don't honestly know." Holden shrugged. "She pulled away but never said why. I kept calling for a while but eventually decided I needed to give her the space she obviously wanted."

"I think it had to do with God more than anything else."

Holden retrieved his menu. "I figured as much. I was happy to see her there at your baptism." A few ticks of the second hand passed. "Has she ever mentioned me?"

Tom grumbled and picked his menu back up.

"I don't mean to put you in the middle. I just wondered."

"You ought to try talking to her again."

This time Holden tipped his menu down so he could glance over it. Tom of the I-know-where-to-

bury-your-body-so-no-one-will-ever-find-it
relationship advice was telling him to talk to Maddie.
"What aren't you telling me?"

"Have you ever had the meatloaf sandwich
here? I love a good meatloaf sandwich."

Holden yanked Tom's menu away, dropping
them both back onto the tabletop. "Spit it out."

The older man's eyes twinkled. "I'm not one
to go telling tales, but a mutual and very dear friend
may have committed her life to the Lord on Sunday."

The air whooshed out of Holden's lungs, and
he sat back, stunned. "Sunday?"

Tom nodded.

"I was there."

A shrug. "It's my not my fault you left early."

Holden stood, threw some bills down on the
table, and called out to the waitress. "I've got to run,
but he wants a meatloaf sandwich."

Thirty-Seven

Maddie ran from Miss Isadore's room to Mr. Rosenthol's, her adrenaline pumping and every sense on alert. His equipment blared out its call. The middle-aged man had been holding steady all day, so the alarms were a surprise. Her eyes flew to the screen that showed his vitals. His heart rate and blood pressure had both dropped dangerously low.

The resident assigned to Mr. Rosenthol and a respiratory technician rushed into the room seconds behind her.

One glance at the monitor, and the resident began barking out orders. Maddie followed each order with precision, paying little attention to the other people who came in and out of the room.

When the CO_2 alarm sounded, the resident slammed his hand against the side of the monitor. "Bag him!"

The intensivist — the teaching doctor in charge — stepped up to the doorway. The respiratory tech cranked the oxygen on and began bagging Mr. Rosenthol as Maddie administered the resident-ordered atropine while another nurse ran to their drug cabinet to get the dopamine. Someone else crowded into the room and silenced the blaring alarms.

"Where's my dopamine drip?" The resident, eyes glued to the monitor, snapped the question into the room like a bullwhip seeking its target.

Maddie ignored the question as she hung the newly-delivered IV bag and began threading the tubing through the pump that would control the drip. Mr. Rosenthol's heart rate was climbing its way back up to normal, but his blood pressure remained low. The dopamine would help the latter while continuing to maintain the former.

The resident moved away from the position he'd been holding near the monitors and pulled out his stethoscope. He listened to Mr. Rosenthol's heart, lungs, and neck. He checked capillary refill and pupil reaction in quick succession, too. Then he turned to Maddie. "He's stable for now. What was he doing when this all started? Any idea what caused it?"

"He's been rock solid all day. We had no warning."

With a nod to the respiratory tech, the resident gave the order. "Stop bagging. Let's see if he can hold his own." Mr. Rosenthol's CO2 level began to climb but then evened out before it could cross over into dangerous territory. His breaths were shallow, but he was breathing on his own.

The resident again skewered Maddie with his eyes. "We need to get a look inside his brain and find out if there's a bleed in there. I'm writing an order for an emergency CT. Call down to let them know it's urgent. And make sure he's ready to go."

She nodded at the command. It would take hours to get him in for an MRI, but CT should be able to fit Mr. Rosenthol into their schedule within the hour. Ironically, it was to his detriment that his vitals were now stable. The folks in CT would get him in faster if he were in imminent danger of flatlining. Sometimes hospital policy defeated the very people it was supposed to protect.

The respiratory technician hung the ambu bag back up but kept it connected to the oxygen. "I'll go get a tank."

Maddie nodded absentmindedly as the tech left. Protocol insisted an oxygen tank accompany any patient leaving the ICU, but even if it weren't standard operating procedure, she would have insisted.

"Good work."

Scanning the room, she found it empty except for the intensivist, still standing in the doorway.

She almost brushed his words off with a *Just doing my job,* but that seemed trite when a man's life had hung in the balance. "Thank you." He smiled his understanding and backed out of the way as Lily came back through with the portable monitoring system they needed to get hooked up so Mr. Rosenthol would be ready to go down for his CT scan.

Mr. Rosenthol's trip to CT was uneventful. His vital signs remained steady the whole time. Not strong, exactly, but still solid. The scan results, however, weren't available yet. Maddie should know. She'd been checking all afternoon.

"Neurosurgery's been called in."

Looking up from her paperwork, she found Mr. Rosenthol's resident standing a foot away. This was the first time he'd ever sought her out for anything.

"Neurosurgery?" She hit refresh on her screen again. Still no results.

The resident sported a frown. "It's not posted yet, but radiology called me. The fourth ventricle is filling with blood, but the picture wasn't clear enough to show us where it's coming from. Has he had any other fluctuations?"

"His heart rate isn't ideal, but it's steady. Same for BP. Is he on the surgery schedule yet?"

"They want an MRI with fiducials so they can map the brain's empty spaces before going in. The PA should be up here soon to put them on."

"Okay." Neurosurgery's idea of *soon* was different than Maddie's, especially when the physician's assistant was involved, but she kept that to herself.

The MRI gave pictures of tissue, but the ventricles were essentially empty space. The fiducials helped the MRI machine to create an image of that empty space. Maddie didn't entirely understand the technology behind it, but she'd dealt with fiducials — and the physician's assistant from Neurosurgery — often enough to have an idea what to expect.

"You did good in there, by the way." The resident's words snapped Maddie out of her short-lived reverie in time for her to watch him walk off without a backward glance.

She'd never much cared for this one. He was too intense, which made it seem like he was always on the edge of anger. His muscles were bunched tight, and his eyes were constantly on high alert, darting around. He didn't laugh with the other doctors or smile at the patients.

Yet he'd complimented her for doing her job.

Maybe he wasn't so bad after all.

Maddie greeted Lyza, her replacement for the night. After giving her the rundown on Miss Isadore, she told her about Mr. Rosenthol's day.

"Neurosurgery said they'd be up soon, huh?" A smirk accompanied the skepticism in Lyza's voice.

"Stranger things have happened."

The older woman clucked her tongue. "I'll just keep on calling until they send someone up. Is he on the MRI schedule yet?"

"They won't put him on until the fiducials are in place."

"Let me guess. The PA won't bother until the MRI is actually scheduled."

"Thomas is coming on duty in two hours down in MRI. If Neurosurgery hasn't made an appearance by then, call him. He'll assign Mr. Rosenthol a timeslot so we can get that PA up here to take care of the fiducials."

"Bless him." Thomas was a favorite among the ICU nurses. He didn't mind cutting through the interdepartmental red tape to make things happen when a patient needed it, and Mr. Rosenthol's situation required some quick intervention.

Maddie collected her lunch bag and headed for the double doors leaving the unit. Some of the nurses congregated, giggling as they peeked out the small windows three-fourths of the way up those very doors.

"Who is he?"

"He's familiar."

"Someone's in the dog house."

"Who's he here for?"

Maddie was too tired, and still too worried about Mr. Rosenthol, to pay much attention. She pushed her way through the crowd and exited the unit. Halfway down the hall, the smell of roses captured her senses. Glancing up, she didn't immediately find the source of the subtle fragrance, so she twisted around to look behind her.

"Uh, hi." Holden waved one hand awkwardly while holding an oversized bouquet in the other. His cane leaned against the nearby wall, but he was uncomfortable. It was there in the stranglehold with which he held the flowers and in the clenched muscles of his jaw.

"What are you doing here?" Her eyes narrowed.

"I came to see you."

"In the hallway?"

A furtive glance at the door to the ICU told her more than his words could. "I didn't want to bring my germs in there. I know how precarious the patients' health can be." He took a step away from the wall. "I saw Tom today. He told me about Sunday. I wanted to do something to celebrate, and flowers seemed like a good idea."

Maddie took a couple steps toward him. "Sunday?"

"I was there, but I left early."

"You're driving?"

He shook his head then brushed his hair out of his eyes. "There's a bus stop in front of the church."

But there wasn't one right by his house. He would have had to walk at least a quarter mile to catch the bus. Being there must have been important to him. Still... "After the last time I saw you, I wasn't sure you wanted anything to do with me."

He shook his head, and color climbed into his cheeks. "The problem was that I wanted *too much* to do with you, and then you showed up at my door wanting to go to the pool, and you are way too attractive in a bathing suit, and all I could think about was how long your legs are, and I tried to make myself focus and pay attention, but then some idiot lifeguard started hanging all over you being everything that I'm not, and I got jealous, and that jealousy turned into self-pity, which sounded a lot like anger..." His next words came out in a mutter. "This would be easier if you were ugly."

A bubble of laughter escaped Maddie's throat. "You'd be nicer to me if I were ugly?"

Holden's shoulders lifted. "Probably not. You're beautiful on the inside, and that's why dealing with the outside is such a problem. Now, if you were ugly on the inside *and* the outside, then we'd be in business." He hung his head. "I'm making a mess of this, aren't I?"

He was, but she wasn't going to say so. "I love roses."

"I know. I bought the ones you like, full-bodied and not too sweet."

That conversation had been weeks ago. "A girl might get the idea you had romance in mind, but you can't."

"Honest, I came here to tell you how happy I am for you and… but…" One of his eyebrows quirked up. "What if I did?"

She took two more steps closer. "I'm all wrong for you."

Holden's eyes scanned the ICU doors again, and Maddie followed his gaze. Their audience was growing. In the middle of the group stood…

The nursing director winked.

"Um." He peered back at her. "What was the question again?"

She turned back around to focus on the man who'd brought her flowers. "You deserve someone who's your equal, and this journey of discovery I'm on is just beginning."

His head bobbed.

"So how did you find out about Sunday?"

"I had lunch with Tom today. Sort of. I might have left him on his own as soon as he told me about your decision. I'm overjoyed for you. Even if you and I never go anywhere, I can't tell you how happy I am that you found your way…"

Their growing audience seemed to be wreaking havoc with his concentration. She took another two steps, bringing her closer while putting her between him and the ICU doors. He could either look directly at her or at the ceiling, but she wasn't leaving him many other choices.

Holden held the flowers in a choking grip. It would be a miracle if any of them were still alive come sunrise.

"I've been confused because what I feel for you is so much deeper than anything I've ever experienced with another woman, but I've been taught my whole life that you don't date a woman unless you… that is to say…" He took a deep breath. "I like you. A lot. More than I should, given the short time we've known each other. It seems to me that these soul-deep feelings for you — they're not a mistake. And you are my equal — or better — in every way that matters."

Maddie released the air she hadn't even realized she was holding captive in her lungs.

His eyes implored her to listen. "I'm not asking for a lifelong commitment here. There's no need to schedule a wedding venue right away."

The words pushed her back a step. Wedding? What?

He held up his hand to stall her. "I'm saying it wrong. Just listen. Please."

She crossed her arms and nodded.

"Let me court you. You know me, and I know you, but allow me the privilege of treating you like you deserve." His eyes fell to the now-mangled roses, and he winced. "I'll do better next time."

Courtship. For such an old-fashioned concept, it kept getting mentioned. "When did you first want to..." She gestured at the flowers.

"The shower," he mumbled. She lifted an eyebrow, but he stalled her. "Never mind. Just know I've been praying about it long and hard. I had to get to a place where I trust God not just with my health, but with my heart. If you break it, I have to believe He'll mend it."

"And if you break mine?"

Holden took a step back, leaning his weight against the wall again. "Relationships are risky. Things don't always go smoothly, and let's face it — you and I aren't always the best at saying what we're thinking. What's in my heart can't be a mistake, though, and I believe it's worth fighting for."

"If you saw Tom at lunch, why did it take you so long to get here?"

He waved the bouquet around. "Finding the right ones wasn't as easy as I'd hoped."

"I like them." She nodded to the flowers before letting her gaze wander over his face again. Warmth started in her middle and spread upward and outward until every part of her tingled with the need to touch him. She was right in front of him. All she'd need to do was lean in a bit...

Holden reached up with the hand not holding flowers and cupped the back of her neck. He ran his thumb along the sensitive skin there as he drew her closer. Their lips met, and sensation exploded in every part of Maddie's body. The thud of her lunch bag and purse hitting the floor barely registered. She reached up to cup Holden's face. Then her hand slid down until she felt his racing pulse against her fingertips. Before she knew it, she was clutching the front of his shirt as sparks continued shooting from where his thumb grazed against her skin to every part of her body. The sound of blood rushing became a roar.

Holden pulled back, his breath ragged, and leaned his forehead against hers. "I think our audience approves."

That roar she'd heard... "It can't be." She tossed a glance over her shoulder. Sure enough, that roar she'd heard was the applause of their ICU audience.

He pulled her close and wrapped his arms around her. "I didn't pick the best place to do this, did I?"

Maddie snuggled into the warmth of his embrace. "You picked the perfect place." She moved her hands from where they'd been resting against his chest and gingerly circled his middle, returning the hug while trying not to trigger a spasm.

His hissed intake of breath washed away the last vestiges of their kiss and reminded her that he'd been standing there longer than was prudent. And she'd rested her hands right where he had the worst part of his nerve damage. "On a scale of one to ten, how much pain are you in?"

He frowned at her. "I'm not asking you to be my nurse. I'm asking you to be my girlfriend, if that's even what it's called anymore."

"You have to be willing to accept me as I am. I'm not much for dumping pretty words on people or going on and on about my feelings…"

His jade eyes started to shine as he finished her thought. "But you'll ask how I'm doing even when I don't want to talk about it. Because you care."

She nodded, unaccustomed shyness tickling the back of her neck.

He stepped back and pushed the flowers toward her, while reaching for the cane resting against the wall. He turned toward the exit as he answered, "I'm at about a seven right now on your pain scale. I might not be able to make it back down to the lobby on my own." Two more steps. "I'd say I'm at an eight now, and I have a feeling it's only going to get worse. I'm a prideful idiot for refusing to bring my walker."

"How long did you stand here?" She collected her purse and lunch bag and walked alongside him.

"Forty minutes." He twisted his wrist to read his watch. Then he winced. "Possibly more."

He shouldn't have stood so long. Foolish romantic man. Maddie breathed in the aromatic flowers. The fragrance was rich and layered with subtle tones of light and dark, much like Holden. "How did you get here?"

"Cab." Short and crisp, the single word told of his pain.

Were they at his house, she'd handle things differently. They were on her turf, though, and she wasn't going to tolerate an argument. She grabbed a hospital issue wheelchair that was sitting abandoned at the side of the hallway. "Sit."

"Maddie." Whatever he was about to say was cut off as he sucked in his breath and stopped moving. He held himself stiffly, the color draining from his face.

"Muscle spasm or nerve?"

"Muscle. It'll ease once I'm off my feet." She locked the brakes on the wheelchair and helped him down into it. His body became rigid enough that bending at the waist to sit proved too great a chore. He fell gracelessly back into the wheelchair as she did her best to guide his momentum without dumping her flowers onto the speckled composite floor. Maddie set her belongings aside and rested the now-mangled flowers on top of them. With a hard pull against the stiff metal, she tugged the footplates down and carefully maneuvered Holden's feet until they were in place.

A spasm that severe hadn't hit him since the early weeks out of rehab. Then again, she'd been around to keep an eye out for the signs and prevent him from acting foolhardy by standing around in hospital hallways for who-knew-how-long.

A tear leaked out the corner of his eye. Should she wipe it away or pretend she hadn't noticed? These issues, though, they would need to be confronted at some point. Now was as good a time as any. She reached out and, with the pad of her thumb, whisked the tear away.

"I hate being so vulnerable in front of you."

Knees bent, she squatted down beside the wheelchair so she could be at his eye level. "You and me, we're the same underneath."

Holden, still in the throes of his back spasm, followed her with his eyes but made no other move.

"Neither of us likes being vulnerable. Both of us wish we were stronger than we are. For you, it's physical. For me, emotional. I don't like to let you see my weaknesses. A part of me always thinks you're going to find a way to use it against me."

"I'd never."

"I'm figuring that out. Just like I'd never use your physical vulnerability against you. You do know that, right?"

He nodded as the pain glazing his eyes began to clear.

Maddie stood and collected her things from the floor and handed them to Holden. Then she released the brakes and moved to the back of the wheelchair. As she pushed, Holden's hand came up and rested on top of hers where she gripped the handle. "We're going to be quite the pair, aren't we?"

She leaned down close to his ear and whispered, "You'd better believe it."

The End

Author's Note

Thank you for taking the time to read *An Informal Arrangement*. I want to take a quick minute to acknowledge the hard work of healthcare professionals across the country in all fields and forms. The work they do is tremendous, and the stress they are under is immense.

I hope you enjoyed Holden and Maddie's story. I had fun getting to know them and the intricacies of their relationship, especially in light of Holden's health situation and how that impacted his sense of self.

If you can, take a minute to tell others about this book by leaving a review on Amazon and Goodreads. I wouldn't mind if you told all your friends about it, too. Or took out an ad in your local paper... although that might get costly. In all seriousness, though, reviews are golden, and I appreciate every single one of them.

As any writer will tell you, gratitude is a common state of being in this line of work. I am beyond thankful that God gives me stories to share and the words with which to tell them. He has allowed me to do something I love, and it's a blessing every single day. Writing isn't a solitary journey, though, and I want to thank the people who have helped pull this story together and make it shine.

They cheered me on when I didn't know which direction to go and didn't hesitate to point out misplaced modifiers and characters that changed eye color mid-story. Thank you to Elizabeth Maddrey, Shari Shroeder, Erin Unger, and J. Gunnar Grey. You're invaluable.

About the Author

Heather Gray writes inspirational romance, including the Ladies of Larkspur western series, the Regency Refuge series, the Informal Romance series and a handful of other contemporary titles.

Heather loves coffee, God, her family, and laughter – not necessarily in that order! She writes approachable characters who, through the highs and lows of life, find a way to love God, embrace each day, and laugh out loud right along with her. And, yeah, her books almost always have someone who's a coffee addict. Some things just can't be helped.

Despite being born into different eras, Heather's characters share a common trait. They're all *flawed...but loved anyway.*

You can sign find Heather online at www.heathergraywriting.com.

Other Books by Heather Gray

Ladies of Larkspur (Inspirational Western Romance)
Mail Order Man
Just Dessert
Redemption

Regency Refuge (Inspirational Regency Romance)
His Saving Grace
Jackal
Queen

Informal Romance (Contemporary Christian Romance)
An Informal Christmas
An Informal Arrangement
An Informal Introduction (May 2016)

Contemporary Stand-Alone Inspirational Romance
Ten Million Reasons
Nowhere for Christmas

Made in the USA
Middletown, DE
18 February 2016